For David

The Englishman

Published worldwide 2013 by Newhurst Press

e-ISBN 978-0-9573711-1-8
Paperback ISBN 978-0-9573711-6-3

Cover design © Simon Wilder

Visit www.helenahalme.com for more books by the same author and for news and reviews of Helena's work.

The Englishman

Helena Halme

NEWHURST PRESS

Acknowledgements

This novel would not have been possible without firstly, the patience of my family; my wonderful husband David, and my children Markus and Monika.

I must also thank my editor, Dorothy Stannard, without whose efficient professionalism I would simply have been lost. I owe a huge debt to the cover designer, Simon Wilder, who took my ideas and translated them into a beautiful image.

Last but by no means least, I want to extend a huge thanks to the many wonderful people who have read and commented on my blog, Helena's London Life, because without you this story would never have been written. Week after week, when I posted chapters online, I was spurred on by you and I can honestly say I would have given up writing long ago had it not been for the encouragement from all of you.

Prologue

KAISA REALISED she'd never felt like this before. This was love. The stuff she'd read about in books since she was a teenager; the films she'd watched. This was how Ryan O'Neal felt about Ali MacGraw in *Love Story*, and Barbra Streisand about Robert Redford in *The Way We Were*. Kaisa grinned. She'd wanted to pose the same question to the Englishman that Katie had to Hubbell, *'Do you smile ALL the time?'*

One

THE BRITISH Embassy was a grand house on a tree-lined street in the old part of Helsinki. The chandeliers were sparkling, the parquet floors polished, the antique furniture gleaming. The ambassador and his wife, who wore a long velvet skirt and a frilly white blouse, stood in the doorway to the main reception room, officially greeting all guests.

When it was Kaisa's turn, she took the invitation, with its ornate gold writing, out of her handbag, but the woman didn't even glance at it. Instead she took Kaisa's hand and smiled briefly, before she did the same to Kaisa's friend Tuuli, and then to the next person in line. Kaisa grabbed the hem of her dress to pull it down a little. When a waiter in a white waistcoat appeared out of nowhere and offered her a glass of sherry from a silver tray, Kaisa nodded to her friend and they settled into a corner of a brightly lit room and sipped the sweet drink.

A few people were scattered around the room, talking English in small groups, but the space seemed too large for all of them. One woman in a cream evening gown glanced briefly towards the Finnish girls and smiled, but most were unconcerned with the two of them standing alone in a corner, staring at their shoes, in a vain attempt not to look out of place.

Kaisa touched the hem of her black-and-white crepe dress once more. She knew it suited her well, but she couldn't help thinking she should have borrowed an evening gown.

Kaisa looked at her friend, and wondered if Tuuli was as nervous about the evening as she was. She doubted it; Tuuli was a tall, confident girl. Nothing seemed to faze her.

'You look great,' Tuuli said, as if she'd read Kaisa's mind.

'I keep thinking I should have worn a long dress.' Kaisa said.

Kaisa's friend from university looked down at her own turquoise satin blouse, which fitted tightly around her slim body. She'd tucked the blouse smartly into her navy trousers. On her feet, Tuuli had a pair of light-brown loafers with low heels. Kaisa's courts made her, for once, the same height as Tuuli.

'What did the woman at the bank say, exactly?' Tuuli asked. Kaisa noticed her blue eyes had turned the exact same hue as her blouse. Her friend was very pretty. Students and staff at Hanken, the Swedish language university to which Kaisa had so remarkably gained entry a year ago, thought the two girls were sisters, but Kaisa didn't think she looked anything like Tuuli. As well as being much taller, her friend also had larger breasts, which made men turn and stare.

'Cocktail dresses…' Kaisa replied.

'Well, I don't wear dresses. Ever.' Tuuli had a way of stating her opinion so definitely that it excluded all future conversation on the matter.

'I didn't mean that. You look fantastic. It's just that she was so vague…' Kaisa was thinking back to the conversation she'd had with her boss at the bank where she worked as a summer intern. The woman was married to a Finnish naval officer whose job it was to organise a visit by the British Royal Navy to Helsinki. She had told Kaisa it was a very important occasion as this was the first visit to Finland by the English fleet since the Second World War. 'The

Russians come here all the time, so this makes a nice change.' The woman had smiled and continued, 'We need some Finnish girls at the cocktail party to keep the officers company, and I bet you speak good English?'

She was right; languages were easy for Kaisa. She'd lived in Stockholm as a child and spoke Swedish fluently. Kaisa had been studying English since primary school and could understand almost everything in British and American TV series, even without looking at the subtitles. She'd all but forgotten about the conversation when, weeks later, the invitation arrived. Kaisa's heart had skipped a beat. She'd never been inside an embassy, or been invited to a cocktail party. The card with its official English writing seemed too glamorous to be real. Kaisa now dug out the invite and showed it to her friend.

'Her Britannic Majesty's Ambassador and Mrs Farquhar request the pleasure of the company of Miss Niemi and guest for Buffet and Dancing on Thursday 2 October 1980 at 8.15 pm.'

'Whatever, this will be fun,' Tuuli said determinedly and handed the card back to Kaisa. She took hold of her arm, 'Relax!'

Kaisa looked around the room and tried to spot the lady from the bank, but she was nowhere to be seen. There were a few men whose Finnish naval uniforms she recognised. They stood by themselves, laughing and drinking beer.

'Couldn't we have beer?' Tuuli asked.

Kaisa glanced at the women in evening gowns. None of them were holding anything but sherry. 'Don't think it's very ladylike,' she said.

Tuuli said nothing.

After about an hour, when no one had said a word to Kaisa or Tuuli, and after they'd had three glasses of the sickly-tasting sherry, they decided it was time to leave. 'We don't have to say goodbye to the ambassador and his wife, do we?' Tuuli said. She'd been talking about going to the university disco.

Kaisa didn't have time to reply. A large group of men, all

wearing dark Navy uniforms with flashes of gold braid, burst through the door, laughing and chatting. They went straight for the makeshift bar at the end of the large room. The space was filled with noise and Kaisa and Tuuli were pushed deeper into their corner.

Suddenly a tall, slim man in a Navy uniform stood in front of Kaisa. He had the darkest eyes she'd ever seen. He reached out his hand, 'How do you do?'

'Ouch,' Kaisa said and pulled her hand away quickly. He'd given her an electric shock. He smiled and his eyes sparkled.

'Sorry!' he said but kept staring at Kaisa. She tried to look down at the floor, or at Tuuli, who seemed unconcerned by this sudden invasion of foreign, uniformed men around them. 'What's your name?'

'Kaisa Niemi.'

He cocked his ear, 'Sorry?' It took the Englishman a long time to learn to pronounce Kaisa's Finnish name. She laughed at his failed attempts to make it sound at all authentic, but he didn't give up.

Eventually, when happy with his pronunciation, he introduced himself to Kaisa and Tuuli, 'Peter Williams.' He then tapped the shoulders of two of his shipmates. One was as tall as him but with fair hair, the other a much shorter, older man. Awkwardly they all shook hands, while the dark Englishman continued to stare at Kaisa. She didn't know what to say or where to put her eyes. She smoothed down her dress. The Englishman took a swig out of a large glass of beer. Suddenly he noticed Kaisa's empty hands, 'Can I get you a drink? What will you have?'

'Sherry,' she hated the taste of it, but couldn't think of what else to ask for.

His dark eyes peered at Kaisa intensely. 'Stay here, promise? I'm going to leave this old man in charge of not letting you leave.' The shorter guy gave an embarrassed laugh and the Englishman disappeared into the now crowded room.

‘So is it always this cold in Helsinki?’ the short man asked. Kaisa explained that in the winter it was worse, there’d be snow soon, but that in summer it was really warm. He nodded, but didn’t seem to be listening to her. She tried to get her friend’s attention but Tuuli was in the middle of a conversation with the blonde guy.

Kaisa was oddly relieved when the dark Englishman returned. He was carrying a tray full of drinks and very nearly spilled them when someone knocked him from behind. Everyone laughed. The Englishman’s eyes met Kaisa’s. ‘You’re still here!’ he said and handed her a drink. It was as if he’d expected her to have escaped. Kaisa looked around the suddenly crowded room. Even if she’d decided to leave, it would have been difficult to fight her way to the door. The throng of people forced the Englishman to stand close to Kaisa. The rough fabric of his uniform touched her bare arm. He gazed at Kaisa’s face. He asked what she did; she told him about her studies at the School of Economics. He said he was a sub-lieutenant on the British ship.

Kaisa found it was easy to talk to this foreign man. Even though her English was at times faltering, they seemed to understand each other straightaway. They laughed at the same jokes. Kaisa wondered if this is what it would be like to have a brother. She had an older sister but had always envied friends with male siblings. It would be nice to have a boy to confide in, someone who knew how other boys thought, what they did or didn’t like in a girl. An older brother would be there to protect you, while a younger brother would admire you.

Kaisa looked around what had been a group of them and noticed there was just the Englishman and her left in the corner of the room. She asked where her friend was. The Englishman took hold of her arm and pointed, ‘Don’t worry. I think she’s OK.’ She saw a group of Finnish naval officers. Tuuli was among them, drinking beer and laughing.

When the music started, the Englishman asked Kaisa to dance. There were only two other couples on the small parquet floor. One she recognised as the Finnish Foreign Minister and his wife, a famous model, now too old for photo shoots but still envied for her dress sense and beautiful skin. She wore a dark lacy top and a skirt, not an evening gown, Kaisa noticed to her relief. The woman's hair was set up into a complicated do, with a few long black curls framing her face. They bounced gently against her tanned skin as she pushed her head back and laughed at something her minister husband said.

The Englishman took hold of Kaisa's waist and she felt the heat of his touch through the thin fabric of her dress. She looked into his dark eyes and for a moment they stood motionless in the middle of the dance floor. Slowly he started to move. Kaisa felt dizzy. The room spun in front of her eyes and she let her body relax in the Englishman's arms.

'You dance beautifully,' he said.

Kaisa smiled, 'So do you.'

He moved his hand lower down Kaisa's back and squeezed her bottom.

'You mustn't,' Kaisa said, not able to contain her laughter. She removed his hand and whispered, 'That's the Foreign Minister and his famous wife. They'll see!'

'Ok,' he nodded and lazily glanced at the other couples on the dance floor.

After a few steps Kaisa again felt his hand drop down towards the right cheek of her backside. She tutted and moved it back up. He must be very young, Kaisa thought. When the music stopped, the Englishman put her hand in the crook of his arm and led her away from the dance floor. He found two plush chairs by a fireplace in a smaller room. It had windows overlooking a groomed garden. As soon as they sat down, a gong rang for food.

'You must be hungry,' The Englishman said, and not waiting for a reply got up, 'I'll get you a selection.' He made Kaisa promise to stay where she was and disappeared into the queue of people. She felt awkward sitting alone, marking the time until the

Englishman's return. She could feel the eyes of the ladies she'd seen earlier in the evening upon her.

Kaisa smoothed down her dress again and looked at her watch: it was ten past eleven already. She saw Tuuli in the doorway to the larger room. She was holding hands with a Finnish naval officer, smiling up at him.

Quickly Kaisa walked towards them. 'Are you going? Wait, I'll come with you.' She was relieved that she didn't have to leave alone.

Tuuli looked at the Finnish guy, then at her friend, 'Umm, I'll call you tomorrow?'

Kaisa felt stupid. 'Ah, yes, of course.' She waved her friend goodbye.

The Englishman reappeared, balancing two glasses of wine and two huge platefuls of food in his hands.

'I didn't know what you liked,' he said, grinning.

He led Kaisa back to the plush chairs. She watched him wolf down cocktail sausages, slices of ham, and potato salad as if he'd never been fed. He emptied his plate and said, 'Aren't you hungry?'

Kaisa shook her head. She wasn't sure if it was the formal surroundings or all the sherry she'd drunk, but she couldn't even think about food. All she could do was sip the wine. She leant back in her chair and the Englishman sat forward in his. He touched her knee. His touch was like a current running through her body.

'You OK?'

Kaisa felt she could sink into the dark pools of the Englishman's eyes. She shook her head, trying to shed the spell this foreigner had cast over her, 'A bit drunk, I think.'

He laughed at that. He put the empty plate away and lit a cigarette. He studied her for a moment. 'You're lovely, do you know that?'

Kaisa blushed.

They sat and talked by the fireplace. The heat of the flames burned the side of Kaisa's arm, but she didn't want to move. While they talked the Englishman gazed at her intently, as if trying to commit the whole of her being to memory. Kaisa found this both flattering and frightening. She knew she shouldn't be here with the Englishman like this.

Once or twice one of his shipmates came and exchanged a few words with him. There was an Englishwoman he seemed to know very well. He introduced her to Kaisa and laughed at something she said. Then he turned back to Kaisa, and the woman moved away. Kaisa liked the feeling of owning the Englishman, having all his attention on her. She found she could tell him her life story. He, too, talked about his family in southwest England. He had a brother and a sister, both a lot older than him, 'My birth wasn't exactly planned,' he smiled.

'Neither was mine! My parents made two mistakes, first my sister, then me,' Kaisa said and laughed. The Englishman looked surprised, as if she'd told him something bad.

'It's OK,' she said.

He took her hands in his and said, 'Can I see you again? After tonight, I mean?'

'Please don't,' she pulled away from his touch.

An older officer, with fair, thinning hair, came into the room and the Englishman got rapidly onto his feet.

'Good evening,' the man nodded to Kaisa and said something, in a low tone, to the Englishman.

'Yes, Sir,' the Englishman said.

'Who was that?' Kaisa asked.

'Listen, something's happened. I have to go back to the ship.'

Kaisa looked at her watch; it was nearly midnight.

The Englishman leant closer and held her hands. 'I must see you again.'

'It's not possible.' She lowered her gaze away from the intense glare of his eyes.

'I'm only in Helsinki for another three days,' he insisted.

Kaisa didn't say anything for a while. His hands around hers felt strong and she didn't want to pull away.

'Look, I have to go. Can I at least phone you?'

She hesitated, 'No.'

His eyes widened, 'Why not?'

'It's impossible.' Kaisa didn't know what else to say.

'Why do you say that?' The Englishman leant closer to her. She could feel his warm breath on her cheek when he whispered into her ear, 'Nothing is impossible.'

People were leaving. Another officer came to tell the Englishman he had to go. Turning close to Kaisa again he said, 'Please?'

Kaisa heard herself say, 'Do you have a pen?'

The Englishman tapped his pockets, then scanned the now empty tables. He looked everywhere, asked a waiter carrying a tray full of glasses, but no one had a pen. Kaisa dug in her handbag and found a pink lipstick. 'You can use this, I guess.'

The Englishman took a paper napkin from a table and she scrawled her number on it. Then, with the final bits of lipstick, he wrote his name and his address on HMS *Newcastle* on the back of Kaisa's invitation to the party.

Outside, on the steps of the embassy, all the officers from the Englishman's ship were gathered, waiting for something. The blonde guy Kaisa and Tuuli had met earlier in the evening nodded to her and, touching his cap, smiled knowingly. She wondered if he thought she and the Englishman were now an item. She could see many of the other officers give her sly glances. It was as if outside, on the steps of the embassy, she'd entered another world – the domain of their ship. As the only woman among all the men, she felt shy and stood closer to the Englishman. He took this to be a sign, and before she could stop him, he'd taken off his cap and bent down to kiss her lips. He tasted of mint and cigarettes. For a moment Kaisa kissed him back; she didn't want to pull away.

When finally the Englishman let go, everybody on the steps cheered. Kaisa was embarrassed and breathless.

'You shouldn't have done that,' she whispered.

The Englishman looked at her and smiled, 'Don't worry,

they're just jealous.' He led her through the throng of people and down the steps towards a waiting taxi.

'I'll call you tomorrow,' he whispered and opened the car door.

When the taxi moved away, Kaisa saw the Englishman wave his cap. She told the driver her address and leant back in the seat. She touched her lips.

Two

THE DARK Helsinki streets whizzed past. The city looked different; it had taken on a magical air. The taxi seemed to fly through the neighbourhoods. As they left the Esplanade Park behind them, the driver crossed the normally busy Mannerheim Street, now deserted, and, rattling over the tramlines, began the climb up the hill on Lönnrot Street. Kaisa loved the Jugendstil buildings in and around the centre of Helsinki. Their ornate facades, built at the turn of the century, and pale coloured walls dominated the landscape. She'd dreamt of living in one of the round towers, like a princess surveying the people on the streets below. She wished all of Helsinki was built in the same style, instead of ugly modern structures in glass and steel. Turning into a small street, the taxi slowed, and Kaisa wound down the window to get some air. Here, on top of the hill, even though you couldn't yet see the sea surrounding the city, you could smell it.

As the taxi crossed the bridge to Lauttasaari Island and made its way towards Kaisa's flat, she wondered what it would be like to live in the city itself rather than in the suburbs. It wouldn't have to be a Jugendstil house, if truth be told, she'd be equally happy to live in the more modern buildings off Mannerheim Street in Töölö, where Tuuli lived. Her flat was close to Hanken and had large windows and tall ceilings. How wonderful it would be to walk up the hill to lectures, or if it was raining, take the tram. The number 3b stopped right outside Tuuli's block. But rented flats were hard to come by in Helsinki. Kaisa was lucky to have somewhere within the city limits. Besides, Lauttasaari was a well-to do area, and she had a separate bedroom, a balcony with a partial sea view, as well as a small kitchenette, so she really shouldn't complain.

At home in the empty flat Kaisa felt inexplicably lonely. Her heart was still pounding when she got undressed and climbed into bed. Suddenly she jumped up and went to put the chain across the front door. For a moment Kaisa listened for steps outside. It was dead quiet. She got back into bed and pulled the covers up to her chin. The streetlight shone through the venetian blinds and formed a familiar zigzag pattern on the walls of her bedroom. What had she done? She'd given a man – a foreigner – her telephone number and she'd let him kiss her. Now sober, Kaisa knew she wouldn't be able to see him again. What she'd done was bad enough already. Not only had she let him think she was free, she'd also betrayed her fiancé. A cold shiver went through her body when she thought what Matti's mother would say if she knew.

PETER HAD hardly slept. The divers hadn't finished searching under the hull of the ship until the early hours of the morning. The excitement had made him sober up pretty quickly after the party at the British Embassy. Perhaps the Duty Officer had been a little jumpy calling them back when it was probably only seagulls fighting over pieces of bread in the water. But, as the Captain had told them, any suspicious activity was to be taken very seriously during this visit. By all accounts, the Russians had a more or less free hand in Helsinki, so who knew what they might try. Peter knew he shouldn't have had so much to drink on the first night ashore, but what could you do when you were required to attend three cocktail parties in one evening?

He stretched his legs over the narrow bunk and smiled; someone had to do it. Who'd have thought the cuts in the Navy's budget would have such an effect on his personal life. The first visit to Finland by the Royal Navy since the Cold War started was supposed to include three ships, but in the event only Peter's had been sent to this small country bordering the Soviet Union. It was pathetic – and embarrassing. I bet the Russians are laughing into their samovars this morning, Peter thought. All the same, this was the closest to visiting a country behind the Iron Curtain Peter would ever get, so he was planning to make the most of it. It wasn't that he'd not taken heed of the Captain's talk about honey traps, but Peter believed in the old proverb, you only live once. This was the most exciting trip of his naval career so far and he was sure he'd spot a KGB agent a mile off, however beautiful she was. And he could keep his mouth shut, he was sure of that too.

Last night Peter almost wished the Russians had planted something – one of those mini-subs they kept hearing about – under HMS *Newcastle*. He could see the newspaper headlines, *'Brave Royal Navy officer Peter Williams discovers Soviet mini-sub in the Baltic'* with a picture of himself from his early Dartmouth days. Of course, it would not have been him – as a sub-lieutenant, he was one of the lowest ranking officers on board. He'd only left Dartmouth a few weeks ago, after all. And he wasn't even a diver. But the image of him as a hero was irresistible. Something like that would have impressed the girl last night.

He got up swiftly and found his mess undress jacket. The napkin was still there in the pocket, with the telephone number scrawled on it. Still legible – just. He took a long, deep drag on his cigarette and blew smoke to the side, away from his bunk.

At noon Peter thought it would be a good time to call the girl. He had nearly an hour until he was on duty again. He walked along the gangway to the wardroom.

'It's the lover boy!' The older officer grinned. Collins was only jealous; his wife looked like a bulldog chewing a thistle. But Peter liked the guy – although not his wife who, at the last cocktail party in Portsmouth, had tried to flirt with him. He grinned at the lieutenant and lifted the receiver. He felt a pleasant twinge in his groin when he heard the phone ringing at the other end. She'd really been quite lovely. He thought back to the night before and knew she'd been smitten by him too. The phone kept ringing at the other end.

'Your bit of foreign fluff not at home?' Collins said.

He dialled again, making sure he got each digit right, and pulling the long cord with him took a step out of the mess and out of earshot of the older man. He tried the number four times, but there was no answer. He was standing in the gangway, and was about to dial again, when Collins passed him a second time and gave him a knowing look. It seemed everyone on board was talking about him and the pretty Finnish girl. There was nothing for it – he'd try ringing again after his four-hour watch on the quarterdeck.

Three

TWO DAYS after the embassy party was a cold autumn day. The single tree outside Kaisa's block of flats had long since lost its leaves – it stood there, desolate, trying to survive the stormy winds from the Baltic that beat its tender trunk. She sighed as she watched its struggle from the narrow window of her kitchenette.

Living alone in a flat in Helsinki had seemed glamorous a year ago. Now the beige walls of the one-bedroomed place in Lauttasaari seemed restricting. The flat, which belonged to her boyfriend's family, wasn't even in Helsinki proper. There was a bus service but it took almost an hour to reach the city centre. While Tuuli could walk to Hanken, she was forced to memorise bus schedules and carefully plan her trips into the city. She was always late for lectures.

When the phone rang she jumped.

'Hello?'

Kaisa heard the familiar voice at the other end of the line and sat down on a kitchen chair she'd placed next to the hall table. 'No Matti, I'm not feeling any better.'

She took the receiver away from her ear and looked at her

reflection in the mirror above the table. Was this the face of a cheat? She listened to her boyfriend talk about the British ship he could see from his office window. Matti worked as a customs officer at the South Harbour. Kaisa tried to sound nonchalant. 'You can see the English people coming and going?' she asked.

'Yes, their uniforms are very smart.'

Kaisa's mouth felt dry. She couldn't speak. The thought of Matti looking at the deck of the British ship and possibly seeing the Englishman walk along it made her feel dizzy.

'You still there?' Matti said. She could hear the irritation in his voice.

'Englishmen are boring,' Kaisa had told Matti when he'd called her the fourth time on the eve of the party. She knew he was desperately jealous of her and would have forbidden her to go if he'd been able to. Now she almost laughed at her own words to her boyfriend. Oh, what a mess she'd got herself into. Perhaps Matti had been right, perhaps she should never have gone to the embassy party.

'Yes, I'm here,' Kaisa said. It took her over ten minutes to convince him that she was still ill. Matti had phoned twice the day before, and she'd had to put on a throaty voice to stop him from coming over. Kaisa just couldn't see him, not yet. She felt bad because she'd never lied to Matti like this before.

When he finally let her go, and she'd replaced the avocado coloured receiver, Kaisa realised the embassy party had been the first time she'd been out without her fiancé since they got engaged. And that hadn't really been going out either – not in the way her friend from university would call going out. When Kaisa first met Tuuli, on the first day of term in the autumn of last year, her friend had been surprised to see the ring on the finger of her left hand.

'But you're the same age as me!' Tuuli had said. Of course, Kaisa was fairly used to that kind of reaction – not many girls got engaged at the age of sixteen – so she just laughed.

Now sitting in the hall, next to the silent telephone, Kaisa looked at the invitation from the British Embassy. She traced the gold lettering with her fingertips and turned it over and gazed at the smudged lipstick on the back. His name and address. For two days Kaisa had sat in her flat waiting for the Englishman's phone call. Like a fool, she'd made only short calls to her friend and tried to get her boyfriend off the line as quickly as possible. She was supposed to be studying before her university lectures restarted on Monday, but all she could think about was the Englishman. Kaisa was furious with herself. Matti had been right; she should never have agreed to go to the cocktail party. Luckily he didn't know what a fool she'd been, so completely taken in by a foreign sailor. Thank goodness all he'd got out of her was a quick, stolen kiss.

She dialled Tuuli's number.

'No call?'

Kaisa tried to listen to the tone of her friend's voice. Was Tuuli getting bored with her talking about the Englishman? 'No,' she said.

'Forget about the Englishman. It was a bit of fun, that's all.'

Of course, Tuuli was right. Kaisa changed the subject. 'Are you going to see your guy again?' Her Finnish sailor had gone back to his barracks at Santahamina, a few miles down the coast of the Gulf of Bothnia.

'I don't know. He was a bit too – correct. You know what I mean?'

Kaisa said she did, but didn't really understand. Matti, her fiancé, was very 'correct'. The Englishman wasn't at all like that, although he was serving in the armed forces. He didn't seem to take anything seriously, he was always laughing. Perhaps that was why he hadn't called; perhaps Kaisa was a great big joke too? Or was it some kind of a game? Was he one of those boys who liked to conquer and then chuck you as soon as they've won you over? But they hadn't done anything; all he'd had was a hasty kiss. It didn't matter now, Kaisa told herself. Why was she here waiting for a call from some foreign stranger when she was engaged to be married anyway? It wasn't right. That was another thing: sooner or later she'd have to come clean to her boyfriend. First she needed to get over her own embarrassment. Matti's questions about the party, the embassy, the foreign officers, the food and the drink could wait.

'YOU MUST have it bad, old chap,' Collins slapped Peter on the shoulder as he passed. He'd lost count of how many times over the last two days he'd tried to dial the number the girl had given him. He'd called it all day yesterday and now on a Saturday it still kept ringing and ringing at the other end. 'Plenty more fish in the sea!' Collins shouted and, turning around, cupped his pretend breasts and pursed his lips in a mock kiss. There was dirty laughter all around him. Peter wanted to tell him to 'Fuck off!' but he was senior to him, so he just laughed half-heartedly. After about ten rings he replaced the receiver on the wall and sat down on an empty sofa in the officers' mess. He ran his fingers through his thick hair. A young steward was clearing away the tea dishes from a table littered with half-filled cups of milky tea and cake crumbs. Peter gazed at the paper napkin under the table, trying to see if he'd missed something in the numbers.

'Still no answer?' Nick, the other sub-lieutenant onboard, was sitting opposite him, reading a magazine. Peter and Nick had graduated from Dartmouth at the same time, but it was really only during the last few weeks on the ship that they'd become firm friends. Peter waited until the steward, balancing a tray full of cups and saucers, left them.

'I don't get it – why would she give me a wrong number?'

'To shut you up?' Nick grinned at him.

Peter didn't look at his friend. He sighed and, leaning back against the hard edge of the wardroom sofa, flicked the now tattered piece of napkin onto the table. He took a packet of cigarettes out of his breast pocket and lit one. Blowing the smoke upwards, he wondered why he was so keen to get in touch with this girl anyway. They were going to sail tomorrow, so there'd be no time to really get to know her, to have her. Still, there was something about her, something different. The way she reacted when he touched her. The hidden passion under that cool exterior. He wanted to know how she looked with the dress pulled down her shoulders, onto her waist. She'd worn no bra and he'd clearly seen the outline of her breasts. God, he mustn't think about it now. He looked over to his friend, who was studying the napkin.

Nick turned it this way and that. 'That last number – is it a seven?'

Peter nodded; he could recount the number by heart now, '245 527'.

'Have you tried it as a one? You know, Europeans put that little slash across a seven and this hasn't got one, so…'

KAISA DECIDED to make some bread rolls. She looked out of the window of her kitchenette. It was snowing; first fall of the year. Light flecks dropped slowly to the asphalt below and melted as they landed. She turned away from the cold scene and started mixing flour with water and yeast. The loud ringing of the phone filled the flat with its urgency. Not Matti again, please, Kaisa prayed, and picked up the receiver with her floured hands.

The Englishman sounded elated when he heard Kaisa's voice.

'You're late,' she said.

'Sorry?' Now there was a serious tinge to his tone.

'Exactly 24 hours late.' Kaisa was surprised by her own tone of voice; she hadn't realised how angry she was.

The Englishman started talking fast. Kaisa balanced the receiver between her neck and shoulder and listened. Even when he was being serious she could hear the smile in his voice. He'd rung the wrong number. The digit 'one' that she'd written in lipstick on his napkin looked like a seven, he explained. A mate had told him Europeans write numbers differently.

'I see.' Could Kaisa believe this foreign sailor? Everyone knew foreigners, and sailors in particular, had loose morals. She thought about her fiancé. How could she tell Matti she'd met up with the Englishman twice? If they didn't do anything and met up just as friends, was it still wrong? If she didn't kiss him again, would that be alright? Kaisa knew Matti would be so angry; he might even leave her. Was she really prepared for that? Then there was the flat, owned by his aunt, not to mention Matti's mother. How would she be able to face her?

'Please, please come and meet me!' Kaisa could hear the Englishman's sincerity in his words. She closed her eyes and thought about the kiss.

'But it's impossible,' she whispered. Kaisa sat down and held tightly onto the receiver now, not caring about the dough sticking to the plastic. She'd have to clean it up later; besides, what did it matter anyway?

There was another short pause. Kaisa held her breath. Was he giving up on her?

Peter looked along the gangway. Involuntarily he crossed his fingers and waited. He could hear her faint breathing down the line. 'If I phone again in half an hour, you'll think about it?' he said.

Four

THE ENGLISHMAN was ten minutes late. Kaisa had been early as usual; she was a Finn, always on or before time for a rendezvous. But as soon as she saw him walking towards her, wearing a dark navy mac, she forgave him his lateness. He didn't know Helsinki after all.

His hair was darker than she remembered, as were his eyes. When he spotted her, he opened his arms, scooped Kaisa up inside his coat and quickly let go of her again. She looked around; it wasn't something people in Finland did on the street, in public. Besides some of her boyfriend's family might see her. Kaisa could just imagine what would happen if his aunt spotted her with a dark-haired man. The old bat would know he was foreign straightaway, with his features and the way he dressed; a summer mac in October! Luckily it was a cold, windy evening and very few people had braved the outdoors.

'So,' he said. They were standing opposite each other, 'You're here.' His dark eyes were again boring into Kaisa.

She looked down at her boots and said, 'Yes.'

'Well, I'm glad,' he said and took her hand. They walked, arm in arm along the deserted North Esplanade. Their steps matched easily, it was as if they'd done this for years and years; sauntered together like this along the streets of Helsinki, looking into shop windows with their bright and inviting lights. But everywhere was shut; it was well past six o'clock. Kaisa suddenly realised she hadn't given a thought to where they should go.

As if he'd read her mind, the Englishman said, 'Shall we go and have a drink?'

Kaisa looked up at him.

'A pub, perhaps?' he said.

She took him to the only place she knew none of her boyfriend's family would go, Kaarle XII. 'Kalle', as the students called the place, was popular with young drinkers – there was a disco on Thursday nights, when it was difficult to get in. Matti hated new music; he only liked the old-fashioned dances, such as tango, Finnish *humppa* or the waltz. Kaisa knew he'd never set foot in a bar like Kalle. For a Saturday night, it wasn't too full; they found a table in the corner and Kaisa went to get two beers from the counter. When she handed the bottle and glass to the Englishman, he glanced behind him, where a group of guys were whistling and pointing in their direction.

'Sailors from my ship,' the Englishman said and poured beer into his glass. He laughed; it seemed to be another joke.

He put his hand over Kaisa's and smiled. She felt inexplicably happy; here she was sitting opposite a foreign sailor, a man she'd met only once before. He was good-looking – in an obvious way, which usually would make Kaisa mistrustful. Yet she didn't want to shift her position even slightly in case he let go of her hand. She smiled at him and he pulled her fingers to his lips and kissed them. 'I'm really happy you're here.'

The noise from the other tables and the music grew louder; they couldn't hear each other. One of the sailors came over to the table and, looking at Kaisa, said, 'Aren't you going to introduce me to the lovely lady, Sir?'

Kaisa couldn't understand what the Englishman replied, but he finished his beer quickly and said, 'Could we go somewhere else?'

Kaisa found another place near the Helsinki train station, where they ordered some food. She watched the Englishman eat a steak, while she picked at a salad.

Over the meal he told her about his childhood, how he didn't do as well at school as he should have done. 'I was very lazy,' he said. His father wanted him to join the Navy, and he did that as soon as he could after finishing school. 'And I love it,' he said, and smiled.

Kaisa in turn told him about her childhood, about all the schools she'd been to, about how her family moved to Stockholm when she was eleven, after which she'd hardly spent more than a year in one school.

'How many languages do you speak?'

'Just Swedish and English, and a little bit of French and German. And Finnish, obviously.'

'Wow,' the Englishman said.

'But my English isn't so good,' she said.

'You speak English wonderfully – I love your accent.'

Kaisa could feel her face grow hot and was afraid she'd blushed. She lowered her eyes. The Englishman took hold of her hands and bent over the table, closer to her. 'I love everything about you.'

'You mustn't say that.' Kaisa could feel the Englishman's fingers over the ring on her left hand.

'Why not?'

'I'm engaged to be married.' She saw the Englishman glance down at her left finger, with the white and yellow gold band on it, and let go of her hands.

There was a silence. Kaisa held her breath. This would surely be it; next he'll say he has to get back to the ship. Kaisa stared at a piece of lettuce on her plate. It had gone brown at the edges.

At last the Englishman said, 'But you're not *married*.'

She looked into his dark eyes; again Kaisa felt like she could sink into them, 'No.'

Kaisa was so relieved the Englishman still wanted to be with her even though he now knew that by being here with him she was betraying another man. She knew she should be strong and go back to her fiancé, but something pulled her back to this foreign man. She knew he'd leave soon and then would never see him again; still she remained there, fiddling with her engagement band, rooted to her seat.

'So…you could come and see me in England?' the Englishman said.

'No, that's impossible,' Kaisa replied without thinking.

The Englishman took her hands into his again. His lips had turned up at the corners into a bright smile, 'I told you – nothing is impossible!'

Kaisa smiled too. The Englishman began to lean towards her, but just then a waiter came over and, looking at Kaisa's half-full plate of salad, asked if they'd finished. 'Yes,' Kaisa said. The waiter turned to the Englishman, pointed at his empty glass of beer and asked in Finnish if he wanted another one. Kaisa exchanged glances with the Englishman. The waiter was being rude on purpose; surely he'd heard them speaking in English.

'We're fine – just the bill please,' Kaisa said in Finnish.

After the meal they did all the things would-be lovers with nowhere to go do. They walked along the Esplanade under the steel-coloured sky, flitted from one Helsinki bar to another. Kaisa was petrified that they'd meet someone she knew, especially as the handsome English naval officer insisted on holding her close to him. So she steered him to places where her boyfriend's posh family were unlikely to go. Of course, they bumped into his shipmates everywhere they went, inducing hilarity and cheering.

In Happy Days, a large bar that had opened only a few weeks before, the Englishman told Kaisa his commanding officer had warned him about her.

'What do you mean?'

'There are honey traps, you know.'

When Kaisa looked at him, not comprehending what he was talking about, he added, 'KGB agents posing as beautiful young women to trap young officers.'

Kaisa laughed. She had to. Her as a KGB agent! In Helsinki! 'But I'm not,' she said and put her hand on his arm resting on the table.

'I know you're not. Very few of these honey traps wear an engagement ring for one.' He laughed and made Kaisa smile too.

'So you noticed the ring from the start!' she said.

He nodded.

'But how, if you knew…'

The Englishman shrugged his shoulders and took her hand between his. 'I couldn't help myself. You're very beautiful.'

Kaisa stared at him. 'Thank you,' she whispered.

'And we sail tomorrow,' the Englishman said. His eyes had grown even darker and Kaisa had to look away to stop herself from leaning over to kiss him.

It became embarrassing to stay inside the restaurant without ordering more food or drink, so they got up and once again braved the cold weather in Esplanade Park. At least it had stopped snowing. They sheltered from the chill wind by the statue of Eino Leino, the Finnish poet. Kaisa tried to remember some of his romantic works, but all she could recall was a verse from a poem about old age that she had to study at school, 'Haihtuvi nuoruus niinkuin vierivä virta'. Kaisa translated for the Englishman, 'Youth disappears as fast as a river flows.' She looked up at the imposing figure, with its heavy cape, and wondered if the great man was trying to tell her something. The park was deserted and they were standing in the shadow of the statue. Kaisa was sure no one would be able to see them, and relaxed a little.

'You're lovely,' the Englishman said, and he took Kaisa into his embrace. She forgot all about the poem, or being cold, or her boyfriend's family. She felt safe in the Englishman's arms. He took Kaisa's face between his hands and kissed her. She kissed him back. He held her tight, kissing her neck, and lips again. His hands, now warmed by her body, were moving around inside Kaisa's jumper; she didn't tell him to stop. Kaisa couldn't resist him. She felt his desire hard against her thigh and she wanted him so much her body ached.

'Can't we go to your flat?' the Englishman asked breathlessly.

'My boyfriend might be there.' Kaisa freed herself a little from his grip, 'He has a key.'

But the Englishman insisted; it felt as if he was expecting her to say no but eventually give in, if he kept at her. At last she had to tell him her fiancé had a hobby: guns. 'He has a favourite handgun, which he sometimes carries.'

The Englishman stared at her, but didn't ask about the flat again.

Kaisa's last bus was due to leave soon, and he said he would walk her to the stop. 'I'll write, and you must promise to write back to me,' he said, and took Kaisa's hand. They walked slowly along the Boulevard, huddled against the cold. The wind swept hard along the tree-lined street and they had to hold each other close to keep warm. When Kaisa saw her bus turn a corner from Mannerheim Street, she felt tearful but swallowed her emotions and forced a smile. The Englishman took hold of her chin and looking into her eyes said, 'We'll see each other again, I promise.' He pulled something out of the pocket of his coat and gave it to her. 'It's a tape of a band I really like, the Pretenders. The best track is *Brass in Pocket*. I want you to have this.'

Kaisa couldn't speak; she held tightly onto the cassette.

'Something to remember me by,' he said and kissed her again.

The bus stopped and Kaisa tried to pull herself away from the Englishman. He held onto her hand and wouldn't let go. 'One more,' he said and they embraced again. Kaisa saw the bus driver shrug. He closed the doors and pulled away.

'That was the last one!' she said, and they both laughed.

When, past midnight, the Englishman put her into a taxi, and Kaisa was alone, she finally let herself cry. She knew she'd never see the Englishman again.

Five

KAISA DREADED going back to her flat. She wondered briefly if she should get the taxi driver to take her to her friend's place in Töölö instead. It was nearly one o'clock in the morning; she couldn't wake her up now. But she wanted to hold onto the image of the Englishman, preserve the feel of his kisses, to not lose the smell of him on her. Yet she knew she had to come clean to her fiancé at some point. When Kaisa opened the door she sighed with relief. There were no lights on. The flat was empty.

She put the chain across the door and leant back against it. She had another night to dream about the Englishman before having to confront her boyfriend.

Kaisa jumped when she heard Matti call her name. He was sitting in the dark on her bed, wearing a pair of brown cords and an Icelandic sweater that Kaisa had knitted last Christmas. Kaisa hung back in the doorway, not knowing what to say, or do.

Matti stood up and grabbed her arm, 'Where have you been?' His brown hair was neatly combed to one side and his eyes looked darker then usual. He wasn't smiling.

When Kaisa told Matti about the Englishman he was quiet. So

she talked more, trying to explain, 'I know he's a stranger, but it feels like I've known him all my life.'

Matti slumped back down onto the bed. He didn't say anything, but made a noise as if she'd stabbed him. Kaisa carried on talking, 'I didn't go to the cocktail party in order to meet someone. It was just an accident.'

'Accident!' Matti's voice was shrill. Suddenly her fiancé, who Kaisa had known for four years to be a calm, controlled man, was shouting at her.

'You saw him again!' he bellowed. 'You're no better than those girls who hang around ports, prostituting themselves to sailors. How much did he pay you?'

'We didn't do anything!'

'Oh yeah? You expect me to believe you!'

Kaisa was scared. She'd never seen her fiancé like this. In spite of his love of guns, he was not a violent man. He was seven years older than Kaisa, and she guessed that had been part of his attraction. While the boys at school drank too much and hardly remembered what they'd done with you the night before, Matti would cook a wonderful meal, or take Kaisa for long walks in the forest, or read her poems. He was never in a hurry and he never did anything without considering the consequences. And he'd never said a cross word to her. Until now.

'You know he'll have a girl like you in every port.'

Kaisa felt sick. She was so tired that tears were running down her face. How long had they been sitting there on her bed, fully clothed?

'And what do you know about him – nothing! I bet you'll never set eyes on him again,' Matti said.

Kaisa sobbed. She couldn't look at him.

Suddenly Matti's tone changed, 'So what are you going to do?'

Kaisa looked at the brown eyes. It was as if the man she knew so well was back again.

'I don't know.'

They were both silent for a long time. Kaisa could hear a solitary car somewhere in the distance. She wished she was in it, she wished she was anywhere else but here.

Matti put his arm over Kaisa's shoulders. 'Let's get into bed.' He was pleading now. Kaisa nodded. It was late. She grabbed her nightdress and went into the bathroom. She needed to be alone. In his fury, her fiancé had expressed her own worries. What did she know about the Englishman? He was young, the same age as her. They had laughed when they found out they were born in the same year and month – just 18 days apart. He didn't have a girlfriend, but he'd been writing to someone. Kaisa hated the girl already. The Englishman was tall, dark and handsome. He loved books and believed that character is fate. He told Kaisa to read Thomas Hardy. His lips were the softest and strongest she'd ever kissed. He laughed a lot, and when he did his eyes sparkled. He looked at Kaisa as if he wanted to wrap her up to protect her, and devour her, all at the same time.

As she sat on the toilet seat, shivering in her thin nightwear, Kaisa couldn't remove the image of the Englishman from her head. His smile, his dark eyes, his warm mouth. She sighed, flushed the empty toilet and ran the water for a second or two. She didn't want her boyfriend to guess what she'd been doing in here – daydreaming about the Englishman.

Matti was already in bed. When Kaisa lay beside him, he turned his face close to her. His breath was hot on her and she knew what he wanted. 'I'm really tired,' she said as gently as she could, and turned her back to him. Kaisa could feel Matti's body tense. He was lying on his back and from his breathing she knew his eyes were open. Kaisa curled herself into a ball and forced her eyes shut. She felt his body move and press against hers, but she remained motionless until his breathing was steady and she knew he was asleep.

In the morning Kaisa woke early and went to make some coffee. She felt as if she hadn't slept a wink. The scene out of the little kitchen window was miserable; a hard drizzle was beating against the window pane. It was almost sleet. There was no one on the street below, and only a few lights shone brightly from the block of flats opposite. It was too early on a Saturday morning. She thought about the Englishman on board his ship. Had they sailed already? He'd said they'd leave early but not at what time.

For a mad second Kaisa thought she'd get dressed and go to the harbour to wave him goodbye. How wonderful it would be to see him once more – she imagined his surprise when he spotted her on the quayside. Then she remembered her boyfriend, asleep in the bed next door. All her clothes were in the bedroom, and he would want to know where she was off to. Kaisa shivered when she thought about what he might do to stop her from meeting the Englishman again. Matti had woken up in the middle of the night, and seeing her awake had said, 'You know if I ever set my eyes on that sailor I'll kill him.'

The coffee machine started making gurgling noises and when Kaisa turned around she was startled by Matti's large, looming figure. He was standing, fully dressed, in the open doorway to the kitchenette. He took a step forward and put his hands around Kaisa's waist.

'Coffee's nearly ready,' she said and turned away from him. She felt his strong grip on her skin and felt sick. What was happening to her? It was as if overnight she'd morphed into another person; a stupid girl who believed a foreign sailor loved her. Kaisa pushed her boyfriend's hands away and fled to the bedroom. She closed the door behind her and got dressed quickly.

Returning to the lounge, Kaisa saw Matti's wide back. He was standing with his arms crossed over his chest, facing the window.

'Breakfast?' she tried to sound normal, cheerful even.

He didn't reply. He didn't even move. Kaisa put out some ham and cheese and sliced the last piece of cucumber she had in the fridge. She'd bought some wheaten rolls from the small bakery opposite the bank a couple of days ago and decided they were still soft enough to eat. She sat down and waited for Matti. Eventually he turned slowly around and sat in his usual place opposite Kaisa, at the small table in one corner of the room.

'So, are you coming to the cottage with us?'

She looked at her fiancé. He was holding half a roll in his hand, delicately balancing the cheese and two pieces of cucumber on top with his index finger. His face was serious, as if he was asking whether, with her new-found career as the local harlot, she'd given up all decent activities, such as taking his mother to the summer place. Every weekend between May and October – if the weather wasn't too bad – Matti would drive to Haapamäki, two hours north, where they'd spend the weekend in the summer cottage.

Kaisa looked down at her plate. She'd forgotten all about the trip. When she didn't reply, Matti said, 'What shall I tell Mother?'

Kaisa shivered. 'OK,' she sighed. All she wanted to do was stay at home and think about the Englishman; perhaps go and see Tuuli and tell her all about the wonderful evening she'd spent with him. But she knew that if she didn't go to the cottage she'd never hear the end of it. Matti wouldn't lie to his mother, so she couldn't even ask him to to say she was ill. (Although she truly didn't feel well.) Kaisa shook her head. What did she think was going to happen with the Englishman anyway? He was in the British Royal Navy and she lived in Finland. He sailed all over the world, met many pretty girls. Kaisa needed to be realistic, to get back to normal. The cottage had to be made ready for the winter, when no one visited. She'd promised to help her boyfriend rake up the leaves, and had told his mother she'd help pack away the fine china and glasses. Every spring his mother brought a box of 'her things' to the cabin, and every autumn she made Matti carry the same box back again. This weekend was the last one they'd spend in the cottage and she had to keep her promise and go.

Six

THE THREE of them drove up north in almost total silence. As usual Kaisa was in the back seat while Matti's mother sat in the front. Kaisa didn't know how to make conversation; all she wanted to do was stare out of the window at the greying landscape. The autumn colours were almost over; when they got out of Helsinki, a few trees by the roadside had crops of yellow leaves still clutching the branches. The sight of them added to Kaisa's sense of hopelessness. Matti's mother sat at the front and for the first few minutes tried to make conversation. 'How are your studies going?'

'I'm not back at university yet.' She knew this; how come she always asked the same question?

'That's a very long summer holiday!' Mother exclaimed and tried to turn to face Kaisa, but could bend her fair head only slightly towards the back seat. Matti's mother wasn't a well woman; she had rheumatism and made few trips without her son. She was quite large, but had very thin ankles and wrists, the way women who had once been slight do when they put on weight in older age. Her hair was carefully coiffured but thin; through the few strands of the up-do Kaisa could make out the pink of her skull. Today she was wearing very little make-up: only dusty pink lipstick and black eyeliner that had been shakily applied. Kaisa often wondered if she should help Mother with her make-up, but was afraid to offer in case she got angry.

At last they drove up the narrow country lane and turned into the cleared bit of land in front of the low-slung building. It was a typical Finnish summer cottage construction; clad with planks of timber and perching on blocks of concrete set to each corner of the cabin. Kaisa hated the dark recess of the house and was sure creepy crawlies, perhaps even snakes, lived in the damp soil underneath. The cabin itself was painted pale yellow and had large windows looking out to the lake. There were three rooms, a largish lounge with a table and four chairs and two small rattan sofas facing each other, with cushions covered in matching pink-and-purple flower-patterned fabric. The whole room had a red tinge in the early afternoon light. The main room had doors to two small bedrooms on one side, and a small kitchen on the other. The front door led directly to the kitchen, so if you were cooking at the old electric stove and someone came in, you had to move to let them pass. Washing-up was equally problematic, but Matti's mother wouldn't hear of using disposable dinnerware. Kaisa often stood at the sink after lunch, when the sun was beaming down outside, wanting to sunbathe instead of watching Matti's mother pass her the dirty plates. Mother's hands were swollen from rheumatism, but her long fingernails were perfectly manicured and painted with pink polish. They made her very clumsy but she wouldn't hear of letting Kaisa do the washing-up on her own. During the whole long procedure Kaisa dreaded there'd be another accident and a broken plate or glass to clear up from the floor.

Kaisa wondered how she could get out of helping to prepare the food. Matti never had to do anything in the kitchen, and since she'd promised to help him rake the leaves she could use that as an excuse. Besides, they were here just to clear up for winter, not to have a normal summer weekend in the country. But when they unpacked the car she noticed there was a cold lunch of mushroom pie and salad already prepared. Mother started immediately to set the table, spreading a white tablecloth. Kaisa sighed and began to help her.

When the food was ready Matti's mother shouted from the doorway to the kitchen, 'Lunch is served!' But there was no sign of Matti.

'I'll go and see where he is,' Kaisa said, but Mother gripped her bare arm with a surprisingly strong pressure, 'No, he should come when called!' Her nails cut deep into Kaisa's flesh.

She couldn't see her boyfriend from the windows; he must be at the back of the house raking leaves or clearing stuff from the space underneath the house, where things like lilos and collapsible garden chairs were kept. Or perhaps he'd gone to the separate sauna cottage, where Kaisa slept.

'He might be getting the boat ready for winter,' Kaisa said to Matti's mother in what she hoped was a soothing tone.

By the sauna there was a long jetty to the lake and a rowing boat pulled up on the shore. Kaisa thought how Matti liked to take her to the opposite shore to pick blueberries in the late summer and mushrooms in the autumn. After they'd filled the baskets he would spread a blanket on a sunny cliff and make love to Kaisa. She shuddered when she thought about the times she'd been certain someone was watching from the other shore. 'All they need is a good pair of binoculars,' she'd tell Matti when he started to undress her. 'Nah, there's no one here,' he'd reply and carry on.

'Where *is* that boy!' Mother now said. Her brown eyes had become dark and her voice shrill. With a large serving spoon in her hand, she struggled out into the garden and shouted her son's name towards the deserted lake.

From the lounge window Kaisa could see a shape slowly approach the house. Matti was still wearing the brown sweater she'd knitted him. Kaisa smiled; as usual Matti was completely unperturbed by his mother's outburst.

Every now and then during lunch, Matti's mother muttered something under her breath. 'I cook and clean but no one appreciates how much I do,' followed by, 'When I was a little girl my mother never did anything – we had servants then, but oh no, not anymore. Not today.'

Kaisa was glad Mother was making a fuss; that way she wouldn't notice she wasn't eating anything. She just didn't seem to need food anymore.

Eventually Matti said, very quietly, 'We're not in tsarist Russia now.'

That Matti's mother had never even been to Russia didn't matter to her. The tales her parents had told her were enough; the grand palaces, the acres of woodland the family had owned, the fine china and silver – 'All of it, left to the Bolsheviks.' But to Kaisa Matti's mother appeared rich still. She wore a mink coat in winter; she lived in a large house in Munkkiniemi, the good part of Helsinki; a huge chandelier adorned the lounge. Kaisa never asked how her fiancé's maternal grandparents had come to Finland, or where the money had come from. Matti tried to tell her about it, but she wasn't interested. As a Finn, Kaisa didn't want to think about the fact that Matti was half-Russian – she was just grateful that, when her own father asked, she could say her boyfriend's father had been Finnish.

When the light faded in the lounge Matti took Kaisa's hand and said, 'I'll take you to the sauna cottage.' She looked into his eyes; they betrayed nothing. This was the usual routine; he'd walk her the few hundred metres to the sauna and, unless Kaisa had her period, they'd make love. Sometimes he'd fall asleep next to her afterwards and not go back to his bedroom until four or five in the morning. On those mornings Kaisa would dread going into the house for breakfast. Yet his mother never mentioned her son's nocturnal escapades. It was as if sex didn't exist for her, or for her son.

'Goodnight, dear,' Matti's mother now said and hugged her.

'I'm really tired,' Kaisa said to Matti when he closed the door to the cabin behind him.

He didn't reply and they walked in silence down the path towards the lake. The sauna cottage was a much more recent addition to the summer place. It was again built on concrete stilts, and had steps up to a small veranda. It was a traditional log cabin, stained dark green. Kaisa remembered watching her boyfriend do the painting on a late summer's day. She was sixteen and they'd been together for just over two months. It was only her second visit to the summer place. Later, Matti told her, his mother had bought the sauna cottage especially so that she'd have somewhere to stay overnight. It didn't occur to Mother that Kaisa would share her boyfriend's bed in the main house. At the time it had seemed endearing, even flattering, this old-fashioned way of doing things. Now it seemed excessive to build a whole new cottage just so that your unmarried son didn't spend nights with his girlfriend under the same roof as yourself.

The sauna cottage had a separate shower room next to it, and a dressing room with a single sofa bed. There was no heating apart from the sauna. That night they hadn't turned it on so the room felt cold when Kaisa opened the door. Quickly she pulled out the trunk from underneath the sofa, where the sheets for her bed were kept. The duvet cover was also flower-patterned and pink. 'I'm really, really tired,' she said again, turning to look at Matti. He lifted his eyes to hers. In the small space his face was so close to Kaisa that she could make out the slight wrinkles around his serious mouth. He took a deep breath in and his nostrils flared. He looked angry and left her without saying a word. Kaisa locked the door from the inside and lay awake for a long time, listening to the pine trees sway in the brisk autumn wind.

When they drove home on Monday through the desolate landscape Matti's mother, too, was quiet. Kaisa asked to be dropped off first. Her boyfriend's dark eyes looked at her through the rear-view mirror.

‘We’re both working early tomorrow,’ Kaisa said, as nonchalantly as she could. All weekend she’d wanted to be alone with her thoughts. Matti turned his gaze on the road and nodded. Kaisa’s stomach hurt when she thought how she’d lied to him again – did he remember that she’d finished in the bank the previous week?

The rest of the day Kaisa spent curled up on the sofa, listening to the Pretenders tape left by the Englishman. She played it over and over, until she knew the lyrics by heart. Kaisa didn’t want to think about her boyfriend, the lies she’d told him, about his mother, or about the future. She just wanted to relive the wonderful few hours she’d spent with the Englishman. Kaisa longed for his touch, for his lips on hers. She wondered if he was thinking about her as he carried out whatever duties he had on that ship. She wished she’d gone to see him off; instead Kaisa had been forced to spend the Sunday at the stupid summer cottage with her stupid fiancé and his stupid mother.

Seven

PETER WAS sitting in the wardroom with his pen poised over a blank piece of airmail paper. He was alone for now, a state of affairs that would be temporary, he knew. So he had to get on with it it – and sharpish. He didn't want an audience for what he wanted to say. For this letter he'd decided to use his fountain pen, which he'd bought for the official correspondence that the Navy required. It was what was expected of an officer, one of his tutors at Dartmouth Naval College had told the whole class. Most guys had later sniggered at the comment, but Peter had taken it seriously. He liked the way the ink flowed from the tip of the feathered pen; it needed control to make the letters on the page legible. He liked to think it took some skill to write a beautiful letter. Now, however, he couldn't begin. As he sat there staring at the blank piece of paper, he realised he wasn't even sure he should write the letter.

'A love letter, is it?' Lieutenant Collins said, and plonked himself on the bunk opposite Peter.

Peter looked at the older officer's grinning face and smiled back, 'No, I just thought I should write to my mother and father.' He screwed the top back onto the pen and closed the writing pad.

He needed to be alone to compose the words he wanted to say to the Finnish girl. The fact was, he did need to write to his parents too, and more importantly reply to Jilly. It was over a week since he'd had her latest letter in which she'd asked when he was next going to be home in Wiltshire. Even thought she hadn't expressly said it, she'd made it clear she was not seeing anyone else. She was saving herself for Peter. Peter bit his lower lip as he watched Collins pick up an old *Sunday Times* off the table and begin to read it. The situation with Jilly was turning into a bloody disaster. His mother had told him in her letter that, 'As a lovely surprise, Jilly popped over for coffee with me last week. She's such a nice girl.' It'd been a mistake to ask Jilly to the Dartmouth Ball, Peter realised that now. But there'd been no one else to ask, and he had honestly thought she understood that it was just a one off. He – in fact both of them – were far too young to tie themselves down. And surely she knew how he felt about the small town he'd spent all his life in? He'd told her over and over that the last thing he wanted to do was to settle down in Wiltshire.

Peter and Jilly had gone to the same local grammar school; they'd known each other since forever, and had been among the first in their year to start going out as a couple in the sixth form. But it had had never been serious. Peter thought back to the last time with Jilly before he left Wiltshire to join the Navy nearly three years ago now. To celebrate his leaving, they'd been to the pub with the group of friends from school. As usual, at closing time, Peter offered to drive Jilly home in his Mini. He'd parked a few streets away from her house, in a quiet cul-de-sac. Jilly had cried, it was true, but to Peter it was clear that it'd been the last time. Afterwards Peter had promised to write. Now after the one evening (and a night, he had to concede), at Dartmouth, she was keener than ever.

Peter opened the pad of airmail paper again and began writing.

"Dear Jilly,

It was very kind of you to accompany me to the Dartmouth

Ball. We both had a great time and now I'd like you to fuck off and leave me alone please."

Reading back the words, Peter swore under his breath, tore the piece of paper off the pad, formed it into a ball and put it into his pocket.

WHEN KAISA entered the Hanken building at the start of her second year at university, she felt almost as nervous as she had on the first day she walked through the famous glass doors. The vast lecture theatre on the second floor was barely full, with no friendly faces. The high ceiling made the hushed voices of the students echo through the hall. The first lecture was on employment law, and the professor spoke quietly and ran through his notes at breakneck speed. Kaisa found it hard to concentrate on the finer points of workers' rights and employers' duties. All she could think about was her handsome Englishman.

Kaisa had agreed to meet her friend in the Hanken canteen for coffee during the first break.

'Back here again,' Tuuli said and bit a large mouthful out of her doughnut.

They both loved the Berlin buns, freshly baked doughnuts filled with strawberry jam and covered with pink icing. The canteen got a delivery only once a week and they'd usually run out by lunchtime.

Kaisa felt like an old timer, watching the first-year students queue up at the counter, umming and ahhing over whether to pick up a bun or not. 'They don't know how rare these are,' she said to Tuuli, who, with her mouthful of doughnut, nodded.

A group of boys walked into the canteen. Kaisa and Tuuli exchanged glances. Two of the guys had hit on them during their first week at Hanken a year ago. They had said they were in their final year, but Tuuli had later found out that the boys had started studying at Hanken in the early seventies, which meant they'd already been there for six years. They all had rich parents, so they didn't need to finish their studies and find work, Kaisa supposed. The leader of the gang was a tall boy, with light-brown long hair.

In their first week at Hanken, and knowing little of the whisper surrounding these boys, Tuuli and Kaisa had plucked up the courage to go and sit at a round plastic table in the Students' Union bar. Quickly they'd been joined by two of the four boys. Both girls had been surprised and quite flattered. The brown-haired boy, who seemed the loudest in the group, had introduced himself as Tom and had asked whether Kaisa ever went to the student disco.

'No, I don't,' Kaisa had said and glanced over to her friend, who was accepting a cigarette from the blonde guy, Ricky, her head bent down to where his hand was cupped around a lit matchstick. Kaisa had felt the glances from the other tables and from people standing about, smoking and chatting. As usual at Hanken, everyone seemed to know one another, so when they, complete strangers, first years at that, had talked to these two boys, it had created a stir. Kaisa and Tuuli had sat and chatted to Tom and Ricky for a while, smoking the cigarettes they offered, until it seemed time to leave. Kaisa had tried to avoid Tom's eyes. The hunger in his face had scared and, as she later came to realise, fascinated her. When the girls left, Tom had given Kaisa a wolfish look. She'd felt his eyes on her backside when they'd walked out into the locker hall.

Later Tuuli found out that most of the boys in the group were titled, with a 'von' in front of their names, and that they were often on the lookout for 'fresh meat'. Kaisa and Tuuli had started referring to the group as 'the rich boys'. After that first time, when Kaisa refused his offer of meeting up at the university disco, Tom had only given her furtive glances when they passed in the corridor, or when the rich boys sat at their regular round table in the Students' Union. Tuuli had been out with Ricky once, but nothing had come out of that either.

The rich boys now made their way noisily past Kaisa and Tuuli in the middle of the canteen, not even making eye contact. They spoke to almost everyone except the two friends. Only when Ricky passed their table, did he give the slightest of nods in Tuuli's direction, and when Tom passed by, he studiously ignored Kaisa. She widened her eyes at Tuuli when the group finally settled on a table on the other side of the room, but her friend's face was expressionless.

'So, have you heard from the Englishman?' Tuuli sounded so calm that Kaisa didn't imagine the incident with Ricky had affected her at all. She must be over him by now, Kaisa thought.

She shook her head, 'I don't think they're back in England yet.'

'What about your fiancé – you're still wearing the ring, I see?' Tuuli raised her eyebrows.

The twisted gold band had been on Kaisa's finger for four years now. Even though she'd thought about taking it off, she hadn't.

'I don't know what to do.'

'Are you still, you know…'

Kaisa lowered her eyes, but said nothing. She fiddled with a napkin between her fingers.

Tuuli gave Kaisa a lecture on how young she was and that she really shouldn't be engaged to be married at the age of twenty. It was a lecture Kaisa had heard many times before. Now Tuuli finished with, 'If it's just sex you want, I'm sure someone else would oblige.' She leant her head towards the rich boys.

They started giggling. After a short while, again serious, Tuuli said, 'Honestly, you have to have a bit of experience – you can't go from being with one guy since you were sixteen straight onto another serious relationship!'

On the following Friday, as usual, Matti used his key to enter Kaisa's apartment after his evening shift at the Customs Office in the South Harbour. They hadn't spoken at all during the week, and she was surprised to see him. But he came in as if nothing had happened, took off his coat as usual and walked into the lounge. He was full of stories of the havoc the English destroyer had caused.

'You told me already,' Kaisa said.

'I was there the morning they arrived. I saw the Finnish girls throw themselves at the foreign sailors. And they were well received, I can tell you!'

Kaisa was quiet. She knew what her boyfriend was doing. But it also made her think how a whole day had been wasted while the Englishman had been trying to decode her telephone number. How he'd been on the ship while she'd been at home, not knowing he was trying to get in touch with her. Had he been tempted by those girls? Of course, Kaisa knew that when foreign ships arrived at the harbour women went to the quayside, although the Englishman hadn't mentioned it.

Kaisa busied herself with spooning coffee into the percolator so that she didn't have to look at Matti. He sat himself down on the sofa his mother had given Kaisa when she moved into his auntie's flat. It was an old-fashioned rococo-style thing covered in green satin with carved wooden legs that perched on the floor like some large bird's claws. When Kaisa had first seen the thing she'd recoiled. She preferred her mother's modern Asko furniture. Of course, Kaisa didn't say how she felt about the foul monstrosity because her fiancé's mother had been kind to give her the three-piece suite.

Matti stretched his arms across the complicated wooden carving on the back of the sofa and said, 'I bet your Englishman sailor took advantage of those girls, too.'

Kaisa walked slowly out of the alcove kitchen, across the small living space and sat on one of the green satin chairs opposite him. 'I can't do this.'

'Do what?'

'I need to sort out what I want.' Kaisa had been looking down at her lap but now lifted her eyes towards her fiancé.

Matti's face was pale and his mouth was slightly open. For once, he looked dishevelled in the pale shirt and dark trousers of his Customs uniform. His tie was loose and the top button of his shirt was undone. He moved his hands down onto his lap and formed them into fists.

Suddenly fear flared up inside Kaisa and her throat felt dry. Was he going to hit her?

She thought about her father.

'It's not fair on you, or on me, if I don't know what I want,' Kaisa said quickly.

'Don't do this, please.' Matti's pleading voice surprised Kaisa. His brown eyes filled with tears. Kaisa got up and went to sit next to her boyfriend. She unfurled his hands and took them in hers, 'I'm really sorry, I didn't mean to hurt you.'

They hugged each other for a very long time. Matti didn't cry, not really, but Kaisa did. Tears just fell down her face and onto his work shirt. She wondered briefly how she'd be able to live on her own without Matti. Would his aunt throw her out of the flat if she broke off the engagement? And would she break it off? If Kaisa didn't hear from the Englishman, would she learn to love Matti again? She held her breath; was she really now in love with the Englishman and not Matti? Is that how easily it happened? She'd only met the Englishman twice – how could Kaisa possibly know he was now the man for her? Kaisa lifted her face up and looked at Matti. 'I think you'd better go.'

Matti put his head against Kaisa's chest. She stroked his thick brown hair. She inhaled the familiar scent of his shampoo. Kaisa hugged Matti and he turned his face towards her and put his lips onto hers.

'No,' she said, and pulled away.

'Please, I love you.'

Matti was very close to Kaisa. He bent down and kissed her neck. His body was so familiar to her. His hands roaming her body seemed natural. Kaisa let him make love to her but afterwards asked him to leave.

'I'll see you soon,' he shouted from the hall. When Kaisa heard the door slam shut she buried her face into her pillow and cried.

***

THE FIRST letter arrived ten days after Kaisa had said goodbye to the Englishman and twelve days after she'd met him at the embassy cocktail party. When she found the blue air mail envelope on the doormat, she nearly screamed. For a moment, Kaisa held it in her hand before opening it. It was thick and silky, and she recognised the handwriting immediately. She ripped the blue envelope open. The first sentences took her breath away.

'It rained when we sailed from Helsinki and the weather seemed to echo my mood. I am sure I've never felt this way about anyone before. I miss you so much.'

The Englishman was a poet. Kaisa read the pages over and over. Then, carefully, she folded the three full sheets of writing back into the envelope and held it against her chest. She thought about the grey weekend after the wonderful night with the Englishman in Helsinki. About the awful hours that followed, which she'd spent awake next to her fiancé, listening to his steady breathing, too afraid to sleep. The days and weeks that followed had been equally hard. Kaisa read the letter over and over; the words became engraved on her mind. The Englishman wrote that he lived in a house in Portsmouth, which he shared with three friends, all from the Navy. He asked if he could phone Kaisa one evening.

She nearly danced to the bus stop and to her lectures in Hanken that day.

'Guess what arrived today?' Kaisa showed Tuuli the blue envelope.

They were standing in the canteen queue. Tuuli looked away from the blackboard. Kaisa knew she was following a strict budget and had been contemplating whether to have the day's dish of fish soup (the cheapest option) or just one of the rye bread sandwiches displayed in the glass cabinet. There were no Berlin buns today.

'Wow!' she said when she saw the letter.

Kaisa smiled and picked up a rye sandwich.

'So, what does it say?' The two girls took their trays of food to the table.

Kaisa leant over the table and whispered, 'He misses me and wants to phone me!'

Tuuli squeezed her arm and said, 'So have you replied to him yet?'

'Of course I did – I posted it on the way here. Imagine that he might call! What will I say to him?'

'You'll know when it happens,' her friend said and picked up a bowl of grey-looking soup from the lady behind the counter.

Kaisa couldn't concentrate on the lecture afterwards. Instead she took out the Englishman's letter and re-read it. He used such beautiful words, but what she kept lingering on over and over was the last sentence, *'Missing you, Yours Peter'*. Kaisa had replied to him in such a rush that morning that she didn't even have time to check for spelling mistakes. She hoped he wouldn't mind.

When Kaisa put the letter down she noticed the other students around her were writing notes. This lecture was on international law, the part of her new course she'd been looking forward to. But Kaisa's mind wandered and she kept forgetting to listen to the professor. She was regretting her choice of second-year subject. She couldn't understand why she'd decided on business law. It was reputed to be one of the hardest subjects to study; there was a labyrinth of rules and regulations that determined how society worked. Kaisa had wanted very badly to be an expert on something, and to be a lawyer in a company had appealed to her. But the study texts seemed frighteningly complicated to her now. There were whole paragraphs just on employment law that she didn't comprehend. On top of that, Kaisa found it really hard to remember legal cases – all the names seemed so similar. During the first seminar with her new tutor she couldn't remember the name of one case. Kaisa was the only student out of the ten at the session who had failed to quote a 'somebody versus somebody'. The tutor, a tall, lean man who always wore a dark suit and a grey tie, looked at Kaisa over silver-rimmed half-moon glasses. He didn't speak to her directly but addressed the group as a whole, speaking into the wall behind them: 'You will notice while you delve deeper into the fascinating subject that is commercial law that it helps if you make sure you learn the relevant legal cases by heart. The sooner you do this the better.'

Kaisa knew it didn't help that while trying to study at home she listened to the Pretenders tape. Instead of the legal cases, her mind would wander to the Esplanade Park and the Englishman's kisses. She couldn't stop listening to the tape.

Eight

WEEKS WENT by without another letter from the Englishman, but Kaisa kept dreaming about Peter. The dreams were not all good. One night she woke with a start. Vividly, as if she'd been at the cinema, she'd seen the Englishman in the arms of another girl. The images of him laughing into the dark-haired girl's eyes, telling her how lovely she was, just like he had with Kaisa, had made her scream into the dark, empty bedroom. That same morning she woke up feeling groggy. It was a Saturday but she had a lot to do; she was falling badly behind in her studies. As she got up and dressed, she decided not to put on the Pretenders tape but to try to study without thinking about the Englishman. After a couple of hours' hard studying, the doorbell rang. On the doorstep was her fiancé. She hadn't seen Matti since she told him to go. He'd phoned a couple of times and asked if he could come over, but Kaisa had told him she was busy studying. Which was true in a way.

'What are you doing here?' Kaisa said. The man standing in the doorway looked different. He was unshaven, and his dark leather coat was open, showing the brown jumper Kaisa had knitted for him.

'Can I come in?' he asked in a low voice.

Kaisa felt sorry for him. She touched the ring on her left hand and opened the door to let Matti in. He stepped gingerly over the threshold and put his arms around her. At first she stiffened in his embrace, but then his familiar scent of pine cones and shampoo soothed her into submission. She relaxed and put her arms around Matti's neck. It was comforting to be held again, to feel safe. Then slowly she moved away from him.

'You OK?' he said.

Kaisa smiled, 'Would you like some coffee?'

That Saturday evening Matti stayed the night at Kaisa's flat. All through their love-making that evening, Kaisa felt as if she wasn't there – as if all the things that Matti always did, kissing her mouth, then her ears, moving slowly but methodically down her body, were happening to someone else. Afterwards, in the small bathroom, she looked at herself in the mirror and tried to discover from her flushed reflection how she felt about it. Making love to Matti seemed right because Kaisa was technically still engaged to him, but even though she hadn't promised the Englishman anything, she felt guilty. And that was mad too; for all she knew he could be in bed right now with his old girlfriend – or a new one. The image of the Englishman was fading in Kaisa's mind by the day. She'd started to doubt whether she'd ever see him again. When Matti left early on Sunday morning to take his mother out for the day, Kaisa decided it wouldn't be fair on anyone if she carried on taking Matti into her bed. But when he turned up on her doorstep the following weekend she was glad to see him. Matti's body was so familiar to her that it didn't seem at all extraordinary to be intimate. Yet it was different from before. Kaisa didn't want to cuddle or kiss Matti afterwards; she didn't feel the closeness she once had.

On the third Saturday, as Kaisa and Matti lay in bed after making love, he said, 'I love you and forgive you.' Kaisa looked into his eyes, but she couldn't tell him what he wanted to hear. She made an excuse and fled to the bathroom instead. She sat on the toilet seat and wondered how her life had become so complicated. It felt wrong to let her fiancé into her bed, yet it also felt wrong not to. Matti kept saying over and over again how much he truly loved her, how he'd loved Kaisa from the moment he'd first set eyes on her four years before.

When Kaisa returned from the bathroom, Matti asked if he could stay Sunday night too.

'I don't think so,' Kaisa said and shook her head.

He sat up in bed and took hold of her waist. She removed his hands and said, 'Please don't.'

Kaisa decided to miss Monday's lectures and stay at home instead, avoiding the Pretenders tape and trying to study. She hadn't heard anything from the Englishman for over three weeks after his first, wonderful letter. She decided he must have forgotten about her. Kaisa touched the thick gold band on her left finger. It felt so familiar, yet heavy and overbearing. She couldn't imagine life without Matti; at the same time she couldn't bear the thought of being married to him. She no longer wanted to be tied down by anybody. But how was she going to tell Matti? And his mother? She shuddered when she thought about what Matti's mother would do if Kaisa broke the engagement. She'd be homeless, that was for sure. She couldn't imagine Matti's aunt would allow her to rent the flat if she left her dear nephew. It was notoriously difficult to find rental accommodation in Helsinki. The student flats went like hotcakes, and were taken up as soon as the universities announced their intakes. But the Lauttasaari flat, just like the ring on her finger, came with a price tag that was too high; Kaisa's freedom.

It was past one o'clock in the morning that night in Helsinki, but only eleven in the UK, when the shrill ring of the telephone, sounding ten times as loud as it did during the day, woke Kaisa up. As if in a trance she clambered out of bed and into the hall, 'Hullo?'

Peter had just come home from the pub with his friends.

At first Kaisa thought she must be dreaming. She'd got out of bed too quickly and had run to the phone in the hall, afraid she'd miss the call. She couldn't tell how long the loud ringing had been going on. Then there he was, talking to her. Peter's voice was low and manly, and when he said he missed her Kaisa nearly fainted. She hung onto the receiver, trying to press the coloured phone as close to her ear as possible.

'I miss you too,' she whispered. Until this moment, hearing his voice, Kaisa hadn't realised how much she had longed for this stranger. How he was the reason for her doubts about Matti. How meeting the Englishman had changed her.

The Englishman was quiet for a moment. Kaisa could hear his breathing, as if he was next to her in the cold, dark hall.

'I wish you were here right now. The things I'd do to you...' Peter's voice had become even deeper. And then he said, 'I think I'm falling in love with you.'

Kaisa tried to control her voice, to keep it level, 'Me too'. What she really wanted to do was shout those words to him.

But international telephone calls were expensive, so Peter had very little time to talk. He promised to phone again soon. Kaisa replaced the receiver and climbed back into bed. The streetlight cast the zigzag shadows into her bedroom.

On the following Saturday, just after six o'clock, Kaisa heard the door to the flat open. She was in the kitchen making coffee. Kaisa met Matti in the hall and kissed him on the cheek. He smelled of the outside and his green jacket was wet with drizzle. Unlike on the other weekends since they'd been together, Kaisa hadn't bought any food. Since Peter's phone call she'd lost her appetite and lost weight. All her clothes were hanging off her, including the black-and-white dress she'd worn when she met the Englishman. Kaisa was now wearing jeans that hadn't fitted her for years. Matti took off his jacket and came close to Kaisa. She turned her face away.

'What's the matter?' Matti said.

'Nothing, I'm just not in the mood tonight.'

'Have you eaten?' he asked and went to open the fridge door.

'I haven't had time to shop,' Kaisa lied.

Matti took Kaisa out to a bar that sold food a few streets away from the flat. The two of them didn't usually go out to eat because Matti was saving money to buy a new car and Kaisa had only her student loan to live on.

'Why doesn't your mother just buy the car for you?' Kaisa now asked. She was pushing the food around on her plate. They'd both ordered minute steaks with French fries. Kaisa had eaten half of hers and was playing with the side salad to buy time. Her stomach seemed to have shrunk – she ate only half the food she'd consumed before she met the Englishman. But Kaisa knew Matti would be upset if she didn't finish the expensive dish.

'Because *I* want to buy this one.' The car Matti was driving now, an old green Opel Kadett, was his mother's car even though she didn't have a driving licence. 'Are you going to eat that?' he asked.

Kaisa lifted her eyes to him, 'Sorry.'

He exhaled heavily and asked for the bill, which he paid with a crisp one hundred Mark note. The girl wearing a pink apron smiled at Matti and wiggled her bum as she walked away from the table. But Kaisa's fiancé didn't even notice. Why can't he be interested in her, she wondered.

'Why did you want to come out and eat if you didn't want the food?' he said. He was putting on his coat when the girl brought coffee: 'You've paid for it – included in the meal.' Again she flashed a hopeful smile at Matti. He sat back down. The place was almost empty; only one other table was taken, by a lonely man nursing a large pint of beer.

This was the same place Matti had taken Kaisa on that first time. It looked dreary now, but then it had been a sunny, hot Midsummer's Eve and Kaisa had been so flattered by the attentions of this older boy – or man. She'd just turned fifteen that same April while he was already 22. He was doing his conscript service in the army and behaved like a grown-up, opening car doors for her and replacing a cardigan over her shoulders when it slipped back. Kaisa looked at her fiancé now. His face looked strained. He must be tired from work. When they'd first met nearly five years ago now, Kaisa had no idea that this boy, a friend of the brother of her school friend Vappu, was interested in her. He'd shown no signs on the few times when they'd met at Vappu's chaotic house. Then, out of the blue, on Midsummer's Eve when Vappu's family – and everyone else in the city – was spending the holiday weekend by a lake somewhere in the country, he'd turned up at the kiosk where Kaisa was working for the summer. He'd driven there at lunchtime to ask when she finished work. She had nothing to do, even her mother was out of town. Kaisa had promised to work because, as usual, she needed the money.

Kaisa now wondered how she'd let this man take over her life so easily. Everyone kept saying that she was too young – even Vappu's mother, who was never around (she was divorced and had to work full-time), had asked to talk to Matti alone. When she'd been satisfied that his intentions towards Kaisa were nothing but the best, she gave her blessing. When Matti told Kaisa about his talk with Mrs Noren, his voice was tinged with pride at having passed the test. It felt strange to Kaisa to have been the subject of other people's conversations. Surely it was up to her, and only her, who she wished to date?

Kaisa's own mother was much more suspicious. She could see Matti came from a very good family, a wealthy one, but after Kaisa brought Matti home one evening for coffee, her mother had asked to speak with Kaisa. Her face was serious and Kaisa thought she must have done something wrong.

'He is very much older than you,' Kaisa's mother had said.

'I know, but he's very kind.'

Kaisa's mother had sighed and hugged her daughter hard.

When, six months later, Matti asked Kaisa's mother if they could get engaged when Kaisa turned sixteen, her mother replied, 'No, she's too young.' She seemed shocked by Matti's request.

In spite of her disapproval, Matti bought the rings ten months after their first Midsummer's night together. It was a sunny and warm Sunday in late April. Kaisa's mother was away at a conference, and Matti took Kaisa to Suomenlinna, a historic island off the coast of Helsinki. She wore a beige mac on the ferry but underneath had a sky-blue dress, which Matti had bought for the occasion. Kaisa had worn rollers in her hair all night and her neck still hurt from the awkward sleeping position. It was only when they arrived on the former military island, and Kaisa saw the old battlements with the guns pointing towards them, that she sensed this was a momentous occasion. For a while they walked along a path that ran around the island; Matti wanted to find the ideal spot – not too crowded by the groups of youngsters who, buoyed by the warm weather, had come out to drink their vodka in the open, yet beautiful enough for the pictures he wished to take. Matti said he wanted the images to look romantic. 'Our three children will want to know where their parents got engaged, don't you think?' He took Kaisa's arm in his. 'You're not cold my little bird, are you?'

'Just a bit,' she said. For some reason Kaisa couldn't stop shivering.

Finally, Matti found a place high up on a hill from where they could see the outline of South Harbour. The riggings of the few sailing boats moored there after winter were rocking back and forth, mirroring Kaisa's own shaking, which had got worse. She tried to stop because she could see it annoyed her boyfriend, soon to be fiancé.

'You can't be cold – it's boiling here!' he said.

Matti wanted Kaisa to take the mac off for the engagement; a coat would spoil the impression of the sunny occasion in the pictures. She tried to breath in and out slowly and took off her coat.

'That's a good girl,' Matti said. 'Sit there on the stone wall.'

Kaisa never liked the pictures from that day – she looked awful, with a forced smile and goose pimples all along her bare arms in the short-sleeved dress.

Now watching her boyfriend slurp his coffee, Kaisa remembered how, when her mother got back from her conference and saw the ring on Kaisa's left hand, she had hit the roof. She threw crockery and threatened to call Matti's mother.

'But it was his mother who insisted we get engaged,' Kaisa said, in tears.

Her mother had stared at her daughter for a moment. She then hugged her. 'It is fine as long as you are sure it is what you want.'

Kaisa nodded and put her head on her mother's shoulder.

Kaisa and her mother never spoke about the incident again, but her mother and Matti didn't really get on. It was, of course, easier after Kaisa's mother moved to Stockholm and she lived alone in the flat of Matti's aunt.

'Ready?' Matti now asked in that same manly tone that had so impressed Kaisa when she was younger. He was staring at her plate, which Kaisa had to admit looked unsightly: a brown piece of meat torn to pieces under a creamy sauce, next to a pile of fries covered in ketchup. She'd only managed to eat about quarter of the food.

Back in the flat, when Matti tried to kiss Kaisa, she moved away from his embrace. Suddenly she couldn't be close to him. There'd been garlic in the food, and his breath stank.

'What's up with you?' Matti moved away from the hall and into the living room. The light had faded outside; without seeming to notice the darkness in the room Matti sat down on the sofa. He tapped the space next to him, 'Come and tell your uncle all about it.'

In the shady living room his presence seemed haunting, even threatening.

'Look, I need to go to bed,' Kaisa said.

Matti got up quickly, 'That's a good idea.'

'No...'

There was a silence. Kaisa knew he understood; he must do. Surely he didn't think they'd be able to carry on like before? That Kaisa would just forget about the Englishman? The velvety voice rang in her ears. 'Look, I need to sleep – alone. I'll call you tomorrow.'

Kaisa watched in silence, rooted to the spot in the middle off the narrow hall, as Matti slowly put his coat on, fastening each button of his Ulster carefully as if he was a child who'd just learned how to get dressed. He'd been wearing a flat cap too – it was nearing zero degrees outside. He picked up his leather gloves from inside the brown cap and held onto them. On the spur of the moment Kaisa took the ring off her left hand and handed it to him.

At first Matti just stared at Kaisa's outstretched arm and wouldn't move to take the ring.

'I'm sorry.' Kaisa pushed her hand out so that the ring touched his coat.

'So this is it, then?'

Kaisa was glad the hall was dark now. She lowered her head and tried to stop the tears. She felt him take the ring from her hand; he snatched it violently away from her as if he'd never wanted her to have it in the first place.

'If you think anything will ever come out of you and that Englishman you must be dafter than I thought.'

Kaisa lifted her head and said, 'It's not just that, you know it isn't. I was too young when we met.'

'Nonsense! Historically girls of fifteen…'

'Don't,' Kaisa had to interrupt him. Why couldn't he just go? She thought of something, 'Can I have your key to this flat, please.'

Matti dug a bunch of keys out of his pocket and began to unwind the silver key from the ring. It seemed to take an age. Finally, the thing came loose and he handed it to Kaisa. It felt hot in the palm of her hand.

'Thank you.'

'Well, goodnight, then.' He kissed her stiffly on the cheek and left.

The next day Kaisa called and asked Matti to collect his things from the flat. There were a few of his LPs left, some shaving cream and deodorant she found in the bathroom, the jumper she'd knitted him the previous winter. Looking at the pile of things, Kaisa couldn't remember how she'd felt before she met the Englishman. She couldn't understand how she'd been able to be with another man. Had she ever truly loved Matti?

Kaisa was making coffee when the phone rang.

'Hello,' the grave female voice said.

When Kaisa didn't reply, it went on, 'Didn't think you'd hear from me, did you?'

Kaisa couldn't get any words out, but her heart was racing. It was Matti's mother.

'So, what have you got to say for yourself?'

'Sorry...?'

'You're a nasty young woman. First you seduce my son, then when it suits, you cast him out like a used dishcloth. But then I knew this from the beginning. Your mother's divorced, after all.'

Kaisa was speechless. She imagined the short, round woman, with piercing brown eyes and carefully coiffured hair sitting in her pink hall in the smart flat in Munkkiniemi. The apartment had high ceilings and the telephone was placed on a dark antique table with a pale-pink satin padded seat next to it. Pink was Matti's mother's favourite colour. She wore the shade nearly every day. Kaisa knew even the telephone was pink.

'Well?' she demanded.

'I'm sorry, I can't do anything.'

'Why not? You don't think the English sailor is ever going to marry you, do you?'

'Well...' Kaisa opened her mouth to speak. She wanted to ask Matti's mother what right she had to interfere in her son's relationship. But she couldn't get a word in.

'You are a very silly girl. If you have any sense, you'll place that expensive ring on your finger again and accept that life with my son is the best you can do with yours. And as far as the flat goes, let's just say my sister doesn't like whores living in her property.'

Kaisa's face grew hot.

She stopped talking. Kaisa heard sniffles at the other end. She remembered how sorry she'd felt for Matti's mother before. Matti was all she had; her husband had died many years ago. After the engagement she insisted Kaisa called her 'Mother'. To Kaisa it didn't seem right and she never called her that. Matti said it made his mother very happy to know she finally had the daughter she always longed for.

'I'm really sorry,' Kaisa said, as calmly as she could. Slowly she took the receiver from her ear and disconnected the call by pressing the plastic buttons down. Her hands were shaking.

When a few moments later the doorbell went, Kaisa took the pile of her ex-fiancé's things and handed them to him over the doorstep.

'Your mother called.'

'Oh,' he said and tried to step inside.

'I'm sorry.' Kaisa kissed Matti on the cheek. 'Goodbye.' She closed the door.

The coffee percolator was making gurgling noises. From the kitchenette window Kaisa watched her old life walk towards his moss-green Opel Kadett. He was holding the pile of things in front of him, like a robot. The sky looked dark; it was about to rain. The first drops fell when Matti's car disappeared from view. Kaisa felt light-headed. The rain didn't matter. The mother's insults didn't matter. Matti didn't matter. All that mattered was that Peter had told Kaisa he was falling in love with her.

Nine

BY MARCH 1981 Kaisa had been exchanging letters with the handsome Englishman for five months. At times she doubted his sincerity. Showing affection seemed to come easily to him. Yet they hardly knew each other.

The fights and recriminations with Matti and his mother had finally come to an end. Kaisa had returned the mink coat Matti's mother had given her as a gift the winter before. The expensive ring her son had given her was no longer on Kaisa's finger. At the end of every month when the rental bill dropped through the letterbox, Kaisa feared it would include a notice to leave. But so far, she'd been allowed to stay in the flat. Kaisa knew they had no right to evict her just because she'd broken the engagement, but Matti's rich family might find a way. During the lonely months following the break-up Kaisa began to realise the affair with the English naval officer might soon also become a memory. Perhaps he'd just been a trigger, making her realise that the relationship with Matti wasn't right. He, and the poet Eino Leino, whose statue she now made a point of visiting when she was in Helsinki centre, made Kaisa understand she was far too young to settle down. What she needed was to concentrate on her studies at the School of Economics and forget about men for a while. On a crackly phone line from Stockholm, Kaisa's mother had reminded her she was still only twenty years old. 'You'll have many, many lovers yet,' she said. Not usual motherly advice, but Kaisa knew she could be right.

In the middle of the stormy spring the Englishman called a second time. Again it was late, two o'clock in the morning in Helsinki.

'I've done it!' he said.

'Sorry?' Once again he'd woken Kaisa from a deep sleep.

'I'm coming to Helsinki; I picked up the tickets from the travel agent today.'

This made Kaisa wake up. In only three weeks' time, in early April, Peter would be in Helsinki for a whole week.

After she put the phone down Kaisa panicked. She needed to go on a diet. She'd been much thinner when they'd met five months earlier. Kaisa must have put on at least three kilos since then. And what would she wear? A new wardrobe was out of the question; her funds were at an all time low. And she needed to clean the flat. Kaisa looked around and her eyes settled on the bed. What if...they didn't get on? She'd never had a boyfriend who'd been the same age as her; Matti had been seven years older. What if he wasn't very experienced? She couldn't bear the embarrassment. What would she do with the Englishman for a whole seven days and nights if it all turned sour?

At the Hanken canteen, Tuuli was much more pragmatic, 'Throw him out if you don't like him.' She'd smiled and added, 'But I know you will.'

On the day Peter was due to arrive Kaisa was agonising over what to wear to the airport to meet him. In his letters Peter had told Kaisa he liked women who wore skirts and dresses. Kaisa lived in jeans and trousers. In her wardrobe she had one skirt and one dress – the summer one she'd worn to the embassy cocktail party. The skirt she'd made herself from a silky fabric with a print of a mountain scene at the hem. In the end Kaisa decided to wear the skirt with a pair of new high-heeled beige boots and a cardigan with small pearly buttons that her mother had given her for Christmas. Standing in front of the mirror two hours before she was due to leave, Kaisa was satisfied. She looked almost like a proper girly girl rather than the boyish, lanky thing who attended lectures wearing old jeans and an oversized jumper.

On the way to the Helsinki Vantaa airport Kaisa felt dizzy. The shiny air-conditioned Finnair bus with tinted windows was nearly empty. A couple of foreign-looking men in expensive dark suits sat at the front. One of them smiled at her when she got on board. Kaisa looked down at the floor. The Helsinki sky outside was grey; it was a cold and rainy April. A few patches of dirty snow were still visible on the side of the road. When the bus pulled up to the terminal, Kaisa let the suited men get off first. She couldn't wait to see the Englishman, but had no photo of him. Would she still recognise him after five months? And would she still like him – love him? And what if he was disappointed when he saw her?

When she finally spotted the Englishman through the glass wall, Kaisa felt suddenly calm. She'd forgotten how handsome he was. The naval officer she'd met at the British Embassy cocktail party six months earlier was real. She hadn't fooled herself into an affection for this man just to have the courage to end her relationship with another. Kaisa hadn't fought with her ex-fiancé and his mother for nothing. Here he was, the man of her dreams, standing a few metres from her, impatiently changing position and staring at the empty baggage conveyor belt. He hadn't seen Kaisa yet. She was grateful for a few moments to observe him without his intense eyes on her. At the same time she was desperate for that look of burning desire.

Peter had had a gin and tonic on the flight, served by a pretty blonde Finnair stewardess. The alcohol steadied his nerves and he could have done with another, but decided against it. He wanted to be sober to meet Kaisa. He could hardly believe he was doing this – going back to see a girl he'd met only twice six months earlier. What if she wasn't as pretty or nice as he remembered? He thought of the words of his captain on HMS *Newcastle*. After the visit to Helsinki, Peter had been teased mercilessly, and during an onboard cocktail party even the captain had asked Peter about the 'Finnish girl'. Peter, though highly embarrassed, had been buoyed by the few drinks they'd all consumed into speaking frankly to the 'Old Man', as the captain was fondly called.

'I can't stop thinking about her.' Peter had said.

The Old Man smiled, creating lines in his high forehead. 'Well then, Williams, it's probably best you go see her. You're only young once.'

Peter didn't see Kaisa until he walked past customs control and through the automatic doors.

Kaisa was standing to one side of the arrivals lounge. Her blue eyes met his. Peter walked towards her, dropped his luggage and kissed Kaisa.

She melted in his arms.

Kaisa had planned a celebratory dinner at her flat, of prawn cocktail, followed by chicken fricassee. Peter ate heartily, praising Kaisa's cooking, while she could hardly face a bite. Her appetite had again vanished. When Kaisa served coffee with the small Pepe cakes she'd bought in the bakery that morning Peter asked if they could move to the sofa.

Instead of coffee they kissed, and kissed. 'You haven't had any cakes,' Kaisa said emerging for breath.

Peter gave her an intense look, 'Can we go to bed?'

They didn't leave the small flat for the next forty-eight hours.

'We have to go for a walk,' Kaisa said on the third morning of their seven days together.

With Peter's arm around Kaisa, the two lovers walked on the shores of Lauttasaari Island. The sea was stormy. Spring was late that year and the chilly wind blew against Kaisa's face. She didn't feel the cold, but the Englishman had not brought the right clothes for the Baltic spring storms.

They took the bus to the centre of Helsinki and bought Peter a waterproof coat from Stockmann's. On the way home, it started snowing and he pulled out his sunglasses. Everyone on the street stared. Kaisa laughed.

'What?'

'There's no sun,' she said.

'The snow flecks hurt my eyes.'

The Englishman had brought music tapes with him. Finnish radio played just domestic hits or a few foreign tracks by Elvis or Frank Sinatra. Kaisa had worn down the Pretenders tape Peter gave her on his first visit. This time his tapes included Billy Joel's *Just the Way You Are* and *She's Always a Woman* and the Isley Brothers' *When Will There Be a Harvest for The World*. They listened to the music and the Englishman sang along.

The day before Peter was due to go back home was Kaisa's 21st birthday and her mother made a visit from Stockholm. She brought a layered sponge, Kaisa's favourite Swedish cake, *Princess Tårta*. It had lots of cream in the middle and was topped with green icing and a pink marzipan rose.

While Peter and Kaisa were waiting for her, the Englishman said, 'She's come to see if I'm good enough for her daughter.'

Kaisa looked at him and laughed. 'No, it's my birthday!'

But when they sat around the small table and Kaisa saw her mother assessing the Englishman, she wondered if he was right, perhaps her mother had planned it?

Kaisa's mother didn't speak English. Before they had the cake, she'd put out some bread, ham, cheese and slices of tomato and cucumber. She'd bought some white bread for the Englishman. Kaisa didn't think he'd like the Finnish dark rye.

'Please,' Kaisa said and nodded towards the Englishman to start. Together with her mother, Kaisa watched as he took two slices of white bread, buttered them both and filled one side with ham and cucumber. Then he put the other on top and pressed hard on it with the palm of his hand. He took the butter knife and cut it in half diagonally. There was a silence.

The Englishman looked up from his plate and smiled. 'What?'

'That,' Kaisa said pointing at the thing he'd made with the bread.

Peter laughed. 'It's a sandwich!'

'Oh,' Kaisa and her mother said at the same time.

'It's what we do in England.'

Kaisa showed the Englishman what they did in Finland, filling just one side and balancing the contents while she ate it. Kaisa translated for her mother. She laughed.

When Peter excused himself and visited the bathroom, Kaisa's mother whispered to her, 'He's so handsome!'

Kaisa nodded.

'When's he going back?' she said.

Kaisa's mother knew her too well. The thought that the week had to come to an end had been on Kaisa's mind since their first evening together. Like a ticking bomb, the last day loomed. How could Kaisa go back to living in the flat on her own, how would she be able to sleep in the same bed on her own? The longing for him would kill her.

'Tomorrow.' Tears filled Kaisa's eyes. Her mother put her arm around Kaisa. When they heard the bathroom door open Kaisa got up and escaped to the kitchen to wipe her eyes.

Back at the airport Kaisa felt a horrible dread. She'd been quiet on the smart Finnair bus when the Englishman held her hand.

'It'll be alright, you'll see. You'll come to England in August, promise?'

August was four months away.

After Peter checked in his bag, they had half an hour before the flight boarded. They stood looking at the large display of flights. The white characters flicked, and moved up the board. Now there were only three destinations before London.

Suddenly the Englishman said, 'Wait here, I'll be back.'

Kaisa stood and watched another flight move forward. An awful emptiness filled her. Every molecule in her body felt Peter's absence. Why did he leave her now when they had so little time left together?

The Englishman came back and handed Kaisa a red rose. 'This is for you'

She started to cry.

Peter took Kaisa's face in his hands and wiped away the tears with his thumbs. 'I love you. Don't ever forget it.' He took her in his arms once more and whispered. 'I have to go now.'

Kaisa nodded.

Peter kissed her and was gone. She couldn't watch him walk through to the passport control, so ran blindly down the stairs, clutching the rose.

The flat felt empty and quiet, too quiet, when Kaisa returned from the airport. She put on the tapes the Englishman had left behind and loaded the coffee machine. She closed her eyes and listened to the music. Kaisa could hear the Englishman's voice when he sang *I love you just the way you are.*' She wondered how she was going to get through the night, alone in the bed they'd shared. The Englishman's scent was everywhere in the flat. On the basin in the bathroom she found traces of his shaving foam. She scooped the small stain up with her finger and inhaled. He'd said some American relatives sent him several cans of the coconut cream because he couldn't get it in England. Kaisa thought how typical that was of him: he always wanted what he couldn't have. She wondered what would happen if the company started selling the product in the UK; would he stop using it. And would he also stop loving her if she, too, became a regular fixture in his life?

Ten

THE FINNAIR flight to Heathrow was almost empty. There were two air hostesses and one steward, who kept Kaisa topped up with orange juice and water. She was nervous. She was used to travelling on her own, but London was a big city in which to get lost. As the plane swung over the Thames, a very blonde male air steward came and sat next to Kaisa.

'Been to London before?'

'No,' she answered, thinking, what if the Englishman is not there to meet her?

'That's Big Ben, and there's Tower Bridge.' He leant closer to point out the rest of the London landmarks through the window on Kaisa's side. He smiled, flashing a perfect set of white teeth. As they left the centre of the large city Kaisa saw rows and rows of houses. There seemed to be no end to them.

KAISA SCANNED the many expectant faces on the other side of the double doors of the arrivals hall. At last she saw the Englishman, tall and slim, wearing a pair of jeans and a navy jumper. She dodged reuniting families and passed an old couple walking slowly in front of her before reaching the Englishman. He put his arms around Kaisa and gave her a long kiss. The steward from the plane came past and waved to her.

'Who was that?'

Kaisa told Peter how kind the Finnair guy had been.

'I bet,' he said.

It was the first time the Englishman had been jealous and it felt good. Kaisa pushed herself closer to him as they walked to the car park. The air outside the revolving doors of the airport terminal was warm. It smelled of sour milk and traffic fumes. There were people everywhere.

'Here, put this on, it'll keep your hair in place.' The Englishman opened the car door and handed Kaisa a Red Sox baseball cap. He'd told her in his letters that he had an open top Triumph Spitfire. *'It's yellow, but that means I won't be missed on the road!'*

The car looked tiny. The seats were black leather and very low. The Englishman rolled down the top and sat beside Kaisa. 'It suits you,' he smiled and kissed her again. 'It'll take us a couple of hours to get to Pompey.'

The warm air rushed past her face. The busy concrete spaghetti junctions were followed by rolling green hills, with occasional cows grazing by the side of the road. Kaisa felt so happy she could burst. With the Spitfire top down, they could only hear each other by shouting, but occasionally the Englishman would lean over, take Kaisa's hand and squeeze it. He'd smile and pull it to his lips.

Suddenly there was water on either side of the road. 'This is Southsea,' the Englishman said and slowed down. They drove past the Common and down along the seafront. At one end was a large Ferris wheel, then a long promenade. People in ones and twos, some with their children or dogs, strolled along the pavement, the couples and families laughing and chatting to each other.

Kaisa realised they were nearly at the house the Englishman shared with his Navy friends. She grew nervous again. What if they didn't like her? She'd chosen what she wore very carefully, but now felt shabby and old-fashioned. What if his friends were very smart?

From the seafront Peter drove down one street, and turned into another, then another. They all looked alike, with rows and rows of the kind of houses Kaisa had seen from the aeroplane. The street names were displayed on white signs attached to low brick walls. Peter stopped on a tree-lined street and said, 'We're here!'

The door to the house was ajar. Peter took Kaisa's hand and led her inside. 'Wait here,' he said. Kaisa stood in a shabby-looking room with a worn-out sofa, a large TV and a stereo with speakers on either side. A stack of LPs stood on the floor. A wooden staircase next to a narrow hall had a strip of carpet on it. The Englishman leapt up the stairs taking two or three steps at a time.

A guy with light-coloured hair in a faded T-shirt walked in from the dark, narrow hallway. He was barefoot. 'You must be the Finnish girlfriend.'

Kaisa took his outstretched hand and smiled. 'Jeff,' he said and grinned at Kaisa. Jeff was followed by a shorter man with tidy dark hair and clothes, whose girlfriend came in too. She had short sandy-coloured hair and dark eyes. Oliver and Sandra both smiled and shook Kaisa's hand too.

Peter tumbled down the stairs. 'Here you all are.' They stood in a circle and for a while no one spoke.

'I'll show you my room,' Peter finally said. His friends sniggered until the English girl, Sandra, looked sternly at them. Kaisa was very embarrassed but allowed herself to be led up the stairs.

DURING THE two weeks Kaisa spent in the UK in the late summer of 1981, the sun never stopped shining and the music never stopped playing. At first Radio One sounded very American to her; all laughter and superficial chatter. But it played the hits she didn't even know to crave in Finland. The station was the only one the Englishman listened to in his car or in the terraced house in

Southsea. He sang along, *'Every little thing she does is magic, magic, magic'*, or *'I'm just a jealous guy'*.

Halfway through the first week of Kaisa's stay in England Peter drove her to the country to see his parents. She wore the now familiar Red Sox cap to keep her hair in place in his yellow sports car.

'How far is it?' Kaisa asked when they pulled into a large-looking town called Salisbury.

The Englishman must have noticed the nervous note in Kaisa's voice, because he squeezed her thigh and smiled. 'I'll let you know when we're ten minutes away.'

The image of Kaisa's ex-fiancé's mother flashed in front of her eyes as they sped past green fields. She thought about what Matti's mother had said to her during that awful telephone conversation. Kaisa looked sideways at Peter. He looked tanned and relaxed, holding the wheel with one hand, his elbow resting on the open window. Surely a nice guy like him would also have a nice mother, Kaisa thought.

Instead of thinking about meeting the parents, she sat back and tried to enjoy the scenery. Peter drove past wooded hills and valleys, where the trees hung over the road, nearly touching the top of their heads. After Salisbury there were small villages with pretty gingerbread houses. Kaisa felt as if she was a character in a TV drama or an old English film. Her head spun with images from *Coronation Street* and *Mary Poppins*, both of which she'd seen in Finland. Kaisa expected a nanny with a large black umbrella to emerge at any moment from one of the chimneys stacked on top of the red-brick houses.

Peter's mother was attending to a flower-bed outside a pink house. She gave a little laugh as she kissed her son and shook Kaisa's hand.

'Hello, so nice to meet you at last.'

She had short greying hair arranged in an old-fashioned hairdo and large-framed glasses. She didn't look as scary as Matti's mother; still Kaisa wanted to be careful. She didn't want to upset her from the start, so she just smiled and said as little as possible.

It was Wednesday lunchtime and Peter's father was still at work. Wearing an apron, his mother cooked home-made chips and served them with thick slices of ham. Peter and Kaisa ate in a large kitchen overlooking a green lawn. The Englishman and his mother chatted about what the two of them had done during Kaisa's two days in Portsmouth. She wanted to know when Kaisa had arrived and when she was going home. She raised an eyebrow when she heard Kaisa lived alone in a flat in Helsinki. Kaisa wondered if she knew Kaisa's parents were divorced.

'I've put you in the blue room.' She lifted her eyes towards her son. 'And you can sleep in the yellow one.'

It was like a scene from Jane Austen. Kaisa didn't dare look at the Englishman. She thought about his bedroom back in Southsea. On his wall he had a large poster of a girl playing tennis, showing her bare bottom. He also had a Pirelli calendar with scantily-clad women on every page. What would his mother say if she saw them?

The Englishman's father was a charming man with a mop of white hair. When he came home his piercing dark eyes fixed on Kaisa.

'Hello,' he said simply, but smiled when he shook her hand and nodded as if to show her his approval.

He put on an LP of Sibelius in the long lounge, which had a green velour three-piece suite. He told Kaisa to sit down on the sofa and said how he admired the Finnish soldiers in the Winter War. 'Brave men. You stood up to the Russians, eh?'

That evening Peter took Kaisa out to a pub in a pretty village called Lacock. The place was dark, with low rustic beams. They sat around a large unlit fireplace and chatted to Peter's schoolfriends. They gave Kaisa furtive glances and were surprised she could speak English.

Late in the evening, as they tiptoed into the darkened house, the Englishman kissed Kaisa softly and said, 'I'll come into your room in the morning when my parents have gone to work.'

During the days in Wiltshire the Englishman took Kaisa to Stourhead. He said it was prettier in May when the rhododendrons were in bloom. She couldn't see how those gardens with deep ponds and sweeping lawns could look any more beautiful. He also took her to Longleat, where they wandered hand in hand through the ancient manor house. And they spent a day in Bath. Kaisa fell in love with the Roman Baths, the Georgian architecture and the smart shopping streets. Cautiously she wondered if one day she might live there.

At the end of the visit, when Kaisa thanked Peter's mother, she said. 'It's my pleasure dear. I try look after all the girlfriends my son brings home.'

Peter laughed nervously.

On the drive back to Portsmouth Kaisa looked at the Englishman's handsome profile. He was negotiating a large roundabout. How many girlfriends had there been, she wondered. Did his mother want to warn her? Was Kaisa taking this relationship too seriously; more seriously than the Englishman? Perhaps all the sightseeing, the introductions to various friends and the love letters were something he did all the time. He certainly seemed practised at making a girl feel special. For once, when the car sped up and the fast rushing of the wind made it impossible to talk, Kaisa was grateful. She was too busy to stop the tears from smudging her make-up.

PETER LOOKED over to Kaisa, sitting there next to him. Her head was held high and she hadn't said a word since they left home. Peter wanted a cigarette, but it was impossible to smoke at this speed with the roof down. He still remembered when, at just seventeen, in his first car, a Mini, he'd flicked a cigarette stub out of the window. A gust of wind had brought it right back and it had nearly burned his crotch. He was more careful with smoking in his car after that. They were coming into Salisbury and the traffic made him stop the car. He glanced over to Kaisa and touched her thigh.

'You OK?'

She turned briefly and nodded, but didn't say anything. So she was upset. Shit. What had his mum been thinking? Perhaps she was trying to tell him that he was too young to settle down? Of course that was true – besides he had no intention of that, and neither had Kaisa. As far as he knew. Peter was glad when they cleared the town with its endless roundabouts and were once again speeding along the A31. Once they were back in Portsmouth, he'd take her into his arms and tell her how much he loved her; she'd be alright. Just the thought of what he'd do to Kaisa later made his groin move.

NOW AND then during Kaisa's last week in the UK, the words of the Englishman's mother – 'all of my son's girlfriends' – rang in her ears. But as soon as Peter took her into his arms, or just touched her, she convinced herself there was nothing to worry about. After all, Kaisa had been engaged to be married when they met. Peter too could have had serious girlfriends before her.

Besides, during the two weeks Kaisa was in England, Peter seemed to want to show Kaisa everything about his country. For her last weekend he took Kaisa to visit his older brother and his wife near London.

'I hear you were put in separate bedrooms in Wiltshire,' Simon said and smiled. Kaisa blushed but was relieved they'd decided Kaisa and Peter were old enough to sleep together in the guest room of the semi-detached house in Surrey.

Simon had the same dark features, but was a little shorter than Peter and his hair had gone grey around the temples. Kaisa knew he was ten years older than the Englishman. His wife, Miriam, a wiry woman with cropped brown hair, kissed Kaisa warmly on both cheeks. 'You must be hungry,' she said and led Kaisa into the kitchen, where four plates, topped up to the rim with ham and salad, were ready to be served.

As a surprise Peter had booked seats at the English National Opera.

'I've never been, so you must tell me all about it,' he said when they were drinking gin and tonics in the bar. They'd discussed Kaisa's love of opera in their letters. Kaisa's mother had taken her and her sister, Sirkka, to see *Tosca* in Stockholm when Kaisa was only eleven years old. On that night she'd fallen in love with Italian opera. The tragic circumstances of Mimi in *La Bohème*, Violetta in *La Traviata*, or *Tosca* spoke to Kaisa in a way no modern film or TV series could. In Helsinki the opera house was so tiny, it was hard to get tickets. And she was always broke.

Kaisa squeezed Peter's hand as the lights dimmed and the first notes of Monteverdi's *L'Orfeo* were played. It was as if the Englishman had wanted her to fall in love with him again. He could not have given Kaisa a better gift than that of live opera.

ON SUNDAY, the day before her flight back to Helsinki, Peter had planned a picnic in Hyde Park. It was a windy but sunny day. Before lunch he drove Kaisa around the sights. The streets of London were quiet. She took pictures of Big Ben, the Houses of Parliament and Buckingham Palace from the passenger seat of the little yellow Spitfire. It felt like a dream to see places and buildings Kaisa had only ever read about, especially after a night when music had flooded all her senses and, at the end of the evening, the Englishman had looked her in the eyes and said, 'You've no idea how much I love you.' He kissed Kaisa long and hard. They'd been standing on a platform at Piccadilly Circus Tube station. 'I love everything about you,' he whispered into Kaisa's ear. She melted into his arms and tried not to think about how they had less than forty-eight hours left before they had to part again.

In Hyde Park they spread a blanket under a large elm. A few young boys were playing football in the distance. The vast lawns were incredibly green and even. The Englishman's efficient sister-in-law had prepared a picnic of sandwiches neatly cut into triangles and arranged into a Tupperware dish. There was a Thermos of tea and one of coffee. The cheese in the sandwiches was strong Cheddar, the pickle vinegary and salty, the ham too fatty. The weak, milky coffee was made out of instant granules. Like most Finns, Kaisa liked black, strong, percolated coffee. But she would have drunk snake's blood if she could have lived in the same country as the Englishman. It was just that, whenever she was close to him, Kaisa had no appetite. Especially when time was ticking so fast.

Lying on the blanket next to Peter, Kaisa tried not to think about the future, although this was the last day they had together. They'd not been able to make plans for the next meeting. Peter had no idea about his schedule in the Navy, Kaisa knew that much. But when he gave her a kiss and whispered hoarsely into her ear, 'I'm going to miss you so much!' Kaisa couldn't wait any longer. She took a deep breath and said, 'So, what are we going to do? About the future, I mean.'

Peter must have known what Kaisa meant, but she needed to be sure he was having the same discussion as her. Peter let go of Kaisa and lay down on the blanket. Suddenly she wished she hadn't said anything. It was as if she'd broken the spell, as if she'd veered off the written libretto and brought the opera down to earth, down to reality, down to the present day. But Kaisa couldn't bear the uncertainty. She watched the Englishman reach out for his sunglasses and speak to the blue sky above him, 'I didn't tell you, but I'm joining a submarine up in Scotland next week.' He turned to Kaisa but she couldn't see his eyes behind the dark glasses. 'And you've got two more years at university?'

'Yes,' Kaisa muttered.

Peter put his arms around her. 'If only Finland was in the EEC, then you wouldn't need a stupid work permit. You could just come and work here – in a pub or something. I'm sure someone would take you on...'

Kaisa moved away from him. She was shivering.

'Are you cold?' Peter removed his glasses and looked at her with concern. He handed Kaisa his jumper. It smelled of his American coconut shaving foam and cigarettes. Then he lent over into the pocket of his jacket and retrieved a packet of Silk Cut cigarettes, and lit one.

Kaisa was grateful for the interlude. Blood was rushing in her head and her heart was beating so hard she could hardly breathe.

Peter blew smoke out the side of his mouth. 'We'll just have to be friends.'

Kaisa looked at his long legs. They were crossed and his white trainers looked shabby all of a sudden. She couldn't look into his eyes, 'What do you mean?'

'When we're not with each other, we can be free to do whatever we want.' His tone was casual, as if he was talking about changing the make of cigarettes he smoked.

It was as if he'd hit Kaisa in the face. 'You mean we'll be free to see other people?'

There was a brief silence. Kaisa listened to the Englishman take a long, final drag on his cigarette. He stumped it out on a small stone near the trunk of the tree and flicked the end away from them. He faced Kaisa again, 'You know I love you.'

'Yeah!' Kaisa got up and turned her back to him. She started tidying the untouched sandwiches back into the container.

'Come here.'

'No.'

From the corner of her eye Kaisa saw how the Englishman lifted himself up into a sitting position. His long hands hung above his knees and he'd put his dark glasses back on. He spoke, gazing at his fingers, 'Look, this has happened to me before.'

Kaisa froze.

Peter continued, 'When I was on a commission in the Canadian navy I met this girl. She...well, we fell in love. But it didn't last. She couldn't work in Britain and I couldn't afford to go to Canada all the time. So we slowly drifted apart. It was very hard.'

Kaisa felt dizzy. She dropped the Tupperware box onto the blanket and sat down. She couldn't talk.

Peter put his arms around Kaisa. In a low whisper he said, 'I just don't want that to happen to us.'

Kaisa looked into his dark eyes, at the straight line of his mouth. She turned around and rested her head on his shoulder and twined her fingers with his strong, long ones. She wanted the world to stop here. They sat like that while Kaisa waited for the tears to come. But there weren't any.

'You OK?' Peter said.

Kaisa turned to him and heard herself say, 'Yes.'

Eleven

KAISA HAD never felt as numb as she did waiting to board her flight at Heathrow after the two weeks with the Englishman. There were just a handful of people sitting outside the gate for the Finnair flight to Helsinki. No one wanted to travel from London to 'Hel' as the label on Kaisa's luggage read. It felt like Hell was just what she was going back to.

Peter and Kaisa hadn't discussed the future since Hyde Park. Kaisa had accepted she was on the losing side. He meant more to her than she did to him. That was one fact Kaisa understood.

It served her right, she thought, as she watched a man wearing a pinstripe suit sitting opposite her read his *Financial Times*. Had Kaisa not similarly cast aside a man who was more than devoted to her? Matti's heart must have hurt as much as Kaisa's did now. What's more he'd been right all along. A foreign man, a sailor, would have a girl in every port. The Englishman didn't care for Kaisa, not in the way Matti did. But the thought of going back to her ex-boyfriend made Kaisa shudder. No, she'd have to learn to be on her own. How difficult could it be? Tuuli was on her own, she'd never had a serious boyfriend. Kaisa felt more alone, sitting on the hard plastic seats of the airport terminal, than she'd ever done in her life.

The man in the suit dropped his paper and gave Kaisa a quick smile. She looked at her watch. The flight was due to leave in five minutes. They should already be boarding, but there was no sign of an official by the gate. She felt shabby in her jeans and a jumper. She should dress more smartly and take an interest in financial matters like the man opposite. Kaisa was a student of economics after all. Instead, she sat there like a lovesick puppy.

Kaisa straightened her back and spoke to the man, 'Is the flight delayed?'

'Looks like it.' He turned a page and lifted the paper again, covering his face.

Kaisa took out her book, Thomas Hardy's *Tess of the d'Urbervilles*, but she couldn't concentrate on the text in front of her. Peter had given her the paperback, saying it was one of his favourite books. Kaisa touched her lips and remembered the long kiss he'd given her by passport control only half an hour earlier. She thought about what he would be doing now. Would he be listening to Radio One, singing along as he drove back to Portsmouth in his yellow sports car? Would he give a thought to Kaisa? On the way to the airport he told her it was the last night he'd spend with his friends in the terraced house in Portsmouth. His face had looked sad then. Kaisa wanted to shout, 'What about me? This is the last time you're going to see me too.' But she said nothing. Instead she listened to him tell her how the four friends were going to go out to the pub for a goodbye dinner.

Kaisa didn't even have a forwarding address to contact the Englishman. He'd told her only the name of the submarine he was going to join. 'I'll write to you as soon as I'm settled up there,' he'd said when they were standing outside passport control.

Kaisa had nodded.

'I promise.' Peter had cupped Kaisa's face into his hands and kissed her. 'I love you, remember that.'

Kaisa hadn't been able to speak. She gave him a last quick kiss and turned towards the man in uniform waiting to check her ticket and passport. And she didn't look back.

HELSINKI WAS cold and rainy. The leaves were already turning yellow and brown. Autumn was here. The smart Finnair bus dropped Kaisa off at Töölö Square and she heaved her heavy suitcase down the hill to Mannerheim Street. She carried her luggage onto the tram and then onto a bus, which took her to the empty flat in Lauttasaari. Kaisa ignored the pile of post, mostly bills, which she'd received while away. Instead, she dug out of her bag two LPs the Englishman had bought for her in Bath. She read *Tess of the d'Urbervilles* while she listened to all the tracks on the Christopher Cross and the Earth, Wind & Fire albums over and over.

KAISA'S LECTURES at Hanken restarted three weeks after Kaisa came back from her holiday in England. It was October and the afternoons were already turning dark in Helsinki.

On the first day of term she got up early, gathered all her bills, including the overdue rent for the flat, and headed into town. She needed to check the balance on her bank account. It was embarrassing being late with the rent, especially now she'd broken off the engagement with her ex-boyfriend. The flat belonged to his aunt after all. She'd tell his mother if Kaisa was late paying, and that would confirm all her suspicions about Kaisa's flaky personality. How unreliable she was. How she could not be depended upon. Just like her divorcee mother.

The ladies in the bank wanted to hear all about Kaisa's holiday in England. They felt responsible for the love affair with the Englishman, especially the Finnish naval officer's wife, who'd organised for her to go to the cocktail party at the British Embassy. When eventually Kaisa tore herself free from their chatter, and asked for her bank book to be updated, she stared at the black printed figures on the small page.

'What's up?' the teller who'd handed her the book asked.

'Nothing,' Kaisa said and left.

At Hanken, she headed straight for the students' advisory office.

'My grant's not been paid into my bank,' Kaisa told the lady at the desk. The woman remembered her from the first year when Kaisa had filled in the forms. There weren't many students who were eligible for a student aid grant at the Helsinki Swedish School of Economics in 1981. Most students were from well-to-do families, not from a broken home like hers.

The woman with pale-blue eyes and messy blonde hair, with grey streaks, looked at Kaisa kindly. 'I'm afraid your grant was denied.'

Kaisa was speechless.

The woman pulled out a sheet of paper and looked at it. She turned it over and pointed at a set of computer printed figures. Kaisa saw her name at the top of the sheet with perforated edges and grey faded print on pale-green-and-white-striped paper.

'You see, you only got 15 credits last term. You need a minimum of 20 to receive the funding.'

'Oh,' Kaisa lifted her eyes to the woman.

The woman tilted her head slightly and opened her mouth to say something. But she closed it again and looked down at the computer print-out.

Kaisa ran out of the office, past the common room where other students were smoking and drinking coffee. Loud chatter and laughter filled the space. She dodged the people, keeping her eyes to the ground. As she got to the door, a dark-haired guy held it open for her. Kaisa looked up and saw it was the guy who'd hit on her last year. He was looking straight at Kaisa for the first time since she turned him down. 'Thanks,' Kaisa said and quickly hurried out onto the cold street.

What was she going to do? Kaisa had ninety-seven Marks in her bank account. That would last for a month, if she was very careful. But it didn't pay for the rent, or for the electricity bill. Both were a week overdue. Kaisa didn't have a job, and even if she got one now, she wouldn't get paid until the end of the month. Besides, good jobs were hard to come by, even for fully-fledged graduates. Kaisa had only passed her first year. How would she explain that in the second year she'd passed only three exams of the eight she'd taken?

On the Number 21 bus to Lauttasaari Kaisa's dread for her future grew. What would she tell her mother? She'd been so proud when Kaisa got the letter from the School of Economics, saying she'd not only passed the entrance exam but also the language test in Swedish. This was compulsory for anyone coming from a Finnish school. Unlike the Finns with Swedish as their mother tongue, Kaisa had learned the language when she lived in Stockholm for three years. She'd been eleven when the family moved and fourteen when they returned to Finland. Kaisa had a Stockholm accent, which made her stand out at Hanken. But she really struggled with Swedish academic text. This is what she would tell her mother. As for her father, Kaisa decided not to contact him at all.

At home, Kaisa was greeted by another bill: the telephone. With dread she opened it: 36 Marks and 79 pennies. Underneath the white envelope was a blue one. A letter from the Englishman. Kaisa felt the silky texture between her fingers and tried to resist the temptation to open it. Of course, rather than the struggle with Swedish, the reason for her failure to pass any exams was the Englishman. Instead of studying, she'd been re-reading his letters over and over again, lying awake at night waiting for his calls, daydreaming at lectures, or not even turning up after a sleepless, lovesick night. When Kaisa should have been studying employment law, she was planning a holiday to England. Instead of making the most of the lectures of a visiting professor in international law, she'd been looking out of the large windows of the lecture hall, remembering the feel of the Englishman's kiss on her lips.

'When I arrived in Faslane it was snowing, can you believe that?

It is so much colder up here in Scotland, just like Helsinki. And I got off at the wrong station and had to wait for another train for ages in the freezing weather. When I finally arrived at the naval base, I met an old mate who I didn't know was also joining a submarine. Of course we had a few beers too many in the Back Bar and now I'm a bit worse for wear while writing to you, my love. I miss you so much. When I saw you walk through to the other side at Heathrow I thought my heart would break. The drive back to Pompey was horrible without you next to me wearing my Red Sox cap.'

Kaisa couldn't read on. She pulled the letter against her chest and closed her eyes. The Englishman did love her. He missed her.

Though it was a short letter, just two sides on one sheet of paper, it was powerful. He gave Kaisa a new address and said he couldn't tell her when he would call, as he didn't know when or where they would sail.

'Even if I knew, I don't think I could tell you, my darling.'

Kaisa put the letter on the little dining table and went into the kitchenette to make coffee. When she opened the tin, she noticed there was just enough for one load in the percolator. Coffee was expensive, but she'd have to go and buy some for tomorrow morning. She'd rather have coffee and starve she thought to herself ruefully. And she'd rather see the Englishman than have coffee. What a stupid, stupid girl she was.

Twelve

THE SMART new ferry smelled of carpet freshener and paint. At the end of a long ramp a large-bellied man in uniform greeted Kaisa with a smile.

'Welcome on board, Miss.'

Kaisa's arm ached from carrying the suitcase and she barely managed a grimace in return. To her relief the luggage store was close by. She placed the heavy bag on a shelf and checked she had all she needed for the overnight crossing: toiletries, a small towel and her purse. She placed the items into a small Marimekko holdall and went in search of the free bunk beds.

Fleeing Helsinki in the autumn of 1981, Kaisa felt like a refugee, escaping her unpaid rent and the wrath of her ex-boyfriend's family. When Kaisa's mother had said on the phone, 'Darling, come to Stockholm,' she didn't hesitate. She had nothing to stay for. No money, no energy to study, no boyfriend.

After the initial elation caused by the Englishman's last letter, Kaisa had begun to doubt him again. She remembered his mother's words about 'all his girlfriends' and the Englishman's own wish to remain free to see other people. However much he missed Kaisa, he didn't seem worried he might lose her to another man. Kaisa wondered whether she should write a reply, but then, the night before she was due to leave, came a phone call.

'To Stockholm, when?' Peter said.

Kaisa told him it was lucky he phoned before she left.

There was a silence.

'What if I hadn't called tonight?' he said. He sounded angry. And tired.

Kaisa didn't say anything. She wanted to seem nonchalant, but his pain was hurting her too.

'I was going to write from Stockholm,' she lied.

DURING THE overnight crossing Kaisa slept very little. She had a prawn *smörgås* and an Elefanten beer in the ship's cafeteria before turning in with a large bar of Marabou chocolate. The taste of her childhood in Sweden.

Not all the bunks in the free sleeping quarters were taken. During the middle of the night a drunk came wandering into the room and for a moment Kaisa was scared; a large man occupying a bed opposite told him to leave.

'I'll call the ship's crew,' he said.

As she lay motionless listening to the drunk's slow but loud departure, Kaisa wondered if she'd always be this poor. Too poor to afford a cabin, like the man opposite her.

Kaisa's mother embraced her at the ferry port in Stockholm. 'Your sister's at work; she'll see you tonight, and she said you can stay with her until you find a place of your own.'

Kaisa relaxed. She wasn't alone; her family would look after her.

Sirkka worked at a large hotel in the middle of the city. One night, a few days after Kaisa had arrived, Sirkka suggested Kaisa meet her after a late shift. 'The staff go out together after we close; the bars and nightclubs are open till very late in Stockholm.' Sirkka smiled at Kaisa over her mirror. She was putting on her make-up in the kitchen at a small table that folded out of the wall. The two sisters were sharing a studio flat. Sirkka had a bed in an alcove, and Kaisa slept on a corner sofa that their mother had bought when they all lived in Stockholm. It was worn out but Kaisa didn't mind. Sharing with her sister was like being teenagers again.

Sirkka had fled Helsinki three years before Kaisa. Not for money, work or studies, but an unsuitable boyfriend. She was two years older than Kaisa. They'd always been close, and spent their teenage years partying and going out together. Kaisa had missed her in Helsinki.

'Just like old times,' Sirkka now said, as if reading Kaisa's mind, and took hold of her arm. She smelled of perfume and her hair was done up in large bouncy blonde curls.

Kaisa had no money but Sirkka told her not to worry. 'Pay me back when you get a job,' she said and laughed. Her job as *maitre d'hotel* paid well.

Kaisa couldn't believe how full the bar was at half-past midnight. The music was playing loudly, and all the tables were taken. Her sister waved at a large group at the back of the room. Two empty chairs were found for them. Kaisa was introduced as Little Sister, her name from the old days. After the bar they went to a disco, and for the first time since arriving in Stockholm Kaisa felt like having fun. She danced with several of her sister's friends, as well as unknown guys who came up and asked her onto the floor. Men in Sweden were so much more approachable than in Helsinki. You could talk to them without instantly being hit on.

'It's because most of them are gay,' Sirkka laughed later in her flat. She was making sandwiches. They were listening to a new Rod Stewart LP, *Blondes Have More Fun*. It was well past 3am. The loud ringing of the phone made them both jump.

'It's the Englishman for you,' Sirkka said, handing Kaisa the receiver. The phone was sitting on a small hall table. There was no chair, so Kaisa sat down on the floor, holding the receiver close to her ear.

'I've tried your number all evening.'

'Sorry, I was out with my sister.'

'Right.'

Sirkka giggled and sang into the receiver over Kaisa's mouth: 'Do you think I'm sexy'.

Kaisa shook her head at Sirkka and she disappeared into the kitchen.

'What was that?' Peter sounded angry.

It wasn't a good phone call. The Englishman seemed cold and distant whereas Kaisa was jolly and a little drunk after such a good night out. They ended the conversation without saying, 'I love you'.

KAISA GOT a job interview with Handelsbanken, the largest bank in Sweden. The offices on the third floor on Karlaplan were bright, with desks separated by low walls. Smiling faces looked up at Kaisa as she followed a friendly woman to her desk. The office staff wore jeans, or casual trousers and tops. It was so different from the bank in Helsinki. There the staff had to wear a shirt and skirt, or a neat dress. Even on a hot summer's day, the dress code was strictly adhered to.

At the end of the interview, which she thought had gone very well, the Swedish woman closed the file on her lap and smiled at Kaisa.

'Can I give you some advice?'

Kaisa was surprised. This didn't sound like a job offer after all.

'Yes, of course.'

'I know you'd make a great employee here at Handelsbanken. And I could quite easily give you the job, and I know you'd be good at it. But...' the woman hesitated for a moment and looked at Kaisa, 'I'd do you a disservice if I didn't turn you down and tell you to go back to Finland to finish your studies.'

Kaisa looked down at her hands.

'This is what you wanted to hear, isn't it?'

Truth was Kaisa didn't know what she wanted. The past two weeks in Stockholm had been wonderful. The Englishman had phoned nearly every night after that first awful conversation. He'd told Kaisa he loved her, and missed her. Each time she wanted to ask why he'd said what he had in Hyde Park, but couldn't. She didn't have the words.

When Kaisa told her mother what the woman in Handelsbanken had said, she took her daughter's hands into hers.

'You think she might be right?'

EXACTLY THREE weeks after the ferry crossing to Stockholm, Kaisa was on her way back in the opposite direction. This time she'd decided to make the journey during the day, and together with a good book, the hours sped past. As she watched the ferry dock at South Harbour jetty Kaisa hoped she'd made the right decision in returning to Helsinki and her studies.

Kaisa had no doubts about this until she saw her father waiting for her just inside the ferry terminal. He didn't smile; just bear-hugged her and took hold of her heavy suitcase.

'We'd better get you into the car then,' he sighed and walked ahead of Kaisa into the already dark Helsinki afternoon.

Kaisa's father, who had two daughters, used to call Kaisa 'My Best Girl'. As she grew up, his obvious favouritism became a burden to her rather than a source of pride. When Kaisa's parents finally split up after years of fighting, it was a relief to both of their two daughters.

Kaisa's parents allowed the girls to choose which side to take when Sirkka was fifteen and Kaisa thirteen. They sat the girls on the plush velveteen sofa and asked them in turn who they wanted live with.

Kaisa's father didn't take the rejection well. 'You've made your bed. There's no more money from me.' He stormed out. That night he came home drunk again.

On returning from Sweden, Kaisa had no choice but to go and live with her father. In spite of the threats, over the last few years he'd occasionally invited his two daughters to lunch. As they parted, he always handed over a few dark-purple 100 Mark notes. When Kaisa told him she was going to study at Hanken, he gave her a small allowance. And when Kaisa eventually phoned him from Stockholm he promised her a temporary home in his house in Espoo, a town of suburbs just outside Helsinki. Of course, Kaisa hesitated, but her mother said, 'It's about time he took some responsibility for at least one of his daughters.'

The Englishman on the phone from Scotland couldn't understand what the problem was, 'But he's your father?'

Kaisa couldn't tell him about the drinking or the violence.

At Hanken, Kaisa was greeted with a hug from Tuuli. 'Coming back to study is absolutely the best decision you could have made.'

The blonde-haired woman at the students' advisory office agreed. 'Why don't you change your subject? Commercial law is a difficult one to specialise in, especially as Swedish is not your mother tongue.' Her kind eyes were fixed on Kaisa. 'The next committee meeting is early December. If you get two exam passes by then, we can re-approve your grant.'

Kaisa became a student of political science at the School of Economics. She lost a year by changing subjects, but her new department was small and homely. She studied the theories of Karl Marx, as well as those of Keynes, and her horizons were widened. While the other students at the university learned how to make money, or account for it, Kaisa's new department taught her the principles behind the desire for wealth and power.

At the house in Espoo, Kaisa's father got drunk rarely now. He'd given up his bedroom for her and was mostly staying over at his new girlfriend's flat in Töölö. Kaisa cooked for him when he was at home, and when he was in a good mood he made *gravad lax*.

While Kaisa tried to forget about the Englishman, his letters wouldn't allow it. He wrote at least once a week and called when he was on dry land. Most often he was away with the submarine, to unknown destinations, for weeks on end, and the letters would dry up.

Then one night, she was woken up with a phone call.

'We've just sailed in, and I've been told I can take leave for Christmas. Can you come to England?'

Kaisa's grant came through in December and if she continued to live with her father she'd be able to afford the fare. She told the Englishman she'd think about it, but Kaisa knew what her decision would be.

At Hanken, Tuuli shook her head. 'Are you sure that's wise? You remember what happened last time you came home from England?' They were standing in the semi-darkness of the Students' Union disco in the centre of Helsinki. After her return from Stockholm, Kaisa and Tuuli had started going out again, most often to 'Ladies' Nights' on Mondays. The disco was full of students from all the Helsinki universities, but mostly students from Hanken. The rich boys were always there, and Kaisa would see them laughing and gazing at her and Tuuli. Kaisa often wondered what would have happened if she'd agreed to go with Tom. Would he now be arm in arm with her instead of the tall red-haired girl he was with that week.

'Look who's here again,' Kaisa now said, turning her head away when the guy looked in her direction. 'Do you think I should have gone out with him that first week?'

'No,' Tuuli said, 'you know exactly what would have happened. He would have fucked you and that's that. It's what they do: as many as possible in as little time as possible.'

Kaisa laughed. But was this what all men were like? Was the Englishman like that too? Was he only so loving and seemingly committed to her because he was lonely up in Faslane, or Faslavatory, as he called it? Where he said there were no pubs or clubs. In other words, no places to meet girls?

When Kaisa got home that night, there was another call.

‘Well, are we going to meet up at Christmas?’

‘Of course we are.’

Kaisa could hear the Englishman take a deep breath, ‘That means I’ll see you in only two weeks’ time!’

Thirteen

WHILE IN Stockholm Kaisa had discovered a company called Fritidsresor, which organised chartered trips from Sweden to London. If she travelled by ferry to Stockholm, a week in a cheap hotel in London, with flights, cost half of a Finnair airfare from Helsinki to Heathrow.

The Englishman said he'd never been to Stansted. When Kaisa arrived, he was the only person meeting the plane full of Swedish tourists, apart from an efficient travel guide wearing a red and yellow shirt and holding a clipboard above her head.

'Stockholm passengers please report to me,' she shouted in her singing Swedish.

Kaisa made her way up to her and said, 'I'm going to be staying with a friend, so I don't need transport to the hotel.'

The tour guide glanced sideways at Peter and crossed Kaisa's name off a list. 'Make sure you're not late for the flight's departure,' she said and flicked her blonde hair.

Kaisa ran into the Englishman's arms. He smelt of the cold outside air. He gave her a long kiss. 'God, I've missed you.'

The airport was at the end of a narrow road that followed the perimeter fence of the runway. With the roof up, the yellow Triumph Spitfire was cosy and warm.

'We're going to my parents for Christmas and then Pompey for New Year, OK?' The Englishman reached over and squeezed Kaisa's thigh. 'We'll be there in about three hours.'

Kaisa relaxed into the low seat and closed her eyes. This time she'd been even more nervous about coming to see the Englishman than last summer. But as soon as she saw him, and felt his lips on hers, all that was said at the end of the last visit seemed like a bad dream. Had the Englishman really told her he wanted to be free to date other people? His letters since, and his behaviour now, were even more passionate and loving than before. It was as if they were a real couple, not just two singles meeting up for occasional sex.

Peter's mother embraced Kaisa warmly. She made a cup of sweet, milky tea and placed a slice of strongly spiced fruit cake in front of Kaisa. The kitchen smelt of her baking. The Englishman sat across the table and smiled while her mother fussed over Kaisa. She didn't dare to say she didn't like tea, milk, or fruit cake, and tried to sip the hot, sickly drink.

Kaisa heard the front door open. The Englishman's sister walked into the kitchen. Nancy kissed Kaisa lightly on both cheeks and sat down. She was dressed smartly in a navy blue skirt and a white blouse. Nancy was seven years older than Peter and had the same dark features, with her eyebrows plucked into a neat shape and her eyes made up with a discreet pale blue. Kaisa hadn't met her before but had seen pictures of her in the house. Her smile was friendly when she looked from Kaisa to her brother.

'I bet you two love birds are glad to see each other at last,' Nancy said and sat down at the kitchen table. Peter's mother had her back to them, making more tea.

Kaisa blushed and the Englishman shifted uncomfortably in his chair. There'd been no time to make love yet. Their yearning to touch each other was overwhelming. It was as if Nancy had sensed it.

Then with immaculate timing, Peter's mother said, 'I've put you in the blue room.'

Kaisa looked from her to the Englishman. Her face felt hot.

'Let's get your things from the car.' Peter got up abruptly and took hold of Kaisa's hand. He led her out of the kitchen. Outside, he kissed Kaisa behind the open boot of the car. 'They've agreed to let us sleep in the same room.'

Kaisa relaxed her body against his. He held her and whispered into her ear, 'The things I'm going to do to you tonight...'

ON CHRISTMAS Eve morning, Peter said, 'I need to do some shopping.'

Kaisa was surprised. He hadn't bought all his presents yet? Peter drove into the nearest town, bought some scented soap for his mother and a book for his father. Then he took Kaisa into a pub on the corner of the High Street. It turned out to be a bar in a hotel and full of people and noise. A large-chested woman approached the Englishman, embraced him and kissed him on the lips.

'How are you, darling?' She was holding a drink and a cigarette above the heads of the other revellers. Her complicated hair-do had ash blonde streaks. A few curly strands fell around her face.

Peter introduced her, 'This is a friend of my sister's.'

'So at last I get to meet the famous foreign girl!' The woman let her gaze wander from Kaisa's high-heeled boots to her tight jeans and cream satin blouse.

'She's very pretty,' she said, and winked at Peter. 'No wonder you're smitten.'

Kaisa could feel her cheeks redden and she lowered her eyes to the floor.

IN FINLAND, Christmas Eve was celebrated with a church service followed by a meal of special Christmas foods, which used to take

Kaisa's mother weeks to prepare. When Kaisa and her sister were small they were allowed to watch a little television, but the highlight of the evening was the arrival of Father Christmas. It would either be their father dressed in his sheepskin jacket turned inside out and wearing a false beard, or one of the professional Father Christmases who roamed the streets on Christmas Eve, going from one household to the next. He brought a sack full of presents for Kaisa and Sirkka and the grown-ups had a drink or two while the two girls played with the toys. But no one went out to a restaurant, or a bar. Even visitors were discouraged until Boxing Day.

Kaisa couldn't believe how different the celebrations were in England.

'Everyone goes out on Christmas Eve,' the Englishman said, 'and then you end up with a hangover on Christmas morning,' he laughed.

Peter and Kaisa exchanged presents on Christmas morning in the privacy of the Blue Room. When she later told Sirkka about their gifts for each other, Sirkka smiled. 'So sweet and so Freudian!' Kaisa hadn't even seen the connection, and was embarrassed; she'd bought the Englishman a leather wallet and he gave her a fountain pen.

On Christmas morning the English house was busy. The rooms were decorated with glittery paper streamers, balloons and tinsel. At around ten, Peter's sister Nancy and her boyfriend arrived, followed by his brother and sister-in-law, who'd driven down from London that morning. His mother was rushing from one room to another, wearing an old-fashioned pinny, waving a tea towel, laughing. One by one the guests arrived for drinks. Soon the large sitting room was filled with cigarette smoke and noise. Kaisa was shy at first, but slowly relaxed when Peter introduced her to the various family friends. Then suddenly, as if by previous agreement, the room emptied and the guests departed, wishing one another a 'Happy Christmas'.

Now there was a rush to get the food to the table. Kaisa had never seen so many kinds of vegetables, roasted, boiled or mashed. The gravy was dark and juicy, and the turkey slices large and white. She felt drunk, but the Englishman poured more wine into her glass.

'It's Christmas,' he said and kissed her cheek.

Everyone around the table smiled at Kaisa.

'How do you like Christmas in England?' the Englishman's father asked. His dark eyes had a spark to them Kaisa hadn't seen before. He too was a little tipsy.

'I like it very much,' she said.

He patted Kaisa's hand. 'We like having you here.' He nodded to his son in the seat next to Kaisa. Peter put his arm around Kaisa's shoulders and squeezed her closer. Kaisa looked through the French windows at the well-tended garden with its green lawn and wondered if being this happy would make up for the lack of snow, or a little quietness, at Christmas.

KAISA WAS back in Finland, at her father's place on a Monday morning in January. She was tired from the travelling. First the late night flight from London, then the overnight ferry from Stockholm. She'd hardly slept on the free bunk bed, even though it had been a quiet crossing.

Kaisa's father was at work when she arrived home. She wondered if he'd forgotten she was coming back that day, because there was no food in the fridge. Perhaps he hadn't been home since Christmas, which Kaisa knew he'd spent with his girlfriend in Töölö. To think of her as a girlfriend seemed strange. She was so much older than her, and yet unmarried. A spinster. Kaisa sat in the kitchen and looked at the thick covering of snow outside. There was a sharp northerly wind and people passing by were huddled against it. She went to bed and put on the cassette the Englishman had given her. The words of '*Every Little Thing She Does Is Magic*' by The Police rang in her ears, just as they'd been sung to her by the Englishman on New Year's Eve. She could still smell his coconut shaving cream on her clothes. Kaisa curled up on her bed and slept.

Kaisa woke up to the telephone. 'I'm coming home later. Is there any food?'

'Happy New Year, Dad.'

'Yes, well, Happy New Year to you, too. So, I guess I have to go to the shop?'

Kaisa put the phone down and went back to sleep. She was so tired she didn't even care about her father's veiled criticism. Or that he obviously thought Kaisa a nuisance. She'd be gone soon enough, and when she left she'd never see him again.

Peter phoned in the evening. 'I love you so much. I can't bear to be without you.'

Kaisa held the receiver close to her ear and listened to his breathing. Her father had been home, eaten some shop-bought raw herring and beetroot salad straight from the plastic container, and then left again. Kaisa was glad to be alone.

'Me too.'

'Listen, I haven't got much time to talk. But, I've got news.'

'Yes?'

'I've just bought a flight to Helsinki!'

Kaisa sat bolt upright and listened in stunned silence. The Englishman was coming to see her in February. 'That means we'll see each other…'

'In just five weeks!' The Englishman was jubilant. Kaisa could hear the laughter in his voice.

Kaisa's father's face fell when she told him the news the next day. 'What, he's coming here?'

'I suppose we could go and stay with mum in Stockholm,' Kaisa said. She was wringing her hands, but stopped and folded them over her chest instead.

'How did that woman manage to get a place big enough for you two to stay?' Kaisa sighed and ignored her father. She wished she hadn't mentioned her mother. They were sitting eating at the kitchen table. Kaisa had made meat balls with a creamy sauce, boiled potatoes and courgettes. He looked at the green vegetables, 'What's this?'

'It's good for you.'

He reached out for the salt and sprinkled it liberally over the food. 'Just like your mother, can't season food.'

Kaisa looked down at her plate and bit her lip.

After a while he asked, 'When is he coming then?'

Eventually Kaisa's father agreed to stay at his girlfriend's place for the week when the Englishman would be in Helsinki.

'But I do want to meet him.'

Kaisa looked up at her father. His pale-blue eyes were serious. For a fleeting moment she could see her old dad, the one who called her 'My Best Girl', and who took her to the park and let her sit on his knee and stroke the soft flesh of his earlobe.

He got up from the table, leaving his plate with the uneaten courgette on it. He belched loudly.

Kaisa looked away.

'I'll teach him how to drink vodka,' he said and left the kitchen. Kaisa heard him sit down heavily in the TV room. 'You tell that Englishman there's no point in coming to Finland unless he's prepared to drink like a man,' he shouted over the noise of the TV.

THE ENGLISHMAN didn't seem at all fazed by the idea of meeting Kaisa's father. 'You've met all my family,' he said and put his arm around Kaisa. He'd just arrived from London and they were walking up from Mannerheim Street tram stop to the bus station to catch the Number 105 to Espoo.

It was strange to meet up so quickly again, after only five weeks, rather than the many months they'd endured without each other before. With Peter's lean, taut body next to her, Kaisa was relaxed and comfortable, chatting about what she'd planned for the week. Again she felt as if they were a real couple. Had she imagined his doubts in Hyde Park? He put his hands inside Kaisa's coat to warm them from the bitter cold of the late February afternoon. When he kissed her in full view of the other people queuing for the bus, she couldn't imagine he'd be with anyone else. But Kaisa couldn't ask. She couldn't even bring up the subject of 'The Future'. She was afraid he'd repeat what he'd said to her last summer. If he did that, Kaisa would surely die. She'd never want to see him again and that alone would kill her. Never mind what the failed relationship would do to Kaisa's ex-fiancé, who still phoned her on any pretext, asking, 'Are you still running after that foreign sailor?'

The cellar of Kaisa's father's place had a sauna with a pool, shared by a couple of other houses in the development. Kaisa had booked it for that first evening.

'I didn't bring my swimming trunks.' Peter stood in his underpants in the middle of the small changing room. After all they'd done in bed, was he shy? Kaisa pulled her top off, and stripped down to nothing.

'Ah,' Peter said. He dropped his pants and followed Kaisa into the hot, darkened sauna.

After a few moments, when their bodies were used to the heat, Kaisa threw water on the coals.

'This is called a *löyly*.'

Peter made a sound and ducked. The steam filled the space and the lovely prickly feeling of the heat touched Kaisa's body. Like all Finns, she loved the sauna. When Kaisa was only three days old her father took her into the sauna in their summer cottage by the lake. Kaisa enjoyed the heat so much they called her the 'sauna baby'.

'You OK?' she said to the Englishman. He was almost doubled over on the bench next to her.

'Yeah, just a bit hot.'

'Sorry, we'll go for a swim to cool down.' Kaisa took Peter into the pool, ignoring his protests about not having any clothes on, 'There's no one there!'

They swam in the cool water of the swimming pool then went back to the warm sauna.

'I feel wonderful,' Peter said after they'd had a few more rounds of *löyly* followed by another swim in the cold pool. Kaisa smiled. She'd make a Finn out of this Englishman yet.

Peter and Kaisa met her father at a Russian restaurant called Saslik. Kaisa had never been there, but her father had said, 'She likes it,' and Kaisa realised he was going to bring his girlfriend.

The place was decorated with dark-red and blue colours, the tablecloths looked like satin, the wallpaper velvet. Lamps were slung low over the tables. As they sat down, Kaisa'a father nodded to an unseen waiter who brought a round of clear vodka.

'To the Finnish ladies,' Kaisa's father said and lifted his glass.

His girlfriend, whose name, Kaisa had learned for the first time earlier that evening, was Marja, giggled. Kaisa took a sip of her schnapps, the girlfriend drank half of hers and both the Englishman and Kaisa's father emptied their glasses. Kaisa's father's eyes did not leave Peter's face. The waiter came around with the bottle to refill the glasses. Kaisa's father nodded to the man, who was dressed in an old-fashioned Cossack's outfit, to leave the bottle of *Koskenkorva* on the table. Kaisa glanced over to the Englishman at her side. Peter put his hand on her knee under the table and gave it a gentle squeeze.

'I'm fine,' he whispered in Kaisa's ear.

'So, you like vodka?' Kaisa's father said, addressing the Englishman, and lifted his glass again.

They hadn't even looked at the menus yet.

Everyone got very drunk very quickly. But no one fell under the table. No one said a cross word or had an argument. Kaisa's father didn't even mention her mother. The food was excellent. Beetroot soup, rare spiced beef with dark sauce, garlicky potatoes, cabbage of some kind. They laughed a lot. Kaisa's father bought two long-stemmed red roses, one for Marja and one for Kaisa. He wanted them all to go dancing together. When Peter and Kaisa decided to leave instead, he looked sad and embraced them both warmly.

'I think I passed,' the Englishman laughed outside the restaurant. Kaisa's father had insisted on giving them money for a taxi and got the Cossack to order it for them.

It was as if the past ten years hadn't happened. It was as if the Englishman had resurrected Kaisa's old father. During the evening he'd even called Kaisa 'My Best Girl' again. Kaisa curled up against Peter on the leather seat of the taxi and fell asleep.

PETER'S VISIT coincided with the annual Hanken Ball. Tuuli wanted to know if the Englishman was going to wear his uniform, but he had told Kaisa on the phone from Faslane that this wasn't allowed. She'd been a little disappointed but thought it must have something to do with the Cold War, and Finland being so close to the Soviet Union. Not that she could see anyone in Helsinki being interested in her British submarine sub-lieutenant.

On the night, Peter looked so handsome in his DJ, just as he did in his uniform at the British Embassy cocktail party all those years ago, that Kaisa didn't mind. Kaisa wore a ball gown, made by an old school friend. It was a strapless white silk dress, with a narrow black belt, which tied with a small bow at the back of the waist. The long ends fell behind her.

This was Kaisa's first university ball, but the Englishman had been to many black tie events during his time at Dartmouth and since. But he said none were quite like this one. According to the Hanken tradition, long tables were served rounds and rounds of schnapps, which were consumed to various drinking songs. There was a Drinks Master, who led the proceedings, and towards the end of the evening some of the top table climbed onto the table to sing. One of them was the Finnish Foreign Minister. He was there without his famous wife this time.

But the Englishman didn't just watch the other people in the room. He took Kaisa to the dance floor. She floated in his arms. She wanted everyone to see, especially the gang of rich boys, how in love they were. Back at the table Peter turned to Kaisa and said, 'You're beautiful, did you know that?' She smiled and felt his warm hands around hers. He looked at Kaisa intently. She burned under his gaze. 'Can I ask you something?' he said.

'Of course.' Kaisa felt out of breath. Was he going to talk to me about 'The Future'?

'Will you marry me?'

Fourteen

KAISA FELT a tap on her shoulder. Tuuli's face looked serious. 'Bathroom, now!'

Kaisa smiled at Peter, 'Sorry, I'll be back.'

He looked surprised but Kaisa didn't have time. Tuuli was already dragging her away from the table. They made their way through the throng of people on the dance floor and passed the bar where Kaisa's eyes met with the rich boy who'd asked her out. He lifted his glass as if to toast Kaisa. He'd loosened his black bow tie and undone the top button of his shirt. He was leaning casually against the bar, with the drink in one hand and a cigarette in the other. Kaisa smiled confidently back at him. She was so happy she didn't care what he thought.

'Guess what?' Kaisa said once they were inside the gleaming ladies' room. The Hanken Ball was held in a smart private club in the centre of Helsinki. Kaisa had never been inside before. Every room was decorated in a thirties art deco style, with black marble and shining chrome. Absentmindedly, she wondered how they could keep a bathroom so clean all the time. Tuuli looked at Kaisa through the mirror where she'd started adjusting her make-up.

'Peter asked me to marry him!' Kaisa said.

Tuuli dropped her hand, 'What?'

'Just now. Isn't it wonderful?'

'What about your studies?' Tuuli's face was blank, unsmiling.

Kaisa looked down at her hands. It was as if she'd splashed cold water over her face from the shiny white sink. 'Yes, I know, I'm not going to drop out – again – but isn't it...'

'Have you ever read Doris Lessing's *The Perfect Marriage*?

'Well, no...'

'I'll lend you the book.' Tuuli turned back to face the vast mirror. She was dabbing at her make-up while tears ran down her face, smudging it further.

Suddenly Kaisa remembered she'd dragged her to the ladies' for a reason. 'What's the matter?'

'He's dancing with another girl!'

'Who?'

Her friend shot Kaisa an accusing glance, 'The Incredible Hulk. I saw them smooching before and just now I saw him kiss her. On the mouth!'

Tuuli's new boyfriend had an incredibly strong physique, and with his spiky dark hair he looked just like the cartoon character. The Hulk was her partner at the ball. Kaisa knew she was really smitten with him, although she said she no longer believed in love.

'The worst of it is, I know her,' Tuuli said between short sobs. Kaisa couldn't believe her eyes. She'd never seen her friend so upset about anything. Especially not about men. 'We went to school together,' Tuuli continued, after she'd blown her nose, 'but she didn't get into Hanken. No brains.'

Kaisa hugged her friend. 'She's a bitch.'

Tuuli nodded and took a deep breath in. 'They can both go to hell. I was getting bored with the Hulk anyway.'

Kaisa watched her friend make up her face again and give a fake smile at the mirror. She thought how strong Tuuli was; how she would never have coped with a betrayal like that.

'How did the bitch get in anyway?'

Tuuli looked down at her purse. 'I think she came as someone else's avec.' She straightened her back and looked at Kaisa, 'But I don't want to talk about it anymore. Let's go back.'

The two friends walked out of the ladies' and through a set of double doors. Suddenly Tuuli turned around and, facing Kaisa, said, 'But, you must promise me that you'll not marry the Englishman. You can't just become someone's wife. You have to finish your studies.'

Kaisa looked at the eager face of her friend. She knew Tuuli was right. Kaisa had been to England; she'd seen how difficult it was to get a job. She didn't want to end up being a barmaid in a pub somewhere. Or worse, have no job at all, and become a Navy wife, bringing up the kids singlehandedly while her husband was away at sea.

'I promise.' Kaisa took Tuuli's hands into hers. They felt cold.

Tuuli nodded and they walked back into the vast dining room.

Peter was sitting just as Kaisa had left him, with one elbow on the table and holding a cigarette. He stubbed it out and got up.

His politeness broke her heart. No Finnish boy would even have known that's what you do when a lady comes back to the table.

'Everything alright?' he said.

'It's a long story.' Kaisa watched as her friend made her way to the other side of the long table. She was glad to see she had another boy, a mutual friend, to talk to. There was no sign of the Hulk.

Peter's gaze was steady on Kaisa. She knew he was waiting for an answer. He took Kaisa's hands into his. She felt trapped and had a sudden desire to pull away from his grasp. She lifted her eyes to him. His dark eyes were wide, his mouth set in a straight line.

'I still have a year and a half left at university,' she said quietly.

The Englishman let go of Kaisa's hands. He leant back in the chair. 'I thought you might say that.' But he was smiling. He gave her a light kiss. The Drinks Master had climbed onto the table. It was time for another drinking song.

When the Englishman left after his week-long visit, Kaisa was heartbroken, but didn't cry. Clutching the red rose he'd bought her at the airport – it was a tradition now – Kaisa sat in the Finnair bus back to her father's place in Espoo, full of determination to do well in her studies at Hanken. She was enjoying her new subject. Learning about political systems, about the workings of the labour market and about the intricacies of parliamentary democracy was a pleasure. And she was safe in the knowledge that the Englishman was serious about their relationship. Kaisa kept thinking: the sooner I get my degree, the sooner we can be together. Though they hadn't expressly said it, Kaisa knew she would have to move to England. Not a big deal. She'd moved countries before and didn't want to stay in Finland, anyhow.

The house was cold and quiet when Kaisa got back. Her father was at home, sitting in a dark room with a bottle of *Koskenkorva* vodka next to him.

'Gone then, has he?' he asked. Kaisa heard the familiar sarcasm in his voice and knew better than to answer. It was in these Jekyll and Hyde moments that she feared him most, so she went into her room, locked the door and put on the latest cassette the Englishman had brought with him. She decided to begin reading Karl Marx's *Das Kapital* for an assignment due in the following week.

Fifteen

AS SPRING arrived, and the snow slowly melted in the small patch of land outside the living room, Kaisa's workload at Hanken grew. Tuuli was still very upset about the Hulk and had immersed herself in her studies. She'd lent Kaisa all of her Doris Lessing books and Kaisa had fallen in love with Lessing's writing. Kaisa had never read a writer whose view of the world was so much like her own.

Kaisa found an old bike in the communal cellar next to the sauna compartment and her father said she could use it. When the weather was a little warmer she cycled to see an old school friend, Tanja, who'd started at Hanken a year after her. She lived with her parents a kilometre away; they'd sit in her bedroom and talk about university, men and fathers. Occasionally Kaisa would go out but she had little money or time.

Peter wrote as often as he could, and phoned when he wasn't at sea. But he was at sea most of the time, now, it seemed.

During that spring, Kaisa's third year at university, she spent a lot of time at the Hanken library, reading or borrowing books too expensive to buy. It was situated at the top of a modern office building, with one lift constantly ferrying students up and down.

The staircase, which was only used when absolutely necessary, was the library smoking room, while the library was the meat market. You could pick up a date for the evening, much like a book you needed. Needless to say, the rich boys spent most of their afternoons in the library. The guy who'd asked Kaisa out now ignored her. If she passed his desk, on which his legs were invariably sprawled, he pretended to examine the text in a book and would not look at her. But if she turned around abruptly she'd catch him assessing her rear. But Kaisa didn't care about him. After all, the Englishman had proposed to her. And she'd see him in April. This time they were going to meet in Stockholm, where Sirkka had promised they could use her flat for the week. Kaisa couldn't wait to show the Englishman her second hometown. Besides, spring would be so much further along there; the city would be filled with greenery, with Easter decorations and sunshine, and it would be the very opposite of grey, cold, windy Helsinki.

On the 3rd of April 1982 Kaisa got a phone call at 3am. 'We've declared war.' Peter's voice sounded grave.

'I know.' Kaisa had seen it on the news, how the mighty United Kingdom, a former colonial power, had been humiliated by a small South American dictatorship. Still, she'd been amazed that they declared a war, in the 1980s.

'It happened on my birthday.'

Kaisa realised the Englishman had had a drink.

'And they've cancelled all leave, I mean ALL leave.'

Kaisa sat down on the floor next to the phone. 'Does that mean..?'

'I can't come to Stockholm.'

The Falkland Islands, a small group of islands Kaisa had never heard of, somewhere off the coast of Argentina, was spoiling her plans to see the Englishman. How could this be? Absurdly she asked, 'What about the flight?'

'Act of War is force majeure. I'm in the Royal Navy; I'll get all my money back.'

Act of War. That was all Kaisa could think about. 'Are you…?'

There was a silence at the other end.

'I mean, are they going to send you to…'

The Englishman interrupted her. 'Please don't ask. I can't say.'

The Englishman didn't tell Kaisa if he went to war. During the Falklands conflict they spoke very rarely. Kaisa felt isolated.

Even his letters dried up.

Kaisa tried to concentrate on her studies and spent most of her time in the Hanken library. As the main pick-up spot, it was ever busier. She kept bumping into Tom in the lift, or on the landing where he'd stand leaning against the steel banister, taking long drags on a cigarette. Once, when Kaisa and Tuuli were chatting in the stairwell, he came out alone from the library and was so startled to see them that he stopped dead. His worn-out leather jacket was undone, and his dark-brown hair flopped over his eyes.

When Tom finally moved away from the door and pressed for the lift, the devil in Kaisa said, 'Can I have a light?' She dangled a cigarette between her fingers. He stared at her for a moment then lit a match and held it in his cupped hands. They were shaking.

Tuuli and Kaisa couldn't look at each other until they heard the lift stop at the ground floor and the outside door open. They both burst out laughing at the same time.

'He's still got the hots for you, you know,' Tuuli said, growing serious. 'I can't believe what I just saw!'

In the bus on the way home Kaisa thought about the rich boy, or rather, man. She and Tuuli had worked out Tom must be at least 26. But the guy intrigued her; Kaisa couldn't help it. She had so little contact with the Englishman she was beginning to forget how his lips tasted when he kissed her. They hadn't seen each other for three months. No one in Finland understood what it meant to have the Englishman at sea, not knowing whether he was involved in the war or not. If a British submarine was lost to the Argentine navy, would Thatcher let the world know about it? Kaisa doubted it. Eventually his parents would be told if anything happened to him, but would they think about letting Kaisa know? They'd be too grief-stricken to even think of anyone else. Had the Englishman told his mother about the proposal? How Kaisa now wished she'd said 'yes' on that magical night at the ball. At least then she'd have an official role in relation to her love, and a right to know if the Englishman's submarine had been sunk.

Kaisa's father was the least sympathetic of all. 'You should find yourself a good Finnish man.' He seemed to have forgotten the night at the Russian restaurant. Kaisa wondered what had caused this change of heart, but wasn't surprised. He'd always been like it: one day he'd say one thing, the next the complete opposite. For the past few weeks he'd spent all his evenings and weekends at home, mostly in a bad mood. Kaisa wondered if he'd had a row with his girlfriend, but didn't dare to ask.

Kaisa was in limbo. She was confused. She was lonely.

The night the news of the sinking of the *Belgrano* was shown on TV, Kaisa's father had been drinking vodka all evening. The bottle of *Koskenkorva* stood on the floor next to his chair. The Finnish newscaster didn't say if there were any British casualties, but who'd know if British submarines were involved? Kaisa had seen enough war movies to know subs hunted ships in packs. She sat on the plush sofa and watched the pictures move in silence. Involuntarily, she put a hand against her mouth. Her father narrowed his eyes and glanced sideways at his daughter.

'You know the Englishman is not there!'

Kaisa ran out of the living room. She cried into her pillow, trying to keep quiet. And then the phone rang. Kaisa heard her father answer. He said, 'Just a moment,' in English.

Kaisa ran out into the hall and took the receiver from him.

'Hello?'

To hear Peter's voice! It sounded as if he was far, far away, but Kaisa knew better than to ask where he was calling from. She sobbed into the telephone; she couldn't help herself.

'What's the matter?'

'Nothing, I was just watching the news, and I didn't know...'

'I'm fine, except I'm missing you.'

Kaisa sighed and sat on the floor in the hall. They spoke for over twenty minutes. Kaisa cried, laughed and whispered into the receiver, not caring how much of it her father heard. When the Englishman said he had to go, Kaisa told him she loved him once more, put the receiver down and walked quickly to her room. Kaisa fell asleep dreaming of her handsome Englishman.

IT WASN'T until June that year of the Falkland's War, in 1982, that Kaisa finally managed to see the Englishman. They'd been apart for four long months, during which she'd feared for her submariner's life her every waking hour. Peter telephoned her very rarely. When the news of the sinking of the HMS *Sheffield* came, she didn't sleep until she had a letter confirming Peter was OK. How, during those war months, Kaisa wished she'd had someone she could call, someone who would understand what she was going through. Instead Kaisa tried to study hard, and by the end of the term she'd passed all her exams with good marks.

Watching the Englishman collect his bag through the glass wall of the arrivals hall at Helsinki airport, Kaisa thought about the two years she'd spent waiting for his letters and phone calls, counting the days until she'd be able to lean against his body again. It seemed strange how her life had changed so dramatically, and so quickly, at the British Embassy cocktail party in October 1980. Before the handsome British naval officer had come over and talked to Kaisa, her path had seemed settled, planned even. She was going to complete her studies, marry her boyfriend, move into a flat bought by his mother in her leafy area of Helsinki. As long as Kaisa didn't upset his mother, she had nothing to worry about. And, of course, the mother and Matti had wanted Kaisa to produce grandchildren, three to be exact.

Instead, she now stood in the deserted arrivals hall, nervously waiting for her Englishman to see her, with no idea what the next year would bring let alone the next month, week or even day.

It was a hot, sunny afternoon, two days before midsummer. In Finland the third Friday in June marks the start of the holidays. Everybody flees Helsinki for the weekend, to go somewhere by the sea, lake or forest. Most stay away for two or three weeks, leaving the city quiet and dusty. Kaisa had booked a room at a lakeside hotel an hour's train journey from town. Her parents had taken the family there when Kaisa was little. It was an all-inclusive package, which Kaisa's father, uncharacteristically, had paid for.

'Show the Englishman how beautiful Finland is,' he'd said.

On the Finnair bus home from the airport, with the air conditioning on full blast, making Kaisa shiver in her thin cotton dress, Peter didn't seem impressed with the plans.

'We're going where?' he demanded.

Kaisa tried to explain, but he just sat next to her on the bus seat, holding her hand, with his face turned away from her, towards the front of the bus. Kaisa looked at his profile, at the dark stubble on his chin. 'Don't you want to go?' she asked nervously.

Peter turned his eyes to Kaisa and kissed her lightly on the lips, 'Of course I do. No problem, let's do it.' But he didn't sound at all sure.

The Rantasipi Aulanko wasn't as Kaisa remembered it. The vast, low-ceilinged lobby was shabby. There was a large mark on the carpet right by the reception desk. The small room, for which a surly woman at reception had handed Kaisa a key, had two single beds arranged head to toe.

When Peter saw the beds he laughed. Kaisa wanted to cry. Instead she went to open the curtains of a large window at the end of the room and saw what they'd come for. The lake, Vanajavesi, opened up in front of her. The sun, still high up in the afternoon sky, was blinding.

Kaisa went to hug Peter and tried to kiss him, but he turned away to put his bag down.

'Let's go, I'll show you around.' she said, grabbing Peter's hand.

***

KAISA WAS eleven when her father took the whole family to have lunch at the newly-built Rantasipi Hotel. It was a drive away from Tampere, on the edge of the Häme National Park, and it was Mother's Day. The dining room was a square space with a high ceiling and large windows, which reached down to the floor; the buffet was laid out on a long table, the various dishes on a crisp, white linen tablecloth. As she led the Englishman through the park to the hotel, Kaisa wondered if the restaurant would also look shabby to her now.

Peter was still very quiet. When they first kissed at the airport, it felt the same as before. When they'd made love that night, it had felt the same as before. But today he had hardly touched Kaisa. Perhaps he really didn't want to come to this place with her. When Kaisa felt a few drops of rain fall onto her bare arms, she began to regret the whole idea herself. She ran into an old, circular-shaped summer house, with chipped paintwork, and sat on a half-rotting bench to wait out the light shower. The warm summer rain fell softly against the old pointed roof. Kaisa felt close to tears. Even the weather connived to spoil the Englishman's week in Finland. Why had she not consulted him before booking this midsummer package? Kaisa looked at Peter's straight back. He was leaning against the railing looking out to what Kaisa thought was the most beautiful view of the lake. But he didn't seem to be admiring it. Instead he turned around and looked at Kaisa. His face was serious. An awful thought entered Kaisa'a mind. Perhaps he was not upset about the hotel at all. Perhaps it was her – them? Perhaps he'd come over to finish it and didn't want to do it in a hotel? That was probably why he hadn't even wanted to do it with her on one of the ridiculous single beds just now. Kaisa shivered.

Peter came to sit next to Kaisa and put his arm around her shoulders, 'What's the matter?' His voice sounded soft.

'Nothing.'

Peter let his arm drop. They sat in silence until the rain stopped. When Kaisa got up, he took hold of her arm and said, 'C'mon, what's up?'

Kaisa sat back down and looked at the shifting clouds. The sun peeked out from behind the tops of tall, dark pine trees on the other side of the lake.

'You know the sun won't even set tonight? It'll never get properly dark. It's supposed to be a magical night.'

Peter said nothing.

'It's a magical, romantic night. Unmarried girls are supposed to put wildflowers under their pillows and dream about their future husbands.'

'Right.'

Kaisa looked at the Englishman's face. He was gazing at his feet, fiddling with a piece of bark. He hadn't heard a word she'd said. 'It's you! Something's wrong with you, not me.' Kaisa was nearly shouting.

Peter looked startled. Now he'll have to say it, Kaisa thought. Now I've made him do it.

'It's this hotel...' he began.

Kaisa couldn't speak.

'It's expensive, isn't it?' He looked up at her with a serious face.

She stared at him. 'Money? You're worried about money?'

Peter looked down at his hands again and said very quietly, 'Yes'.

Kaisa wanted to laugh. 'Oh, that,' she said lightly. 'I've already paid for it, or rather...'

Peter looked at Kaisa, surprised, 'How...?'

'My father paid for it.'

Peter's face changed. His jaw became more square than it already was, and his eyes became even darker than they had been.

'Your father has paid for me to stay here?' he asked with a steely voice.

That midsummer's night was far from magical. Peter told

Kaisa he would pay her father back for the hotel, and then refused to discuss it further. Kaisa couldn't understand him. As far as she was concerned her father owed her big time for all the years Kaisa's mother had to scrimp and save for the school fees and food bills, when all he contributed was the occasional 50 Marks for a birthday or Christmas present. And even those he often forgot. But Peter wouldn't let Kaisa explain. They left the hotel without speaking to each other. Kaisa felt as if he'd suddenly turned into someone else.

BACK IN Helsinki, at night, Kaisa's old Englishman returned. As long as she didn't look into his eyes, where something had changed, he was as before. He whispered lovely things into her ear as before, his touch was as wonderful as ever and his kisses as sweet as always.

On the Monday after midsummer Kaisa had to go back to work in the bank, where her annual summer internship had already begun, and leave Peter alone. He didn't seem to mind; he stayed asleep in the morning when Kaisa tiptoed out of the house. In the evening, she cooked him steak and salad while he read his book. They watched Finnish TV, which he thought was funny, and retired to bed, where Peter was his old self.

The night before Peter was due to fly home, he told Kaisa he was joining a new submarine at the Scottish base in Faslane. 'It's a nuclear sub,' he said. Kaisa had been reading about the women at Greenham Common protesting against nuclear weapons and was against them too. As a Finn, she felt vulnerable between two superpowers wielding nuclear armaments. She shivered at the thought that Peter would be part of that deadly weaponry.

'Don't you think the nuclear arms race should be stopped?' Kaisa said.

Peter regarded her for a moment. 'It's not for me to decide,' he said firmly and continued packing his things.

When they parted at Helsinki airport, they didn't discuss the future. Peter bought Kaisa a red rose, but she didn't cry when he waved her goodbye.

THAT SAME Sunday night, after Kaisa had said her tearless goodbye to Peter, she started to be sick. When two days later she still couldn't keep a glass of boiled, cooled water inside her, she phoned the student health service in the centre of Helsinki. They told her to come and see them straightaway.

The doctor wore a white coat. He had round gold-rimmed glasses and grey thinning hair. Kaisa sat on the examination table while he took her temperature, tapped her knees, looked into her eyes and felt her glands and stomach. She hurt all over, but was so tired after two days and nights of diarrhoea and vomiting that she had no energy to even utter a sound. He took two steps back and wrote something on his notes.

'I think you might have salmonella poisoning.'

Kaisa nodded. All she wanted was to be allowed to sleep.

The doctor regarded Kaisa for a moment. 'Did someone bring you here?'

'No.' Kaisa suddenly realised it was the journey from Espoo, with a bus, a walk to the tram stop and then another long walk to the health centre that had exhausted her.

'You need go to bed; take these and sip a mixture of this.' He gave Kaisa a packet of tablets and a few sachets of something. 'If you don't improve within the next 24 hours, get an ambulance to take you to hospital.' The doctor had kind eyes. 'Can you phone someone to come and get you?' He nodded at his desk phone. 'You can use that.'

Kaisa couldn't think of anyone to phone. Tuuli was travelling around Europe for the summer and her mother and sister were in Stockholm. She hadn't seen her father since midsummer, and didn't know if he was back at work. Kaisa dug in her handbag for her address book.

'Yes?'

'It's me. I'm not very well, I'm in Töölö Health Centre. The doctor said I should have someone to pick me up.'

'What?'

'There's no one else I can call.'

'Can't you take a taxi?'

Kaisa was close to tears. Her father sounded irritable.

'I haven't got any money.'

Kaisa's father inhaled loudly. 'Of course not,' he said dryly. 'What's wrong with you anyway?'

When Kaisa told him, he said he'd come and meet her at home and pay for the taxi there. 'I don't really want to catch it, so I'll stay away until you're better.'

Kaisa was ill for two weeks. She slept for most of it and had nightmares about sinking U-boats, nuclear mushroom clouds and men in uniform laughing at the suffering women and children. She didn't go anywhere, or see anybody. Her father phoned half way through the second week; when he heard Kaisa was still not able to eat anything he said he'd stay away for another week, just to be safe.

'You do that,' Kaisa said and decided she would never forgive him for abandoning her like this. Kaisa's mother didn't know how ill she was. Both her sister and mother were too far away to help anyway.

During those summer weeks in 1982 Kaisa didn't hear from the Englishman either. There was no letter, or phone call. She didn't even know if he had reached the nuclear submarine in Scotland, or whether he was away at sea, or on dry land at the base. Kaisa didn't know if they were still together, or if his disastrous week in Helsinki had finished the two-year romance. It was strange, but Kaisa wasn't sure she cared one way or the other. Not worrying about him, not longing for his touch or hearing his voice, or reading his letters seemed oddly liberating.

When Kaisa returned to her internship at the bank in mid-July, she'd lost five kilos in weight. All her clothes hung off her and she loved it. Something good had come out of the suffering. The nice doctor at the health centre had signed her off the sickness register and given her a note to take to the bank manger.

'I was quite worried about you, young lady,' he said and smiled. All Kaisa could think was why couldn't her father, or Peter, be worried about her if a doctor who doesn't even know her was?

Finally three weeks and three days after Peter had returned home, he called.

'You OK?' he asked after they'd said the usual hellos. Kaisa noticed he hadn't said he missed her.

Kaisa told him about the salmonella poisoning. 'You didn't get it?'

'No.'

Hearing Peter's voice made Kaisa realise how angry she was with him. Angry for spoiling their week together, angry for being an officer in the Royal Navy, angry for not being there when she needed him, angry for not understanding how angry she felt. But Kaisa said nothing.

'So…' Peter said.

'Yes?' Kaisa replied. Her anger was spilling over and made her unable to even speak.

'You OK now, right?' he tried again.

'Yes.'

'Right.'

Kaisa had had enough. 'Look, I've made a decision.'

It was Peter's turn to be quiet. Kaisa could hear noises in the background. Was he phoning from a pub?

'Where are you phoning from?'

'The mess. I couldn't get away, we've been at sea all this time and I couldn't even get a letter to you.'

'Oh.'

'Hold on,' he said, and Kaisa heard him talk to someone. 'Five minutes,' he said.

Now there was a time limit, of course. Foreign calls were expensive.

'Anyway, as I was saying, I've decided it's probably best if we stop this,' Kaisa tried to keep her voice level.

'What?' Peter sounded absentminded, then his voice sharpened. 'What did you say?'

Kaisa inhaled deeply and repeated the words, even though as she said them a strange lump formed in her chest, as if a heavy weight had been placed against it. It made her struggle for breath.

'You can't say that.'

'I just have,' she said.

There was a silence. 'Oh my God.' He sounded truly shocked and Kaisa felt dizzy. Surely she was only saying what he thought, too? Or…?

'We never see each other. I've got another year at Hanken. There's no guarantee I'll get a job in England when I'm finished. Or a work permit. And you're always away at sea. And…' Tears were running down Kaisa's face. She sniffled.

There were more voices behind Peter. 'Look, I have to go, but please don't cry. We have to talk about this, OK? Can I call you tomorrow night? Please.'

Kaisa could never say no to the Englishman.

With shaking hands, she replaced the heavy receiver on the hook and sat down on the floor. Her heart was racing against her ribcage; it felt as if the lump had now engorged and was crushing the whole of Kaisa's upper body with its weight. Her heart had no space to beat and no air was reaching her lungs. What had she done? What if Peter didn't call back, what if, having thought about it, he knew Kaisa was right? The relationship was doomed, their future together hopeless. Kaisa put her head in her hands and howled like an animal into the empty house.

Sixteen

PETER DIDN'T phone the following day, or the day after that. On the Saturday morning, three days after Kaisa had told him she wanted to finish it, she was woken up by a knock on her door.

A strong light filtered through the half-closed venetian blinds in the bedroom window. The weather was continuing to mock Kaisa. The summer was the hottest she'd ever seen in Helsinki. It made everyone smile on the streets and in the bank, where Kaisa was processing people's mortgage applications. She had no desire to join them in their happiness. She just wanted to go to work, come back home, watch TV and go to bed, where she'd lie awake trying not to think about the Englishman.

This weekend the temperatures were supposed to reach new heights and, by the looks of it, the sun was already high up in the sky.

Kaisa climbed out of bed and opened the door.

Even her father looked happy. 'We're taking the boat out to the archipelago. Do you want to come?'

Kaisa thought for a moment, then nodded to him and closed the door.

'Don't forget your swimming trunks or whatever you women wear,' he shouted through the door.

Without wondering too much about his good humour, or the strange desire to include her in the first outing in his latest purchase, Kaisa got ready and was soon on board the legendary *Paula*, as her father had christened his new speedboat. Marja and Kaisa sat at the rear while her father, proudly wearing a blue seaman's cap, steered the thing at high speed under the bridges on the western shore of Helsinki. He was behaving like a child with a new toy, veering it this way and that, making the women scream as he accelerated and made the boat bounce on the surface of the sea. Kaisa was relieved when at last he chose a small island and moored the boat under a steep cliff.

Marja had made a picnic. 'Did you have a nice time in Aulanko?' she asked when they were all sitting around a checked tablecloth that she'd placed on the ground. Kaisa didn't know what to say, and instead looked down at the food: there was a plateful of her father's *gravad lax*, a packet of thinly sliced smoked ham, a loaf of rye bread, butter and salted gherkins. As she spoke, Marja handed Kaisa a paper plate and her father picked up slices of ham with his fingers and stuffed them into his mouth.

'Don't talk about that Englishman,' he mumbled to Marja.

She stared at him, the sea breeze making her messy hair blow over her dark brown eyes. 'I just wondered, because the weather…'

'She doesn't want to talk about it – can't you see that?' Kaisa's father barked.

Here we go, Kaisa thought. She lay down and shut her eyes. The rock was warm against Kaisa's bare back. She was so tired. She hadn't slept through for one night since the phone call from Peter.

'Give her a *Lonkero*,' she heard her father say.

Marja handed Kaisa a cold bottle of the gin and bitter lemon drink. She smiled at the girlfriend. Kaisa felt sorry for her. She had no idea what she was taking on with Kaisa's father. And Kaisa felt a pang of guilt – should she warn her about his drinking and his moods? Should she tell her that he'd hit Kaisa's mother? But Kaisa knew all men were pigs. Marja was well over thirty; old enough to have figured out that herself by now. As Kaisa lay in the warm sunshine, she wondered how it was that all through her life she'd let herself be completely steered by men. First by her father, then by her fiancé, and now by the Englishman. Wasn't it high time she took decisions about her own life without considering a man?

They stayed on the small, rocky island for the rest of the day. The sun was bright in the sky, and to cool down they all swam in the sea. Kaisa's father was in one of his good moods and talked of old times. He told Marja stories about when Kaisa was little. How he had to buy her a large box of chocolates to stop her crying when Sirkka started school, leaving Kaisa to play alone at home all day long. How, lying on his back, he used to rock Kaisa on his belly when she was a baby, and how then Kaisa's hair had been wispy and thin. How Kaisa had been ill with diarrhoea and vomiting and nearly died when she was only four. How useless Kaisa's mother had been, just crying, and how he was the one to take Kaisa to hospital.

When he'd finished his long narrative, Kaisa shaded her face with her hand to look at him. Her father's large frame was splayed on the rock, the round, smooth shape of his belly mirroring that of the cliff. Kaisa wondered if he remembered what happened just a few weeks ago when she was sick with a similar virus. But there was no sign that he'd made the connection. So she continued to listen to her father, now talking about someone in his office, smiling and laughing when required. But Kaisa knew this brief interlude of good humour with her father would not last. After the Jekyll, there'd always be his Hyde.

At the end of the day, when the sun was moving down towards the horizon, and Kaisa's father steered the boat into harbour, she was glad she'd spent a day out on the water with Marja and him. After he'd moored the boat, Kaisa's father pressed a few hundred

Mark notes into her palm and said, 'There's a bit of money for a *Lonkero* or two. Go and enjoy yourself!'

He'd decided to stay with Marja for the rest of the weekend. On the bus home, Kaisa thought for once her father was right; she should enjoy herself a bit more. But how did he know about her and Peter? He wasn't at home during the fateful telephone conversation. How, when he didn't even remember that Kaisa was seriously ill a few weeks ago, did he notice that she was in need of cheering up now? But Kaisa took his advice. When she got home it was only seven o'clock. She looked at herself in the mirror and noticed how the day spent in the sun had bronzed her face and limbs. There was no one around to go out with, so Kaisa decided to do something she'd never done before.

Wearing a bright green miniskirt, with a matching scoop neck top and black lace-up sandals, Kaisa walked alone into the university disco. It was half-full even though it was a Saturday night. Most students were either travelling around Europe on InterRail or at their parents' summer places. That was why all of Kaisa's friends were out of town. She went up to the bar and ordered a *Lonkero*. As soon as she turned around, she spotted him. Leaning against the railings of the bar upstairs on the mezzanine floor was the rich boy. He was looking at the dance floor, but hadn't spotted Kaisa. She ducked out of his sight. Her heart started to race. She realised it was him she'd come out to find. But now she didn't have the courage to go and talk to him, or even invite him over with a covert glance or gesture. Kaisa lit a cigarette and tried to look cool. She gulped down the drink and ordered another. She needed to get drunk. Fast.

'What's the hurry?' the guy at the bar said when he handed Kaisa the second bottle.

She stubbed out the cigarette and said, 'No hurry, I'm just thirsty.'

The barman smiled and in his eyes Kaisa saw that she looked good. She smiled back, and, holding an unlit cigarette and the drink, headed for the stairs to the mezzanine level.

***

KAISA WOKE up with a dry mouth and a screaming hangover. She felt constrained, and realised she was pushed against the wall in a narrow single bed. The shape next to her moved and she looked around the room. A studio flat somewhere in Ullanlinna. There was a window draped with a see-through curtain, a sofa covered with discarded clothes, a table stacked with books. She was incredibly thirsty.

Kaisa felt a hand on her waist, then a bulge against her back. His hot mouth closer to her ear. She froze.

'Sorry, I feel a bit sick.'

He removed the hand and got up. Kaisa closed her eyes.

'Fair enough,' he said and slapped Kaisa's bum. She saw his strong hairy legs disappear into the bathroom.

The sound of his peeing reverberated against the water in the pan. Then the noise stopped and started again. Kaisa shuddered, got quickly out of bed and found her clothes. She cursed her stupidity. Why had she agreed to come home with this guy? Because he was a tennis player, third in the Finnish rankings? Or because the rich guy hadn't even looked at her when she'd stood next to him at the bar upstairs in the university disco? Because the tennis player, with his strong thighs, was the only one showing any interest in her short skirt and sexy sandals?

Kaisa was sitting on the edge of the bed, fully clothed when the guy came out of the bathroom. He looked surprised to see her, as if he'd forgotten she was there.

'Can I?' Kaisa nodded towards the bathroom door.

'Sure.'

The bathroom smelled bad. Kaisa held her breath and splashed cold water on her face and wiped it dry with paper. She must get away, quickly.

When she re-entered the room, the tennis player was on the phone. He was talking into the receiver, balancing it between his neck and ear, while holding onto the base with his hand, its long cord snaking over the discarded clothes on the floor. Looking out of the window, wearing just his boxers, he laughed at something the other person said. Kaisa tiptoed towards the bed and found her handbag. She opened the front door. 'Bye then.'

Startled, the tennis player swung around; a brief recognition passing over his face, he nodded and turned back to face the window.

The bus driver looked down at Kaisa's short skirt and sandals. It was obvious she was still in last night's clothes. He knew her. Kaisa took this same bus into work and university every day.

She felt so ashamed. Is this what she wanted – to feel cheap, used, not loved, just fucked? Is this what it was like to be free from a fiancé, who was obsessive but, as Kasia knew, at least loved her. Or from the Englishman who was forever absent? Was this the alternative? Skulking back home in the morning after a cold, senseless one-night stand? Kaisa looked at the people taking Sunday walks in the heat of the day, normal people with normal lives, not sluts like her with a hangover and wearing dirty knickers.

When the bus stopped in Tapiola, a woman in her thirties or forties, wearing a stylish white jumpsuit and pretty white espadrilles, got out of the bus. Kaisa had seen her before, though never with a man. Still, she looked happy, always smiling even to the miserable bus driver. She didn't seem to need a man, so why should Kaisa? It was 1982 not 1882 after all.

When she got home Kaisa realised the tennis player hadn't even asked for her phone number. She must have been very disappointing. He was probably used to women like the one in the tennis girl poster in Peter's room. Slim things with tiny pert bottoms and no fat on their thighs.

Kaisa was in the shower, washing away her shame, when the phone rang.

'I've been trying to ring you all night!' Peter sounded angry. He had a nerve!

'I was out.'

'Must have been a late night?'

'I stayed over with a friend.'

'I see.'

Silence.

'So…how are you?' Peter sounded hesitant now.

'Fine.'

'Please don't be like this.'

'Like what?'

'Look, I've got more leave, and I've decided to come and see you. To talk. That is, if you want me to?'

Kaisa's heart started beating very hard. 'When?'

'Week after next. Is that OK?'

There had never been such a short amount of time between Kaisa and Peter seeing each other. Only four weeks! When Kaisa told her father the news, he just grunted and shot her a quick glance. 'Guess you want me out of the way again then?'

But Kaisa didn't care about her father's grumpiness, not now. She had only ten days to prepare for Peter's visit. She decided not to arrange anything special. Helsinki was still basking in glorious summer weather, so she decided to take him to Seurasaari, the open-air museum where those with no summer cottage went for midsummer. Or they could go to Suomenlinna, the sea fortress built by the Swedes to keep the Russians away from Helsinki in the late 18th century. That kind of historical site might appeal to Peter, especially as the English had been fighting the Russians in the same place during the Crimean War. Or they could just walk in the Esplanande Park, as on that first wintry evening two years ago.

They'd do just as much or as little as Peter liked, but they would talk. Kaisa would tell him how much she missed him, how lonely she felt, how she worried about him being in the Navy, operating nuclear weapons, and how she feared she'd never get a job in England. And she would have to tell him about the tennis player. Kaisa knew she should have told him over the phone, but then she thought they were finished, didn't she?

Kaisa felt so guilty, and for what. Why had she been so stupid? What if he wouldn't forgive her? What if he never wanted to see her again?

AN HOUR after Peter had arrived at Helsinki airport Kaisa and Peter were sitting on the edge of her bed. At the airport Peter had hugged Kaisa tightly and kissed her for a long time. But now, before they'd even made love, he was sitting next to her looking down at his hands.

'What's the matter?'

He lifted his head and his eyes rested on Kaisa briefly, before he turned and looked away, 'I've got to tell you something. I've been so stupid.'

Kaisa waited. What was he talking about?

'I've slept with someone else.'

Kaisa heard the words even though they were whispered in a low tone. They were like daggers piercing her heart. This is what he had come all this way to tell her? She couldn't speak for a long time. Then anger surged inside her.

'Me too,' Kaisa said, quickly.

'What?' Peter turned around and his eyes were black.

And then Kaisa couldn't face him. She lowered her eyes and looked down at her hands. But Peter wouldn't let her be. He took hold of Kaisa's shoulders and shook her, 'What did you say?' His grip was strong.

'You're hurting me.' Kaisa sobbed. She couldn't help herself. She wiped the tears from her face with the back of her hand and stood up. 'This is it. We're both as bad as each other. What kind of a start is this to a relationship? We might as well stop here.'

Peter followed Kaisa into the dark kitchen. A lonely street lamp was shining against the August twilight. The refrigerator hummed in the silence between them. Kaisa didn't know how long they stood there, either side of the small kitchen table.

'Come here,' Peter said.

Kaisa turned around and looked at Peter's face. He'd been crying too. She ran into his arms and started sobbing again.

'Shh, it's OK, we'll be OK.' Peter stroked her hair, then took her face between his hands and looked deeply into Kaisa's eyes. 'Let's go to bed. We'll talk after?'

PETER AND Kaisa spent the week playing happy families. They stayed in every night, cooked together, and smiled into each other's eyes. In the mornings Kaisa went to work at the bank, and Peter went shopping for food. He told Kaisa how the women at the meat counter in the supermarket in Tapiola laughed at him when he tried to use the Finnish phrases she'd written down for him.

When Kaisa came home from work he poured her a gin and tonic. They sat outside on the small patio at the back of Kaisa's father's house and had 'sundowners'. Peter said that's what the officers called the first drink of the evening on a naval visit to somewhere hot. They'd sip their drinks while watching the sun set against the horizon before disappearing into the sea.

'It goes, *psshht*,' he made the noise of a lit match dropped into water.

Kaisa watched the children who lived in the surrounding houses playing on the swings in the middle of the communal gardens. There was a small area of neglected grass in front, patchy and yellow in the scorching dry summer. The sun was still high up in the sky. This far north it didn't set until much later in the evening. Still, in her mind, sitting next to Peter, Kaisa was in Gibraltar or the Caribbean, smoking a cigarette and drinking a smart cocktail.

After that first night Peter and Kaisa didn't talk much about serious things. Or not enough. At the end of the week when they said goodbye at Helsinki airport, Kaisa nearly pulled Peter back, wanting to start the week all over again. Later in bed, alone, her mind turned to what they hadn't talked about, and a chill spread over her. She wrapped the thin summer duvet tighter around her body. She tried not to think about the girl he'd slept with. Peter said it was a 'stupid accident' that just 'happened'. When Kaisa asked if it was someone she knew, he vigorously shook his head and didn't look at her. Kaisa ransacked her brain for anyone, any girl, who'd shown signs of being smitten with her Englishman. But she hadn't met many of his friends; she'd only been to Britain twice.

Peter had blamed the drink. But how drunk did you have to be to accidentally sleep with someone? Kaisa had been drunk too; too drunk to realise that she shouldn't have a one-night stand with a stranger, but she didn't call it an accident. She'd been fully intending to do what she did before she even set out that night. Did that make it better or worse? Had Peter, like Kaisa, decided that they were finished before he had his accident? If so, what had changed his mind?

The other thing that disturbed Kaisa was that Peter had asked very few questions about the tennis player. As if he pretended it hadn't happened. But surely he must have been curious?

Jealous?

None of it made any sense and now he was gone Kaisa couldn't ask him. Perhaps she should write to him? No, the wait for a reply would kill her. Perhaps when Peter phoned? Would Kaisa have the courage to spoil a telephone conversation with her doubts? She, too, had been unfaithful, so why not just forget about it and plan for the future?

At least they had planned when to see each other again. During the week together Peter had told Kaisa that in the New Year he was going to be based in Rosyth, near Edinburgh. He said she should come over for a longer visit.

THE DAYS and weeks after Peter left passed even more slowly than usual. His phone calls were more frequent now, as were his letters, but they were poor substitutes for his presence. In October, Kaisa continued her political science course at Hanken and negotiated a postponement of her December exams with her professor, a rare Finnish Anglophile. He organised a pass to Edinburgh University library for her, and recommended books she should seek out there.

Kaisa could stay in the UK for six weeks. To save money she travelled to London by train and ferry. The whole journey would take four days, but Kaisa broke it up a little by staying over at her mother's flat in Sweden.

Sirkka had started a job running a hotel in Lapland, so Kaisa was sorry not to see her too.

'I can't believe you're still going strong with your Englishman after two years,' Kaisa's mother said, as she helped carry her bag to Stockholm's railway station, T-Centralen. 'Must be love.' She hugged her daughter hard. Kaisa didn't want to tell her how much she still doubted the relationship.

On the first leg of the journey, Kaisa had a bunk in a four-berth sleeping compartment. In mid-December Stockholm had a thick covering of snow, but as the train made its way south the landscape turned dull and brown. It soon became dark and there was nothing to see out of the window, so Kaisa climbed into her bunk.

Woken sharply by loud clanking noises, she didn't at first remember where she was. From the small window she saw the train was in Helsingborg, about to cross over to Denmark. Kaisa glanced at her watch and saw it was 1.30am. Struggling to sleep for the rest of the journey, she tossed and turned under a scratchy thin blanket, wondering what made her travel so far to be with a man. She wondered if Peter did truly love her, and even if he did, was he to be trusted? Would this 'accident' of his be one of many? But Kaisa kept reminding herself she was just as bad. At the end of the night she'd convinced herself there was no future for the two of them, and that they'd find this out during the next six weeks – the longest time they'd ever spent together.

Early next morning, when the conductor made his way through the compartments, knocking on doors and giving a wake-up call in

Danish, Kaisa was already up and washing her face. Tired after the sleepless night, she entered the busy Hamburg station. There was an hour to kill, so she found a place to have a cheese roll and a coffee. Afterwards she hauled her suitcase up a set of escalators and boarded the train to Ostend. She was to arrive there late afternoon and then take an overnight ferry to Dover.

Finally, three days after Kaisa had said goodbye to her mother in Stockholm, she was on British soil. She took in the warm sea air, and followed the line of equally exhausted passengers from the ferry to board the train to London. The carriages were full and the only free seat was in a smoking compartment, full with noisy football fans.

A guy opposite Kaisa opened a fresh can of beer and winked at her. 'Fancy a drink, love?' She shook her head and looked out of the window at the green grass. She longed for Peter's touch, and closed her eyes, willing the train to move faster. She suddenly realised she knew what loving someone more than life itself meant. If Peter would ever leave her, Kaisa wouldn't survive. She had to make this work at all costs. It didn't matter about the 'girl' or the 'accident'. Kaisa had to make him want her, only her. There was no other option. She was going to be like Chrissie Hynde, tough and sexy. Kaisa started to hum a Pretenders track that Peter had given her two years previously. The very first of the many tapes he'd left with her.

Seventeen

PETER DROVE Kaisa up to Scotland on Boxing Day 1982, after a lovely, jolly Christmas with his parents in Wiltshire. The journey took a whole day. Peter had bought new tapes for the trip, ABC's *Lexicon of Love*, *Night and Day* by Joe Jackson and *East Side Story* by Squeeze. They sang along to the tracks and Kaisa tried not to think how apt the lyrics of *Tempted* were to the two of them.

They stopped for lunch – scampi in a basket – at a pub somewhere in the Lake District, in the shadow of an imposingly dark mountain. The sun didn't make an appearance that day, and Peter and Kaisa arrived in Edinburgh in the dim light of a Scottish winter afternoon.

It was raining, but the warm welcome given to Kaisa by Peter's friends made up for the bad weather outside.

Lucy, the wife of Peter's friend, was the first naval wife Kaisa had ever met properly. Her husband, a balding man with a permanent smile on his face, immediately went to 'mix the drinks'. Then he took the bags upstairs. Kaisa was embarrassed by the amount of luggage she carried. She wanted to explain that there were heavy text books in the suitcase, but Roger just smiled and said, 'Don't worry your pretty little head about it.' He winked at the Englishman. 'You've done well there.'

Kaisa was glad the man had turned towards the stairs and didn't see her blush.

Lucy was heavily pregnant.

'I'm at the waddling stage,' she said the next morning when she poured hot tea into two brown glass mugs from a large teapot. Kaisa smiled at her and looked down at the steaming milky stuff in front of her. She turned her face away from the smell. How could Kaisa possibly tell Lucy she didn't drink tea?

'The boys' as Lucy called Peter and Roger, had left early for work at the Rosyth base. Kaisa had not seen Peter in uniform since she'd met him at the cocktail party at the British Embassy in Helsinki two years before. Peter looked even taller than usual in his black trousers and navy jumper with gold lapels. His eyes appeared darker. When he kissed Kaisa goodbye, she got a whiff of diesel from the scratchy wool.

'You girls can natter to your hearts' content,' Roger smiled. Peter had winked at Kaisa and placed the white cap on his head.

Trying to drink her tea, Kaisa looked over to the communal garden between the semi-detached houses that made up the naval quarters. The patch of grass was lush and green, but the grey concrete of the houses opposite and the steely skies above made the space look oppressive. She glanced at her watch. It was only nine o'clock, eight hours till she'd see her Englishman again.

'It's laundry day today,' Lucy said and sighed, lifting herself heavily from the chair. 'I like to have a daily routine; makes time pass quicker.'

Kaisa looked at her. Lucy reminded her of the female character in Doris Lessing's books; she was just like Martha Quest, before she left the oppression of her marriage. Just as Kaisa had imagined Martha, Lucy, too, had a pretty face, with large pale-blue eyes and a luminous complexion. Her long hair, which she kept in an old-fashioned, loose bun, was very fair, almost grey. Her vast tummy had spread around her hips and towards her backside. The middle of her body looked out of place with her slender wrists and small ankles. Kaisa wanted to ask how long she'd been married, and if she'd had a career. Or what she'd done before dealing with washing and ironing, dusting and tidying. But Lucy liked to talk, not to answer questions. She wanted to show Kaisa how to become an efficient naval wife.

Kaisa vowed never, ever to be like Lucy, and never, ever have children.

Peter and Kaisa stayed two nights in Lucy and Roger's quarters, until a room in a flat became available in Edinburgh on the day before New Year's Eve.

Peter and Kaisa drove to a part of Edinburgh called Leith in the dark. 'It's an old tenement building,' he said, but Kaisa didn't know what that meant. 'Where poor people lived,' he explained, turning to smile at Kaisa, 'but don't worry it isn't like that anymore.' He didn't sound convinced, though. He parked the car on a narrow street, overshadowed by tall buildings on either side, and hauled the luggage out of the boot. All Kaisa could think about was that they'd have their own place for five weeks. It didn't matter what the place looked like. They could come and go as they pleased; they could stay in bed all weekend if they wished.

The vast hallway had a wide, stone staircase. There was a strong smell of disinfectant. On the second-floor landing Peter stopped in front of a door, one of many that looked exactly the same, and rang the bell. A slim dark-haired girl appeared, and immediately flung herself into Peter's arms. He kissed her cheek, and freeing himself from her embrace, pulled Kaisa to his side. 'This is my girlfriend.'

'Kaisa, meet Frankie.'

'Hi,' the girl said and took Kaisa's hand. Her slim fingers felt bony and cold. 'Come in!' she said, moving aside to let them pass. She nodded to Kaisa and smiled into Peter's eyes.

The flat had high ceilings and smelled musty. The room that

Frankie showed Peter and Kaisa was as big as Kaisa's living room in Lauttasaari. It had a large bay window overlooking the street, a set of heavy brown curtains hanging either side of the glass, with yellowing net curtains obscuring the view. There was a single mattress on the floor, an electric heater in front of a small fireplace, a table with two chairs, and a single comfy chair covered in dark-green fabric.

'This is great,' Peter said.

'How do you know her?' Kaisa asked, as casually as she could, after the dark-haired girl had left them alone in the massive room. The lyrics of *Tempted* by Squeeze again rang in her ears. Was this slim girl with cold fingers Peter's 'accident'? Would he really bring Kaisa under the same roof as 'the girl'?

'Frankie? She's the sister of a friend.' Peter took Kaisa in his arms and kissed her neck. Kaisa closed her eyes and decided not to think about anything else but the sensation of Peter's body against her own.

KAISA AND Peter spent their first full day, New Year's Eve, in the flat in Edinburgh, kitting out the room with missing essentials. Their street was just off Leith Walk, where small shops sold everything from light bulbs to loaves of bread.

On the corner was a place called Naz Superstore. In there, Peter and Kaisa bought a cheap reading lamp, a travel alarm clock and a small transistor radio. Kaisa felt like they were a young married couple buying the first supplies for their new home. An Asian man rang the till, then with a heavy Scottish accent told Peter what they owed. They walked out of the shop hand in hand, carrying their purchases back to the flat. It was cold and rainy outside but inside it felt even cooler.

Frankie, the landlady, the dark-haired girl, was standing in the hallway as Peter and Kaisa entered. She wore a short skirt, long leather boots and a black waxed jacket. Around her neck she'd tied an expensive looking silk scarf. Kaisa felt shabby and inappropriately dressed in her new suede jacket, which wasn't standing up very well to the rain. Wet streaks had formed in the front and back, soaking through to the padded lining.

'I'm off to a party tonight. You guys doing anything?' Frankie asked.

'I'm on duty tomorrow morning,' Peter replied. The girl kissed him on the cheek, nodded to Kaisa, and disappearing out of the door, shouted, 'Too bad. See you in 1983!'

'How come she's got a big flat like this?' Kaisa said, scrutinising Peter's face. She still wasn't sure about Frankie, though she just couldn't believe Peter would be as stupid and unfeeling as to bring her to the home of someone he'd been to bed with. However much of an 'accident' it had been.

'I think it belonged to her aunt or something.'

Peter had spotted a small pub opposite the tenement block and thought it would be a good place to see in the New Year. But when they entered, he instantly regretted his decision. The pub was full of middle-aged, chain-smoking men.

When Peter asked what Kaisa would like to drink, she said 'A pint of 80 shillings'. In Finland, girls always drank what the guys did, and the Englishman always had a pint.

Peter turned to her, away from the bar, and said quietly, 'I'll get you a half.'

Kaisa looked around the brightly lit pub. She noticed she was the only woman there. Peter drank his pint quickly; the men, who'd stopped talking as soon as Peter and Kaisa had entered, didn't start again until he handed the empty glasses to the barman and headed for the door. When Kaisa asked what it had all been about, Peter said, 'They hate the English.'

Kaisa didn't understand any of it; she took his arm and started running towards the door of their block of flats. It was bitterly cold and the air hung heavy with rain, or even snow. Kaisa and Peter opened a bottle of red wine they'd bought earlier and drank it in bed, huddling against the warmth of each other's bodies as 1982 turned into 1983.

DURING THE weeks in the cold room in Leith, Kaisa and Peter fell into a routine of sorts. On the mornings the Englishman was working at the base in Rosyth, he'd get up first and put on the electric heater, before Kaisa could even think of getting out from under the blanket. To keep warm in bed, she wore Peter's thick submarine socks and long white uniform shirt. Kaisa would lie in, watching Peter get washed and dressed. She'd hear him start his car each morning, and if it wasn't playing up, listen to him drive off along the road. She was amazed how the noise, echoing between the tall tenement blocks, travelled up to the third floor. She'd wait until the room got a little warmer, not getting out of bed until gone ten. Then she'd either walk into town or take the bus to the university library. The room was too cold for her to concentrate on anything but trying to keep warm and she just couldn't study like that.

Besides, she didn't feel brave enough to use the lounge in the flat in case she'd bump into Frankie.

It rained every single day of the five weeks Kaisa and Peter spent in the cold, dark flat in Edinburgh. Kaisa realised early on that she'd brought the wrong clothes. The suede coat, of which she'd been so proud, was ruined, and the beige leather boots looked dirty. But Kaisa fell in love with Edinburgh in spite of the cold and the rain. The city was dominated by the imposing castle, which at night was lit up and looked like a fairy tale fortress. It bewitched her. The people she met in shops along Leith Walk or on Princes Street, in the more affluent part of the city, or at the university, were friendly, in a direct, almost Finnish way. This was Viking country after all, she realised.

Peter and Kaisa had so little money they had to count up coins for their drinks in the pub. They bought food every day, and always overspent. But being poor didn't matter. They laughed about it and promised themselves they'd be rich one day. The most important thing was that they were together. It seemed the longer she spent with Peter, the more in love with him she became. Kaisa tried not to think about the future, or that, as always, time was ticking away; her return home getting closer by the day.

Peter introduced Kaisa to blue cheese in an Italian delicatessen on Leith Walk. They ate the Gorgonzola with water biscuits and a bottle of cheap red wine on the floor of the cold room, laughing and listening to Radio One on the small transistor radio. In the tiny kitchen at the other end of the flat, Peter cooked new foods that Kaisa had never heard of: beef kebabs, shepherd's pie, chilli con carne.

Some nights they would meet up with Peter's many friends in the small, dimly-lit pubs scattered around the old part of the city. Its cobbled streets and low buildings were as charming and enchanting to Kaisa as the castle. She felt she was living a dream.

The evening before Peter was due to drive Kaisa down to Newcastle to catch a ferry to Gothenburg, the first leg of her long journey back to Finland, she cried. The shoulder of Peter's shirt was soaked with tears.

'I know this is the end,' Kaisa sobbed. She had no idea when she'd next see him. Peter didn't know where he'd be based next, or even when that would be.

'This is just the way the Navy is. You must trust me,' Peter said, taking Kaisa's face between his hands. 'You know I love you.'

Kaisa looked into his eyes. Before she knew what she was saying, the words came out of her mouth. 'But what if...what if there's another girl, just like our landlady, and another accident?'

Peter stared at Kaisa. He dropped his hands and walked over to the large bay window. He formed his hands into fists and looked down at the dark street below. Kaisa held her breath. She wanted to take the words back, yet at the same time she wanted to hear what he had to say. Kaisa couldn't bear another long journey across Europe, not sleeping, thinking about this girl. She had to know the truth. Who was she? What had she meant to him? If, as he claimed, it was nothing, a mere mistake, what then of their future? Did Peter still want to spend it with Kaisa; did he still want to marry her one day? Or would Kaisa return to Finland without a boyfriend. To carry on as if they were together, but not bound to each other: 'free'. Kaisa had to know before she left. She just had to.

'You know I love you,' Peter said, not turning around. He folded his arms across his chest.

Kaisa got up and went to stand next to him. She put her head on his shoulder. 'And I love you.' She burrowed herself between his chest and his hands. He laughed, briefly. It was a dry sound, almost a cough.

'I need to know,' Kaisa said quietly.

'It wasn't Frankie. How stupid do you think I am?' Peter said, freeing himself from Kaisa's embrace. He walked to the other side of the room.

'Who was it then?'

'I told you, nobody.'

Kaisa thought for a while. 'So what are we going to do?'

Peter came over to her and took Kaisa's hands into his, 'We'll find a way. I promise. You know I'm going to miss you so much. Being here on my own in this flat, in this room…'

'I know,' Kaisa said. His eyes looked sad, his hands were trembling. She knew he was speaking the truth.

'I'll never be a naval wife like your friend, you know. Never,' Kaisa looked into Peter's dark eyes.

Peter laughed, relieved now. 'I know that. And I bloody well hoped you wouldn't.'

THE DRIVE from Edinburgh to Newcastle was much shorter than the journey from Wiltshire to Scotland had been five weeks earlier. Sitting next to Peter in his yellow Spitfire Kaisa wished time would stop and they'd be on the road south forever.

'You must take one of these,' Peter said. They were onboard the musty-smelling ship, standing in a four-berth cabin she'd booked for the crossing to Gothenburg.

'Why?' Kaisa looked at the packet of Stugeron.

'It's going to be choppy.' Peter put his arm around her, 'the North Sea in winter.'

It hadn't even occurred to Kaisa she might be seasick. She'd never been sick on the ferry between Finland and Sweden but when she tried to explain this to Peter he laughed and said, 'Just take them; believe me you don't want to take the chance. There's a saying in the Navy, "When you're seasick, first you fear you're going to die; then you wish you would."'

Kaisa put the packet into her handbag. She didn't need to be seasick to wish to die. The tannoy announced that the ferry was leaving in fifteen minutes. She lifted her eyes to Peter, trying not to cry. Peter took her face between his hands.

'Your eyes are very blue today.' He looked at Kaisa for a very long time and whispered, 'I love you.'

They kissed.

And then he was gone.

KAISA STOOD in the middle of the large space wondering if the ache for her Englishman would ever go away. A woman in her late thirties came into the cabin, dragging two heavy suitcases. She introduced herself, but Kaisa couldn't talk. She nodded to her and mumbled her name. Kaisa sat on her bunk and pretended to look for something inside her bag, hoping the woman would not see the tears running down her face. Kaisa tried to control herself but all she wanted to do was scream. Her stomach ached; her chest felt as if it had caved in.

As she watched the ferry pull away from the dock, with the afternoon light fading, it felt as if Kaisa's heart was left on the jetty, a part of her body being ripped away.

Kaisa went to the cafeteria, which was full of lonely men – lorry drivers, she presumed. She bought an egg-and-anchovy open sandwich and a bottle of Elefanten. Long ago, when they still lived in Sweden, Kaisa's father had told her this was the strongest beer you could have, and Kaisa wanted to be anaesthetised. She spotted the packet of travel sickness pills in her bag and swallowed two, downing them with gulps of beer. After the meal Kaisa walked around the ship. She went up to the deck, or the 'Upper Scupper' as the Englishman called it. She smiled and fought the tears again. It was only six o'clock, but she felt tired and drunk from the beer so she decided to go and lie down in the cabin.

Kaisa slept for twenty-three hours. She woke once or twice to the movement of the ship and to people coming in and out of the cabin.

'We were worried about you,' said the woman whom she'd met when the ship was still docked at Newcastle. She had bloodshot eyes and smelt strongly of alcohol. 'Thought you'd died on us!' she giggled.

The woman told Kaisa the sea had been heavy during the long crossing and that many people had been seasick. Kaisa wondered how she could tell the difference between being sick from alcohol and the motion of the sea, but said nothing. The woman told her she'd spent the time in the bar and had met a great guy. Why is she telling me all this, Kaisa wondered wearily. She felt slightly odd herself, as if she'd been drugged. Then Kaisa remembered the seasickness pills. Perhaps she shouldn't have taken alcohol with them.

The short train journey up to Stockholm passed quickly. Kaisa's mother greeted her warmly and Kaisa spent two nights with her. Sirkka was home from Lapland and the two sisters slept on the floor of the living room, on two thin mattresses side by side. Kaisa told her sister everything about the trip to Edinburgh, and Sirkka told Kaisa about a man she'd met up in Rovaniemi.

'He's Swedish and the same age as father!' she whispered.

Kaisa could hear the faint sounds of her mother snoring in the room next door. 'I've never felt like this about anyone, not even the bastard in Finland.'

Kaisa hugged her sister. Suddenly she was alarmed, 'He's not married is he?'

Sirkka told Kaisa the man had three grown-up children but was divorced. He had his own restaurant on the Swedish side of the border and drove a huge Mercedes.

'But what will father say?' Kaisa asked.

Sirkka shrugged, 'Why should I care about him?'

After two nights talking with her sister about everything, and planning weddings that hadn't even been spoken about with the prospective grooms, Kaisa had to return to Helsinki. Her father met her at the ferry terminal, together with the girlfriend. It was a Sunday morning and the sun was bright against the white snow at South Harbour.

'The wanderer returns!' Kaisa's father said. He hugged her and she felt as if he was truly glad to see her. Marja giggled, and Kaisa's father said, 'I'm going to take you both out to lunch!'

Kaisa nodded and thanked him, though she wasn't at all hungry. In her ruined suede jacket Kaisa felt the cold and shivered. They walked towards her father's dark-blue Saab.

'Happy New Year,' Marja nudged herself close to Kaisa, 'How did you celebrate the arrival of 1983?'

'We went to the pub.'

Marja launched into a long tale about a language course she'd attended years ago in Eastbourne. How she'd survived the month on Mars bars because English food was inedible. But she'd loved the pubs, and the beer in particular. Kaisa was bored and tried not to listen. Besides, this woman knew nothing about England, not the real England. There was no proper coffee, that was true, and the whole country seemed to smell of milk that had gone bad, but there was some good food. Kaisa had never had chips that tasted as good as the ones Peter's mother made, or the cabbage salad, called coleslaw, served with ham in pubs. And the ham was thickly sliced and tasty, not like the thin over-salted stuff that Kaisa's father bought from the local shop. And there was no Cheddar cheese in Finland. Kaisa closed her eyes and thought about the Gorgonzola she'd eaten with Peter, sitting on the floor of their temporary home in Edinburgh.

Next day at the School of Economics, Tuuli was glad to see Kaisa, too, 'I thought you might not come back,' she said when she hugged her.

Kaisa looked at Tuuli's serious eyes. That must have been what everyone thought. Her mother, even Sirkka, her sister, her father, his girlfriend. That's why everyone was so glad – relieved – to see Kaisa back in Finland. What did they think, that she'd just stay, marry Peter and abandon her studies for good?

The possibility hadn't even occurred to her. Or to Peter.

Why hadn't it?

Eighteen

IN FEBRUARY 1983 Kaisa got a part-time job at Stockmann's department store, selling fabrics on Friday evenings and Saturday mornings. She was short of money after all her travelling the previous winter. In spite of all the time spent away, her studies at the School of Economics were going well and she'd passed the exams she took on her return from Edinburgh. Kaisa continued to get good marks for the coursework, even though she had less time to study because of the new job. Every week Kaisa also went out with Tuuli to the university disco. Once or twice she bumped into the fourth year guy who'd been flirting with her, but his attentions didn't bother Kaisa anymore. Once Kaisa even saw the tennis player there; he'd walked towards her and their eyes met. Trembling, Kaisa just nodded and turned her back to him. She'd feared he would come and talk to her – Tuuli was on the dance floor and it looked like she was alone again, just like in the summer – but Kaisa held her breath and was glad when he didn't. 'Well, at least he recognised me,' she thought, and smiled to herself. But Kaisa had no desire to speak to him, or see him ever again.

Kaisa missed Peter wherever she found herself.

He wrote nearly every week, his words full of longing and love for her. Occasionally there'd be a late-night phone call. Sometimes a fortnight would pass without any communication, and all Kaisa could assume was that he was away at sea, onboard his nuclear submarine. Kaisa replied to each letter, but often their messages to each other would cross in the post, and a question would take two or three letters to be answered. They didn't write about the future or anything important though: just what happened to each of them during the week. Kaisa told Peter how Russian customers at Stockmann's would try to buy dress fabric with a bottle of vodka, or what marks she had got in her exams. Peter told Kaisa about nights out with his mates, and about a trip down to Portsmouth to see his old friends. He said very little about his work, merely referring to 'refits', 'work-ups', or 'programmes'. Kaisa didn't understand what the 'boat', as he referred to the submarine, did when it sailed, nor what Peter's job was. She assumed she wasn't supposed to know or understand.

In April, Peter told Kaisa he'd visited his parents and they'd given him money towards a new car for his birthday. He sold the yellow Spitfire and bought a more reliable car, a Ford Fiesta. Kaisa mourned the open-top sports car and couldn't imagine her Englishman at the wheel of anything else.

Kaisa spent her twenty-third birthday later the same month with her father and sister, who'd travelled down from Lapland to see Kaisa.

'If I were you, I'd move to England now,' Sirkka said.

Kaisa asked her about the new boyfriend, but she said it was finished.

'Why?'

'Oh, I don't know, Little Sister, I don't think he's the one for me after all.'

They were sitting in the Happy Days Café, where their father had taken his two daughters for a buffet lunch. The place was full of memories of Kaisa's first date with Peter. It seemed an age ago now. For once, her father's girlfriend wasn't with them, even though it was a Saturday. Kaisa looked at the uneaten *gravad lax* and pickled herring on her plate and sipped at the half litre glass of beer Sirkka had insisted she should have. 'It's your birthday and he's paying, for goodness sake,' she whispered in Kaisa's ear when she'd hesitated about what to order.

'But it's different for you, you're in love,' Sirkka now said and took hold of Kaisa's hand, 'so move to England!'

'But I won't be able to get a job without a work permit.' Kaisa said.

'Get a work permit, then.'

'You can't get one. There's huge unemployment in the UK, just like here, and no one outside the EEC gets a work permit. Unless you're a brain surgeon or something.' Kaisa looked at her sister's blonde curly hair and dark-green eyes. Living in Lapland obviously suited her. She looked slim and athletic in her short black skirt and stripy jumper with a deep v-neck. Kaisa continued, 'I'd have to marry him to be able to live and work there.'

Sirkka smiled broadly. 'So, what's the problem? You love him, he loves you.'

'I know.'

'Besides, he's already asked you to marry him once, so just say yes!' Sirkka lifted her glass and clinked it with Kaisa's.

Their father sat down heavily next to Kaisa in the leather booth. He'd brought a plateful of food from the buffet. 'Yes to what?' he said, looking suspiciously at Sirkka.

'I think someone should marry and leave this godforsaken city and country for ever.'

Their father's nostrils flared as he took a deep breath in. Kaisa wondered if she could ask them not to fight on her birthday. But it was already too late.

'You'd think that, wouldn't you! You, who scarpered over to Sweden to follow that bitch of a mother of yours. Foreign men, that's what you're after, just because no Finnish man would have you. I bet you'll marry some soft, milk-drinking Swede.'

There was a silence. The little appetite Kaisa had had vanished. She didn't know what to say. Sirkka was looking down at her plate. She glanced at Kaisa. Her eyes were dark, dangerous-looking. Father was staring at Sirkka, holding his knife and fork upright. Like a man-eating giant about to pounce, waiting for the retaliation. But Kaisa's sister was silent, for once not rising to the bait.

A waitress came to the table. 'Any schnapps here?'

Father's eyes lit up with anticipation. 'Yes, we'll have a round of *Koskenkorva*.'

Kaisa glanced at her watch. It was barely 11.30am.

'I DON'T care what he thinks,' Sirkka said later. They were walking along the Esplanade to a restaurant where a friend of Sirkka's was working. In the restaurant business everyone seemed to know each other, even in different countries. It was a sunny, almost warm day. Trees along the park were beginning to bud; spring was definitely on its way, at last.

They'd left their father to drink himself stupid at Happy Days Cafe. Luckily his mood had improved with the first round of *Koskenkorva*. After they'd eaten, he told Sirkka and Kaisa to go out and have fun, pressing a few hundred Marks into each of their hands.

The same old routine.

'Might as well use the money as His Pisshead Lordship wishes,' Sirkka laughed and took Kaisa's arm.

Peter phoned later that night, to wish Kaisa a happy birthday. She very nearly told him what Sirkka had said about moving to England and marrying him, but at the last minute she hesitated. It was for the man to ask the woman, not the other way around.

'I've only got three weeks of term left,' Kaisa said instead.

'Right, and then what?' Peter said.

'I start at the bank on Monday 23rd May.'

'Ok.'

That was it. Kaisa couldn't get any more out of him. She tried not to worry that he had stopped loving her or that he'd 'accidentally' slept with another girl, or even the same mysterious girl. In bed that night, Kaisa reread his last letter, in which he'd sworn undying love for her. Perhaps he truly didn't know or couldn't tell Kaisa what he was doing in the next few months, or even weeks. There was a Cold War on after all. Goodness knew who might be listening in on their telephone conversations. It always sounded as if several lines were open when the overseas connections were made, and Kaisa often heard a click or two, like someone putting the phone down during their call. The Englishman's jokes about sleeping with a spy, or the famous 'honey traps' that the ship's company had been warned about when they met, still rang in Kaisa's ears. Surely Peter didn't suspect her of being a Soviet spy after all this time? After two and a half years?

A MONTH later, when Kaisa had already started her fourth summer internship at the bank, a letter from Peter was waiting for her on the doorstep at home. Just that day, she'd discovered the British Council Library in a building next to the bank and had borrowed Graham Greene's spy novel *The Human Factor*, in English. She was looking forward to curling up in bed reading about England in English, but first Kaisa ripped open the thin blue envelope.

'I have been so miserable here without you all this time. But now I finally know what my schedule is going to be for at least the next few months. As you know, our refit has been delayed so many times now, and as a consequence they've decided to send me on an OPS course in Portsmouth. I'll be on dry land and away from Scotland for six months! The course starts early June and ends at Christmas.'

Peter was going to live in his friend's house in Southsea again, and he wanted Kaisa to come over *'for as long as you can, as soon as you can make it.'*

Kaisa sat down on her bed. Her father was still at work, or perhaps he wasn't going to come home that evening. Kaisa was glad, she needed to be alone to think. She had no idea what an OPS course was, but it didn't matter. How could she ask for time off at the bank when she'd only just started? Would they understand she needed to go and see Peter? For once Kaisa had some money; she'd saved up from the part-time job at Stockmann's. At the end of the month she'd have her first pay cheque from the bank. Even though it was just for one week's work, it would cover the cost of the flight.

The next day Kaisa went to see the manager at the bank.

'Young love,' he muttered and smiled. Kaisa had known him since her first summer internship. He'd graduated from the same university as Kaisa ten years earlier and kept calling her 'The Lady Economist'. He thought Kaisa very smart and she feared the day when he'd find out the truth about her academic abilities. 'Take two weeks paid leave. I'm sure we'll manage without you.'

Kaisa was amazed. It was unheard of for summer interns to get leave, paid or unpaid. The interns were there to cover the permanent staff's holidays, after all. Kaisa shook the manager's hand and thanked him. She danced out of his office.

That afternoon, walking back to the bus stop along Mannerheim Street, Kaisa hummed to herself. Straight after work she'd gone to the Finnair travel agent in the corner of Aleksanterinkatu and reserved her flights to Heathrow. In only two weeks' time she'd be on the plane, on her way to London. In only fourteen days' time Kaisa would be in the arms of the Englishman.

KAISA ARRIVED at Helsinki airport only twenty minutes before the flight to London was due to leave. She'd missed the bus from Espoo, where it stopped outside her father's house, by a whisker. The nasty old bus driver had, she was sure, seen her running for it, dragging the heavy suitcase, but had driven off anyway, leaving her breathlessly cursing the bloody man. Kaisa saw his face through the side mirror as he sped away from her. He had something against Kaisa, even though she'd barely exchanged one word with him during the two years she'd been living with her father. After that, Kaisa had to wait twenty minutes for a Finnair bus at the terminal in Töölö.

'The flight is full,' the heavily tanned, red-haired woman at the check-in said. Her bright-pink lipstick clashed with her colouring, and with the sky-blue Finnair uniform.

'Really?' Kaisa said, not really comprehending how she could be booked onto a flight and not have a seat reserved. An awful sensation came into her stomach: did this mean she'd miss the flight?

The woman revealed a set of white teeth, 'But, you've been upgraded to Business Class.'

Kaisa looked at her. She was still feeling dizzy.

'Have a good flight, Miss.' She handed Kaisa the boarding pass and nodded politely, as if she'd suddenly become a more important person.

Kaisa was wearing jeans and a T-shirt under a pale-blue jumper. Everyone else in business class wore a suit, and she was the only woman in the whole compartment. Apart from the air hostesses, of course, who surely knew Kaisa didn't belong there.

Even the business class compartment was completely full. Kaisa had a window seat next to an older Finnish man, who started talking to her as soon as they took off. 'Going to London for work?'

'No, I'm a student, going to see a friend.'

'Do you study at Helsinki University?' The man smiled to Kaisa in a kindly way, like a father to a daughter. She guessed his children were her age.

'No, at Hanken, the Swedish School of Economics.'

This really seemed to impress the man, 'Oh!' he said.

Kaisa turned towards the window. They were hovering above white clouds. The air hostess brought a meal and Kaisa asked for orange juice. She looked at her watch: only two hours fifteen minutes until they'd land at Heathrow and she'd see Peter.

'You must be excited about the elections then?' the man said. He was chewing a piece of chicken and Kaisa wasn't sure she'd heard him correctly.

'The elections?'

'Yes, Margaret Thatcher! You must like her radical views on the economy?'

Kaisa looked at the man. His thin hair was going grey at the temples. Kaisa didn't know much about the politics of the newly re-elected British Prime Minister, only that she was very right-wing. But she agreed with everything the man said, trying to avoid further questions. Eventually he gave up when Kaisa dug the latest Graham Greene novel she'd borrowed from the British Council out of her handbag.

Peter was waiting for Kaisa with a dark-red rose in his hand. He kissed her for a long, long time. Kaisa had forgotten how he smelled of cigarettes and the coconut shaving cream, and how his mouth tasted minty. She felt breathless; her heart beat so hard she felt sure everyone around must have heard it.

The new car was on the second level of a concrete parking lot. It was a grey-and-black Ford Fiesta and looked dull compared to Peter's old yellow Spitfire, but Peter told Kaisa how the old sports car was always breaking down.

'I remember all those freezing cold mornings it wouldn't start in Edinburgh!' Kaisa said. Peter squeezed Kaisa's shoulders and smiled at her. It felt good to be able to share something that had happened in the past. Something they had both experienced.

The new Ford started like a dream. Peter kissed Kaisa on the mouth and drove the car out of the dank car park and into the bright sunshine. They headed down to Portsmouth and Kaisa was struck by the bright-green colour of the fields they passed. It was a hot June day. Some farmers were already cutting their crops of hay. In Finland they didn't start doing that until at least a month later. Summer was so much further ahead here, she thought, and wished she could stay in England forever.

'You didn't forget your dress, did you?' Peter said.

'Sorry?'

'For the Dolphin Summer Ball?'

'Yes, I remembered.'

'Great. It'll be good fun!'

Peter had told Kaisa about the ball, which was held each summer at the submarine base in Portsmouth. She was nervous about meeting a new set of his friends. She'd brought the same dress (the only ball gown Kaisa owned) that she'd worn to the Hanken Ball in Helsinki a year and a half ago. Kaisa was afraid it would be far too ordinary-looking. She was sure the other girls would be wearing designer gowns, not ones that were made by a friend from cheap material.

Peter and Kaisa were the only ones out of the old group of Navy friends who stayed in the terraced house in Southsea that summer. It belonged to Peter's best mate, Jeff, who was now serving in Northern Ireland. The girl, Sandra, who had lived there two years previously, when Kaisa had been to stay the first time, was working for NATO in Brussels, and her boyfriend, Oliver, was in Faslane, where Peter had been. It seemed strange for everyone to be scattered around Europe, but as Peter put it, 'That's the Navy for you.'

Again Kaisa and Peter fell into a routine. Each morning during Kaisa's two-week stay in the little house in Southsea, after Peter left for work, looking handsome in his uniform, she walked down to the shops at the end of the street. Kaisa wanted to cook Peter Finnish dishes, and searched for the right ingredients at the small butcher's and greengrocer's.

Kaisa made Karelian stew out of diced beef, pork and lamb's kidney, pea soup from a hock of ham and dried peas, and fish chowder from cod and new potatoes. She struggled to work the gas oven and hob in the little kitchen at the back of the house, often burning her fingers with matches. It seemed so old-fashioned and dangerous to cook with gas, but Peter said it was much better and cheaper than electric. Kaisa felt like a little wife, but strangely this didn't bother her anymore. What was most important was that Peter and she could spend every evening and night together, as well as the long weekends, when there was just the two of them and they could please themselves.

THE LONG-awaited Dolphin Summer Ball took place two days before Kaisa was due to return to Helsinki. She'd been dreading it, and trying not to think about it.

The invitation was written in the same kind of gold lettering, on a similar card, as the invitation to the cocktail party in Helsinki all that time ago. Looking at it took Kaisa back to the days before she'd met Peter. This time it was issued in Peter's name. Underneath there was space for an *avec*, where he'd written Kaisa's name.

Peter wore his summer dress jacket, white with the gold lapels. When he was ready and Kaisa was still getting dressed, he kissed her on the cheek and said, 'No rush, darling. I'll go and fix you a gin and tonic.'

He sounded so domesticated, or husbandlike, as if he'd just stepped off the set of an English TV series, like *Bouquet of Barbed Wire*, which Kaisa had watched in Finland with her shocked mother. Kaisa smiled to herself, took a deep breath and looked at herself in the mirror. She didn't want to wear too much make-up but her reflection looked so pale that she added more blusher to her cheeks. It was another hot summer's evening. It had rained only once during the whole two weeks Kaisa had spent in the house in Southsea. But tonight Kaisa felt a chill run through her body. She couldn't understand why she was so nervous about this evening. Was it the fear of perhaps seeing the girl, Peter's 'accident'? They hadn't discussed the past, or the future. But still, that girl had to be part of Peter's social circle. She had to be someone Kaisa had already met – otherwise why would Peter not tell her who it was?

The past two weeks had gone by in a blissful haze of domesticity. It was only now, when Kaisa knew they had to go out together, to meet other people, that it occurred to her that she still didn't know if they were a proper couple. She'd again not been brave enough to talk about anything important with Peter and she certainly couldn't do it right now.

Peter drove the Fiesta to the jetty in HMS *Vernon*, where Kaisa and he boarded a pass-boat over to Gosport on the other side of the harbour. Peter went aboard first and gave Kaisa his hand to guide her onto the small vessel. She felt as if she'd entered the last century when she sat down next to two other women. The ladies in their evening gowns, made out of luxurious velvet and silk, and wearing long satin gloves, smiled. The men stood, holding onto the side of the boat. They took off their caps and nodded to Kaisa.

'Good evening,' one said.

'Good evening,' Kaisa replied. It was still warm, but she was shivering.

Peter sat down next to her and put his arm around her shoulders. 'You OK?'

'Are Lucinda and Roger going to be there?'

Peter laughed. 'No, I don't think you'll know anyone, but don't worry. I'll look after you,' he whispered into Kaisa's ear as the loud engine of the boat started and headed towards the other shore.

The Dolphin Submarine School knew how to organise a party. There were different areas for food, dancing or just socialising. There was a disco, a Caribbean steel band, and a live group called The Smugglers, who played old-fashioned music from the Sixties. It felt appropriate to be listening to the Beatles' songs in England, although the sound of *Love, Love Me Do* reminded Kaisa of her childhood summers spent in the wooden-clad cottage by a lake in Finland. One year, Sirkka and Kaisa played this same single, bought by their father in Stockholm, over and over. Kaisa felt as if those summers in Finland had happened to her in another life.

Peter led Kaisa to a vast balcony overlooking Old Portsmouth and Southsea. He handed her a drink and introduced her to a string of his friends and their wives or girlfriends. As soon as they told Kaisa their names, she forgot them. She struggled to follow the conversation over the music, which flowed from the different rooms. Everyone was happy; the men were making jokes and the women laughed out loud. Kaisa smiled, too, trying to pretend she'd understood the punch lines.

'You stay here, I'm going to check where we're sitting for supper,' Peter said and left.

A slightly older man, who seemed to be on his own, came to stand next to Kaisa. He had watery eyes and thinning pale hair. His jacket had several gold rings on it so Kaisa guessed he must be more senior than Peter.

'He's not given you a set of Dolphins yet then?' the man said, bending down to look at the top of Kaisa's dress.

Kaisa placed a hand over the low-cut cleavage. She felt very exposed, and cursed her decision not to buy a proper ball gown after all. Hers was made of very thin fabric and had narrow straps, making it impossible to wear a bra. Kaisa had asked Peter if he thought it too revealing but he'd just smiled and said she looked good.

'Sorry, I don't understand?' Kaisa now said. The man pointed at a small brooch-like pin on his uniform jacket.

'No, he hasn't.'

Peter had, of course, told Kaisa about the Dolphins, the emblem of the submarine service. Once you passed your exams and had done the sea time in a boat, you had to earn your Dolphins by catching the pin between your teeth from a glass of rum. She remembered how proud he'd sounded when he told her about the ceremony. But Kaisa didn't realise the women could have them too.

The man laughed at Kaisa's confusion and said, 'I don't suppose he's told you he can't marry you, either?'

Kaisa looked at the man's red, flushed face.

Just then Peter reappeared by her side. 'C'mon, darling, there's someone I want you to meet.'

Kaisa was still staring at the man.

'Excuse us, Sir,' Peter said, and led Kaisa away.

Nineteen

KAISA'S EARS were ringing. Peter took her to the end of the long balcony. She saw how the lights from the other side of the harbour reflected against the dark water. The floor beneath her felt uneven, as if she was still on the boat. Or floating in the water. Noises around her seemed muffled. Had she gone deaf? Peter rested one hand on Kaisa's waist, drinking a pint of beer with the other. He was half-leaning over the low balcony wall, talking to three other officers, who'd appeared from nowhere. Kaisa wondered if she'd met them before. Their laughter seemed to come from somewhere far, far away.

Kaisa shook her head and slowly regained her hearing. She finished her drink in a few large gulps and asked Peter to get her another one. They were still standing by a low balcony wall at the Dolphin mess. Music was flowing out from the rooms beyond, and people were moving in and out of the long, wide outdoor space overlooking the harbour mouth. Lights from Old Portsmouth opposite flickered against the dark water. Men were handsome in their pressed uniforms and polished boots, women glamorous in their long ball gowns.

'Alright darling, what would you like?' Peter asked with a puzzled look on his face. Ladies weren't supposed to ask for a drink, they were supposed to wait to be asked, Kaisa thought. But she didn't care. She saw the large beer glass in Peter's hand and nodded towards it.

'A pint? Are you sure?'

Kaisa said nothing; she just looked at Peter.

'I'll get these, it's my round,' said one of the other guys Peter had been talking to as he walked inside the noisy mess. He too was on the OPS course and had also been with the Englishman at Dartmouth Naval College. 'He's really, really rich,' Peter whispered into Kaisa's ear.

She might have been impressed, but all Kaisa could think about was what the old man had said to her.

'Who was that man I was talking to before,' Kaisa said, trying to sound nonchalant, as if she was just making conversation.

'He's Commander SM; he sort of runs this place. Why, what did he say?'

But Peter didn't really want to know. He wasn't even looking at her. He was surveying the crowd. He waved his hand to someone. The buzzing sound returned to Kaisa's ears. A pretty girl wearing a salmon-coloured silk satin gown, cinched in at her tiny waist, with a huge bow at the back, was walking towards them. She was flanked by three men in uniform.

'Hello, handsome,' she said to Peter and kissed him on the cheek.

Peter introduced her. 'This is the lovely Tash. The girl we were all in love with at Dartmouth.'

Kaisa managed a smile, although her ears were buzzing ever louder and her face seemed to have frozen into an unmoveable stare.

'Nonsense,' Tash said. She dipped her chin and looked up at Peter, feigning shyness.

The drinks arrived. As Kaisa was handed the pint, there was a silence. All eyes seemed to follow the glass of beer as it travelled from the tray to her hand.

'Well, cheers,' Peter said.

'Cheers!' all said in unison.

'You know, I once knew an Australian girl who drank pints,' one of Tash's entourage said, nodding kindly to Kaisa.

'Yes, and I've heard all the girls down under do!' said the other.

'Do girls in Norway girls drink pints, too?' asked the man who'd bought Kaisa the drink.

'I don't know,' she said, 'I'm from Finland.'

Another silence.

Peter took hold of Kaisa's waist and said, 'She can drink any of you under the table, though she hasn't grown a beard yet.'

Laughter.

I'm now the butt of a joke, Kaisa thought, and she drank her beer quickly. When asked, jokingly, by the rich friend if she wanted another one, Kaisa nodded.

When it was time to sit down to the meal Kaisa was drunk, but all she wanted was to drink more. Occasionally Peter took hold of her hand under the table, and asked if she was alright, but for the most part he laughed and talked loudly with the other people at their table, one of whom was the famously lovely Tash, or Natasha, as Peter said her full name was. 'But everyone calls her Tash,' he'd added.

She was sitting on the other side of the round table, attended by a handsome naval officer on either side of her. Kaisa felt sorry for a dark-haired girl who sat next to one of Tash's adoring fans. Her purple dress had a deep cleavage, showing off her plump breasts. Occasionally Kaisa would catch one of the guys around the table staring at her assets, but for the most part she was ignored, leaning across her partner to catch what Tash was saying.

As soon as Peter left her side, or she went to find the ladies', other uniformed men approached Kaisa as if she was fair game. She thought somehow they'd guessed she was foreign, and therefore thought her inferior, even desperate. Just like their famous nurses. Peter had said there was a joke among young naval officers, 'There are only two certainties in life: death and nurses.'

They weren't home in the little house in Southsea until gone two o'clock. Kaisa was sick in the bathroom all night. Even after she'd brought up everything she'd eaten and drunk that night, she couldn't sleep and sat at the edge of the bed. She felt like crying. The alarm clock on the side table said 5.30. Sleepily, Peter put his head on her lap and said, 'You got room spin?'

Kaisa looked at his square face, 'No.'

Peter closed his eyes and lay back against the pillow, 'Come to bed then.'

Kaisa knew she should have done as he said. She should have lain beside him and slept. She should have waited until the morning to talk. It was a Saturday and they'd have the whole day together. Their last whole day before Kaisa was going back home to Helsinki. But, still drunk, she couldn't help herself.

'You're never going to marry me, are you?'

There was no response. Kaisa turned around to see if Peter had gone back to sleep. If he'd dared…Anger surged inside her.

But he was lying on his back, eyes wide open, looking at the ceiling. Kaisa turned away from him again. She felt such rage at him for putting her through the evening. He must have known what the people would be like, looking down their noses at her, a foreign girl daring to dream that an Englishman, a British Naval Officer, would ever marry her. Introducing Kaisa to a girl like Natasha, who, she'd learned later in the evening, was the daughter of an admiral and would be the perfect wife for Peter. She'd know how to behave at cocktail parties and naval dances. She'd not wear a dress that was obviously cheap and too revealing, or drink pints.

'Well?' Kaisa said.

'Come here.'

Oh, how she wanted to go and lie next to him. To feel his strong arms around her, to put her head against his warm chest, to cry about everything in his embrace. But she couldn't. She wasn't going to be charmed by his empty words, by his warm kisses, or by sex. Kaisa had to be strong, and not be seduced. She had to know if they had a future together.

'No.'

Kaisa heard Peter sit up. He yawned loudly. She waited, with her back to him. She heard him breathe heavily, deliberately, in and out. 'You know how much I love you.'

Kaisa turned around, 'You don't even mean that any more!'

'But I do, darling, please, I'm so tired...You've been sick all night and...'

'Oh yeah, it's because I'm so uncivilised, foreign girls do that you know. Especially we Finns, we're barely human, so we can't really be trusted to attend fancy balls like tonight. Unladylike freaks, we drink pints of beer, not tiny glasses of sherry like the lovely Tashes of this world.'

Peter got up. 'What's the matter with you?' He looked angry, standing there in his boxers, his arms by his side, his fists tightly bunched.

Tears started to run down Kaisa's face. She wiped them away with the back of her hand, swallowed hard and said, 'That man, the Commander, he told me you knew you'd never be able to marry me.'

Peter came to sit at the edge of the bed, next to Kaisa. He put his arm around her shoulders, but she shook it off. She didn't want his pity. She was shivering, thinking and hoping he'd soon tell her it wasn't true. That he loved her and would marry her as soon as she wanted, that he'd never been in love with that pretty Tash, that he would die rather than lose Kaisa forever.

'Look, I wasn't going to tell you...'

Kaisa couldn't believe this. It was true, or was he talking about something else? 'Tell me what?'

Peter was looking down at his hands. Kaisa couldn't see his face when he spoke. 'I wrote to my Appointer and asked him if there was a problem with marrying someone from a near-Communist country.'

Kaisa could hardly breathe. She stood up and shouted, 'Finland is not a Communist country!'

'I know that, but as far as the Navy is concerned...'

Kaisa was speechless. She was staring at Peter, at the Englishman, sitting there with his head bent. How long had he known about this? How long was he going to string her along, without telling her that she would never be able to move to England and be with him?

Peter came up to Kaisa and took her into his arms. She was stiff in his embrace while he spoke, 'I was told by someone that marrying a girl, from, you know,' Peter took a deep breath, 'You've got to admit Finland is a bit different, so close to the Soviet Union. Anyway, they told me marrying you may end my career in the Navy.'

Kaisa wriggled out of Peter's grip, but he took hold of her arm and held onto it. She was losing her hearing again. To Kaisa Peter's words sounded as if he was speaking in a cave, or a deep tunnel.

'So I thought I'd ask directly, you know from the one person, my Appointer, who makes the decisions on my career.'

He stopped there.

Kaisa looked at his face. His lips were in a narrow line, his complexion pale. 'So what did he tell you?'

'I'm still waiting for his reply.'

IT WAS raining when the plane landed at Helsinki airport. The goodbye at Heathrow with Peter had been even more difficult than usual. Kaisa lost count of how many times they'd said, 'I love you.'

On the last day together they didn't get out of bed until the afternoon. They talked about how they met all that time ago. The two and a half years Kaisa and Peter had known each other seemed like an eternity.

Kaisa had been sitting on the double bed, trying to pack. Sheets were strewn everywhere, her clothes mingled with Peter's. He came out of the shower, with a towel around his angular hips. His hair was wet and he smelled of the special coconut shaving cream that his relatives in America sent him. He sat next to Kaisa and took her hands into his. 'I wanted you so much that evening we spent wandering in the cold park in Helsinki. But you kept saying, "It's impossible"'

Kaisa remembered the passionate kisses, the way Peter had looked deep into her eyes. And here they still were. Still in love, still longing for the day they could be together forever. 'Our relationship is still impossible,' Kaisa wanted to say, but she didn't utter a word. She didn't want to go back to the discussion about the future when it seemed they had no control over it.

'I thought I was going to die if I couldn't make love to you.' Peter took Kaisa's face into his hands and kissed her. He promised to phone as soon as he heard from the Appointer.

After a brief silence, he said, 'I heard there is an engineer who married a Czech girl, but I think he's a skimmer.'

Kaisa looked at him, 'A skimmer?'

'A lieutenant on surface ships. They skim on top of the sea, not under it, like us.'

'And why is that different?'

'It just is,' Peter kissed the top of Kaisa's head. She didn't want to ask any more.

SITTING IN the Finnair bus, Kaisa now realised submariners must have a higher security clearance. But she could see he didn't want to talk about it. Instead, during those last 48 hours he held Kaisa close and said he couldn't imagine life without her. Peter kept taking Kaisa's face between his hands and kissing her, telling her she was beautiful.

But was that just because he felt bad about putting his career before their future together? Or because he thought it might be the last time they saw each other?

Kaisa remembered Peter telling her sometime in the beginning, perhaps at the embassy cocktail party, how he loved the Navy even if it meant being away at sea for long periods. 'Even if it means being away from loved ones; it's what I've always wanted to do,' he said. In his eyes Kaisa saw loving what he did, being good at his job, meant a lot to him. It was what he lived for. The Royal Navy was his life.

So what if the Navy said he couldn't marry her?

If they didn't get married Kaisa wouldn't get a work permit in the UK. And she couldn't just move to England and not work. She needed to be good at her job too. One of the many things they had in common: they were both ambitious.

The rain ran down the windows of the Finnair bus. There was a lightning strike. How Kaisa wished she could be back in Sunny Southsea, as the Englishman called the part of Portsmouth where they'd been staying. When Kaisa said she thought it true, Peter laughed at her and said, 'It rains a lot here!'

'But you call it "Sunny"' she protested.

'It's called sarcasm, or British humour. You'll get the hang of it,' he'd said and pulled Kaisa close to him.

The bus driver was listening to a sports programme on the radio. Barbra Streisand came on singing *A Woman in Love*. The way the Finnish announcer pronounced both the artist and the song, in his heavily accented English, made Kaisa smile. She thought how it would make Peter laugh. She allowed herself to listen to the soppy song and dream of life in England, together with Peter. How could she bear being without him?

Kaisa looked at the wet Helsinki streets, through the sodden bus window. People were walking fast, with their heads hidden underneath black, sombre umbrellas. No one was smiling, no one holding someone else's hand, everyone just on their miserable own. Kaisa couldn't believe she was back here again. The city, with its tall, utilitarian buildings, its unhappy people, oppressed her. None of the people she saw on the street can have known love like she had, she was sure of it. The Barbra Streisand song got cut off halfway through when some sports results were announced. Kaisa looked at the front of the bus and noticed the luggage tag dangling from her suitcase in the rack at the front of the bus – 'Hel'.

She was back in Helsinki, 'Hell' for short.

THE REST of that summer in Helsinki was again glorious. The second warm summer in a row. But the weather didn't suit Kaisa's mood. If it hadn't been for her good friend Tuuli at Hanken, she wouldn't have survived the latter part of that year. By the end of July Tuuli had finished her finals and submitted her thesis, which she'd written in record time. Now she was ready to party. So party they did. During the day Kaisa worked at the bank and at night the two friends were out in the university disco, or in the Helsinki Club, or a popular summer place called the Pikku Parlamentti. It was near the Finnish Parliament and only open from June to August. With some tables outside and sliding glass doors facing the park, which sloped down to the sea, it was a perfect place to celebrate a graduation. There, and elsewhere, Tuuli and Kaisa often bumped into the old gang of rich boys, and sometimes exchanged a few words with them. Who spoke with whom didn't seem to matter so much anymore, although, unlike her friend, Kaisa would still have to see everybody at Hanken in the autumn. She had a few exams to take, as she'd lost time with the change of subjects in her second year. But, as usual, her future depended on the Englishman.

The 'If we can marry, I can have a work permit and move to England, but if we can't, what then?'question was always on Kaisa's mind. But when Peter phoned, which he did at least twice a week, they skirted around the issue. At first, she asked him every time if he'd heard from the Appointer. But when after a few times the reply was a short 'No' she didn't ask again. Peter was in the middle of a tough course and he, too, had exams to study for. He told Kaisa it was very important for him to do well, so she let him be.

But he kept telling Kaisa how much he missed her and loved

her. How much he longed for the day she moved to England. They speculated whether she might get a work permit through the bank where she'd been a summer intern. The bank was opening a commercial branch in London, and she got an interview with the man heading the new venture. But when Kaisa attended the interview, in plush offices just a few blocks from where she'd worked, it was clear she had no idea what the job entailed. The man, with dark hair, combed back and shiny, asked Kaisa what she knew about hedge funds and Eurodollars. Kaisa had never heard these terms before and couldn't deny it.

There was still no word from the Navy. Whether they'd allow a marriage to a girl from a country so near the Eastern Bloc, or whether it would prove too much of a security risk to an English Naval Officer, Kaisa didn't know. It was as if her life was hanging in the balance. She couldn't even decide on a subject for her thesis. Kaisa had narrowed it down to three choices. The one she really wanted to do was about British party politics. But for this she needed to be based in England. Handy if she was living there, impossible if it all fell through.

As the nights drew in and Helsinki descended into its depressing winter hibernation, Kaisa returned to lectures at the School of Economics. Her professor pressed her on a decision on her thesis, but Kaisa kept putting off meetings with him. It was October 1983; Kaisa was 23 years old and had no idea what was going to happen to her life.

Twenty

A LITTLE over a month later, in the middle of November, Peter called.

'I have Christmas and New Year off! Can I come over to see you?'

Kaisa spoke to her father the next day. 'Christmas? Here?'

'Yes, I thought we could get a ham and I'd cook the Karelian stew and the swede bake, and you could make your *gravad lax...*'

Her father didn't hesitate, 'I'm not having any guests here. Christmas is a commercial invention anyway, for shops to sell more stuff.'

He'd been in an unusually bad mood for weeks. Kaisa guessed he'd had a fight with his girlfriend again, because he was spending all his evenings and nights at home, drinking *Koskenkorva*, monopolising the TV and complaining if she watched anything after he'd gone to bed.

Kaisa looked at him. She wanted to say, 'What about me?' or 'Please can we have a family Christmas here, just like we did when I was little?' but she didn't. What if he sneered at her or worse, started to complain about her mother. Tell Kaisa some story or other about how awful Christmas was with her. Kaisa wanted to hold onto her childhood memories and not have them spoiled by her bitter father.

Kaisa spoke to her mother instead. She was delighted and said it would be a special Christmas with the Englishman in Stockholm.

There was no snow in Helsinki when Peter's plane landed on the Saturday before Christmas. The city looked grey with the lights over Aleksanterinkatu, reflecting on the black pavements instead of the sparkly whiteness of snow. Kaisa took the bus to the airport and prayed the weather would turn colder. Everything looked so much prettier with freshly fallen snow. Peter had two weeks off and flew first to Helsinki. Their plan was to fly together to Stockholm for the holidays and then back again to spend New Year with Kaisa's friends in Helsinki.

When she saw him through the glass at the arrivals hall, giving her a shy wave and rushing towards her with a bag over his shoulder, Kaisa didn't give a thought to the distant future. The next fourteen days were all that mattered to her.

Kaisa's father was waiting in the kitchen when they arrived. In front of him was a half-full bottle of *Koskenkorva* and an empty tumbler. He shook Peter's hand and took another glass out of the drying cupboard. With a nod to the Englishman he filled the two glasses up to the brim and lifted one to his lips. Peter glanced at Kaisa and emptied his glass. He made only the slightest of sounds as the strong vodka flowed down his throat.

'We're going out tonight,' Kaisa lied and took Peter's hand. He coughed.

'Even more reason to start the evening off with style,' Kaisa's father poured another round of drinks. She looked at the clock on the kitchen wall. It was just past four o'clock in the afternoon.

'It's OK,' Peter said. He'd placed his hand on Kaisa's knee under the kitchen table. With his free hand, he lifted the second glassful to his lips.

'C'mon we have to go,' she replied.

Her father looked up. His eyes looked very blue and he smiled, 'You don't have to go. I'm off to Lapland today.'

'What?' Kaisa said.

PETER LOOKED from one face to the other. Kaisa and her father had switched to Finnish. After three years, he still struggled to understand the most basic words in Kaisa's mother tongue. He'd tried – he'd even managed to order a Linguaphone course in Finnish through the Navy. But, however much he practised by listening to the tapes with the dead-pan female voice, he just couldn't get to grips with the language. He could say, *Kiitos*, which meant 'thank you', and *Anteeksi* for 'sorry', and, of course, the inevitable, 'I love you', or *'Minä rakastan sinua'*, but as far as understanding anything anyone said in conversation he was at a loss.

It didn't help that when you tried to talk Finnish to them, most people, in Helsinki at least, immediately spoke English back to you.

Peter sighed. The vodka was beginning to have an effect on him. He surveyed Kaisa's profile. Her small features looked so delicate, those rosy little lips so beautiful, made even more attractive by her pale skin and blonde hair. He wanted to move his hand further up her leg under the table, but was afraid her father might see. If only he'd leave them alone, so he could take her to bed. He'd been thinking about nothing else but sex during the long journey from Scotland. Now Kaisa's father's *Koskenkorva* made him fit to burst. There was no way he could wait until the evening.

'I won't see you until next year,' Kaisa's father said, again in Finnish, and took a wad of hundred Mark notes out of his wallet. 'Have a few drinks on me, or even a meal.' He laughed, bear-hugged Kaisa and shook Peter's hand.

When the door shut behind her father Kaisa shook her head. Peter's face was a question mark. She told him what her father had said. 'He didn't tell me he was away for Christmas. They must have made up and are going up to see his girlfriend's family in northern Finland.'

Peter pulled Kaisa close to him. His eyes looked cloudy. He kissed her and said, 'Can we go to bed now?'

THEY WOKE late the next morning, the 21st of December 1983.

'What do you want to do today?' Peter asked.

'Go into Helsinki for some Christmas shopping?'

It was drizzling with cold rain, almost sleet. They spent an hour walking around Stockmann's department store, holding hands. Peter kept stopping to kiss Kaisa. He didn't seem to mind how people everywhere stared when he did that. And he didn't speak much. Suddenly, when they were queuing up to pay for some Fazer chocolates for her sister, he said, 'So your father. Am I going to see him again?'

Kaisa looked at him. Peter was wearing a thick Puffa jacket, jeans and a thick jumper. Even when he wasn't kissing her, with his dark hair he looked foreign and attracted sideways glances from other shoppers. 'Again?' she asked.

'Yes, before I go back.' Peter looked uncomfortable. A man in front of them in the queue turned around when he heard English being spoken. His eyes wandered from the Englishman's dark features to Kaisa's blonde head. There was strong disapproval in his gaze. Kaisa stared at him and eventually he turned back to face the till. Peter widened his eyes and directed them towards the man's back. 'What's his problem,' he mouthed to Kaisa silently.

She shrugged and said out loud, 'No, don't think so, my father's away for the whole of the holidays. Why?'

'Nothing,' Peter said and pulled Kaisa towards him for another kiss.

'Can we go for lunch somewhere?' Peter said when they were walking out of the store.

The sleet was still falling and even though it was only twelve o'clock, and in spite of the bright Christmas lights, the street looked dark. Kaisa spotted the sign of the new American hamburger bar opposite and started running towards it, dragging Peter behind her.

'It's not McDonald's but they do a rye burger.' she said.

Inside Peter looked around the small space. 'You sure this is OK?' he said.

The place was called Hesburger and being new, it was fairly full. As usual people stared when Peter and Kaisa entered. She looked at Peter. 'Yes, we just want a quick bite, yeah? And it's raining.'

After some translation of the menu, they got the bags of food.

'Let's sit by the window,' Kaisa said and nodded to one of the red plastic tables and chairs.

Peter looked at Kaisa across the table. He hadn't touched his burger.

'Aren't you hungry?'

He reached across the shiny tabletop and took her hand. His fingers felt cold against her skin.

'You know I love you.'

Peter's mouth was a straight line. His eyes were wide. He looked almost scared. Kaisa's heart sank. Had he heard from the Navy Appointer? Was this bad news?

'I know.'

Peter pulled something out of his pocket. It was a small black box. 'This isn't quite the kind of place I imagined I'd do this, but...' He looked deep into her eyes and opened the box to show her the contents.

Kaisa saw gold and glittery stones. She looked up at Peter.

'And I really wanted to ask your father first.'

Kaisa's mouth was dry; she couldn't speak. She wanted to throw herself at Peter. Kiss him, hug him, feel him close to her. But the people around them, munching on their burgers, loudly sucking at their straws in their near-empty paper cups of Coca Cola, with the smell of French fries everywhere, made her stop.

'So, what I'm asking, is...'

Still Kaisa couldn't speak. And Peter was struggling to say the words. She wanted to help him and say, 'Yes, yes, a hundred times yes,' and very nearly did, but then realised he hadn't actually asked her yet. What if by some awful mistake she'd completely misunderstood? Kaisa looked down at the ring in front of her, then at his straight mouth. How she wanted to kiss those narrow lips, taste the cigarettes and mint, feel the roughness of his always unshaven-looking face.

'Would you please marry me?'

Kaisa smiled and said simply, 'Yes.'

ON THE day before Christmas Eve Peter and Kaisa took their first ever flight together from Helsinki to Stockholm. Though there was no snow on the ground, and the landscape looked dark and miserable, it was magical.

To be standing together in the passport queue, rather than saying goodbye on the other side, seemed unreal. Then walking through the airport terminal holding hands, looking at the tax-free shops, selling furs, china or wooden goods to tourists, felt so wonderful that Kaisa wanted to pinch herself. Surely she was dreaming? Peter bought a bottle of gin, although he said it would have been half the price in England. He'd fretted about not having any presents for Kaisa's mother and sister but she gladly put both their names on the little cards to go with the gifts. These were their first Christmas presents given together.

The new ring burned on Kaisa's finger and she couldn't stop touching it, or gazing at the sparkling diamonds. Peter said he'd bought it as soon as he heard from the Appointer. The letter had been short but to the point, 'The Royal Navy cannot see any reason why one of its officers should not marry a Finnish passport holder.' He hadn't told Kaisa before because he wanted to surprise her with the ring.

As soon as they arrived in Kaisa's mother's small flat in Lidingö, she announced there was going to be an engagement party on Boxing Day. Kaisa blushed, thinking what Peter would make of her mother's friends, some of whom were a little eccentric. There'd be the Polish dentist, who called herself Kaisa's aunt, even though there was no family connection, and who had been telling Kaisa to sit up straight and beware of Communists ever since she was a teenager.

There would be Kaisa's mother's childhood friend, with whom she'd lost contact until a chance meeting on the ferry 20 years later. Kaisa must have heard the story a hundred times, about how they'd discovered they both lived in Stockholm only a few miles apart. She was lovely but her husband was a self-proclaimed alcoholic who couldn't stop drinking in spite of loud protests from his wife. He always ended up passing out during any get-together, sparking a loud marital row.

Then there was the dog.

Having been nagged for years, Kaisa's mother had eventually succumbed and got Jerry for the girls right after the divorce. Now, 12 years later, the cocker spaniel was old and frail. He could no longer control his bladder and often ended up peeing in the hallway of the smart block of flats where her mother lived. Once outside, the dog immediately wanted to come inside again, having already done its business. So whoever was unlucky enough to take him for a walk would have to drag the stubborn animal around the streets, appearing ridiculous at best and at worst cruel to any bystanders.

With all the Christmas cooking to be done, Kaisa's mother felt the Englishman would be perfect for this task, especially as he kept offering to 'do anything to help'. Kaisa tried to warn him but to no avail. He just smiled, kissed her on the lips and said, 'Don't worry, I'll be fine.'

'He's stronger than he looks,' Peter said when he returned with Jerry. He told Kaisa how the dog had done a 'number two' in the middle of the zebra crossing, in front of a bus full of people. He said he'd never seen so much angry glaring and head shaking as he tried to drag the squatting animal across the road.

On Christmas Eve, after the long meal had been consumed and the presents distributed, Kaisa joined Peter and Jerry on their nightly walk. She'd wanted Peter to experience a snowy Nordic Christmas, but the weather was still mild and so far only rain had fallen from the sky. At least it was now dry, and when they reached the dark end of the road, where there was a narrow path down to the sea, stars twinkled in the night sky. Kaisa lifted the shivering dog up and Peter traced the galaxies with his gloved hand. 'There's Venus, look, and that's the Plough.' Kaisa looked up into the black sky and wondered how someone could ever be this happy.

'And that's the North Star.'

Peter was quiet for a moment. Then he put his arms around Kaisa, while she placed the dog gently on the ground. 'I'm very happy,' he said and kissed her. Then, looking into her eyes, in his faltering Finnish, he said, '*Minä rakastan sinua*'.

Kaisa replied, 'I love you too.'

KAISA'S SISTER had come back from Lapland and was now working in a hotel in Stockholm again. She was again in the same rented flat, in the same block where Kaisa's mother lived but one floor below. She'd offered the flat to Kaisa and Peter for Christmas, so they had lots of time alone at night and in the mornings. Had it not been for Kaisa's mother's strict timetable and all the cooking that needed to be done, the newly engaged couple would never have left the warm studio flat.

On Boxing Day, an engagement party was scheduled for 2pm. Kaisa's mother's schoolfriend and her small, bearded husband arrived half an hour early. She was twice his size and wore a large paisley-patterned poncho. Peter and Kaisa were lost in her warm embrace. She'd brought along her daughter, who was a friend of Sirkka's. Kaisa looked at her with relief, even though she'd met her only once before. She was waiflike and wore faded jeans with a pretty layered top. Kaisa was glad that at least there'd be one more person near their age at the party.

The Polish 'aunt' arrived half an hour late. Just as Kaisa's mother started to worry that she wouldn't come, through the door she flowed, wearing a tight black satin skirt and a frilly cream blouse.

'Stand up straight, girl!' she said in her strongly accented Swedish, as she hugged Kaisa. Turning to the Englishman, she said, 'Let me see.' There was an awkward moment when she started to rummage around in her handbag with one hand, while holding onto Peter with the other. Peter gave Kaisa a look of panic, but finally her 'aunt' found her glasses, put them on and started to examine the Englishman more closely. Kaisa looked at her mother, imploring her to stop the examination, but Kaisa's mother just shook her head. There was nothing they could do but wait for the verdict, hoping it would be an agreeable one.

After what seemed like an eternity, Kaisa's Polish 'aunt' exclaimed, '*Dobry*!'

'Good?' Kaisa's mother said in Swedish. '*Tak*!' The 'aunt' smiled broadly at Kaisa and Peter. 'See, your mother speak Polish fluently!'

Kaisa translated her Swedish words to Peter. He looked a little pale, so she took his hand and led him to the lounge, where the small bearded man was already drinking vodka and Coke. He lifted his glass and smiled. He very rarely said more than two words. During the twenty years that the couple had lived in Sweden only her mother's friend had learned a little Swedish. Their daughter translated necessary forms and other official documents for them. Kaisa's mother disapproved of this. 'All their friends are Finns,' she'd said to Kaisa. 'So they don't learn the language. I'm not going to be like that. Besides, I already speak Swedish very well.'

As the odd group of people sat around the small coffee table and ate the *Princess Tårta* sponge cake, which her mother had somehow hidden from her during Christmas, the conversation ran more of less smoothly in three languages. Kaisa did most of the translating, while sitting close to Peter, holding onto his hand.

The Finnish man got drunk, and as usual he and his poncho-wearing wife had to leave early to avoid a huge argument. 'See what I have to put up with!' Kaisa's mother's friend said, as she led her family into a waiting taxi. The daughter just smiled and shrugged her shoulders.

Kaisa's Polish 'aunt' spent most of the time gazing at Peter and Kaisa, sometimes wiping the corners of her eyes. When she left, she held onto their hands and said, 'Ah, you both so young!'

Kaisa was surprised by her words. She felt terribly old and experienced. Certainly old enough to be engaged and soon married.

One thing everyone wanted to know was the date for the wedding, but Peter and Kaisa hadn't even discussed that yet. Peter's course in Portsmouth had ended before Christmas and he didn't know what his next job in the Navy would be. 'The Appointer is aware I'm getting married in the summer and I hope he won't send me to a submarine that's due to sail before then.' he'd told Kaisa while they lay in bed in Sirkka's flat that morning.

Twenty-one

'GETTING MARRIED in the summer,' rang in Kaisa's ears as she waved goodbye to Peter at Helsinki airport a week later, clutching the red rose he'd bought her.

'This will be the last time we have to do this,' Peter had said before going through passport control. He stroked Kaisa's hair. She tried not to cry. Knowing they'd soon be together didn't make saying goodbye any easier. Kaisa felt the ring on her finger and prayed that her last few months in Helsinki would pass quickly. As she watched him disappear from view, it suddenly occurred to her that she'd have to organise a wedding, too. She ran out of the airport terminal and into the waiting bus. There was so much to do!

KAISA'S FATHER was due home from his travels that evening. When they'd kissed by passport control, Kaisa felt closer to Peter than ever before. She'd assured him it didn't matter that he hadn't asked her father for her hand.

At home, she put the red rose into a vase next to her bed and went into the kitchen.

Kaisa had planned to cook her father's favourite meal: meatballs in a creamy sauce with boiled potatoes. She made a salad, too, but knew he wouldn't want any. He called it 'rabbit food'.

'Did you have a nice Christmas?' she asked.

Kaisa and her father were sitting opposite each other at the small kitchen table. She wondered if he'd spotted the ring on her left finger.

Kaisa's father lifted his head from the food and looked at her from under his light-coloured, unruly eyebrows, 'In Oulu?'

'Yes.'

He put down his knife and fork, 'In Lapland they don't even know how to bake a ham properly. They're not really Finns; they're too close to the North Pole.' He paused, then a smile flitted across his untidy face. He looked tired. 'But the Christmas tree didn't cost anything. We felled it from one of the forests her family have. They're big landowners up there.'

'That's nice,' Kaisa said and rested her chin on her left hand. But her father went back to eating, ladling the food into his mouth as if he'd never been fed. Kaisa sighed. 'I got this,' she said, stretching her arm across, shoving the hand with the sparking diamond ring under his nose.

It took him a little while to comment. He looked at the ring as if it was on fire. Or infectious. His eyes moved slowly from Kaisa's hand up to her face. She smiled. He went back to the food and cleared his plate in silence.

Kaisa sat and waited. She couldn't eat.

'You're getting married and moving to England then?' he said finally.

'Yes.'

'Getting married in England?'

'I...I don't know. We haven't decided yet. It all depends...'

'I'll pay for it all if you get married in Finland,' Kaisa's father interrupted her.

'Oh.'

Her father's eyes were squarely on Kaisa. He coughed and said, 'Anyway...are you happy?'

Kaisa was so surprised by this question, she didn't reply for a while. He'd never asked her such a thing. She didn't think 'being happy' entered his consciousness. He scoffed at the modern disease of stress, thought any psychiatrist was a conman, worse if they happened to be female. He called anyone who belonged to a cult, religion, or had any beliefs, 'one of the Happy People'.

'Yes, very.'

'And, of course, your mother has met the young man, and approves?'

'Yes.' Kaisa realised her mouth was still open. She closed it and tried to remember the last time her father had called her mother anything other than 'that woman', or worse, 'that bitch'. Had he undergone some kind of personality change?

'Good, good,' he said, nodding vigorously.

There was a long silence. Kaisa looked out of the window. It had started snowing at last. Large flakes hung in the air, slowly falling onto the ground. The single lamppost gave an orange glow to the small patch of dead grass outside the house.

'I think this calls for a celebration!' Kaisa's father got up and took a bottle of *Koskenkorva* out of the fridge. He filled two tumblers and lifted his glass. '*Kippis*!'

Kaisa nodded and lifted her own glass. Still she couldn't speak. They sat in silence drinking the neat vodka. It burned Kaisa's throat, as it always did. She took small sips and tried not to grimace.

'There's a lovely church in Espoo, you know,' her father said.

Kaisa didn't know what to say, the conversation was getting more and more absurd. 'Yes?'

'Have a look and tell me how much it's all going to cost. I've got the funds, so don't worry about that.' Kaisa's father downed the rest of his drink and walked into the living room. She heard him put on the TV, sit down in one of the velour-covered comfy chairs and fart loudly.

***

ESPOO OLD Church stood at the end of a country lane, set aside from a newly-built shopping centre. In the distance lay high-rise blocks on one side and a wide motorway on the other. Kaisa and her father went to see it for the first time one Saturday in January 1984. It seemed odd to plan a wedding in a church she'd never been to, but her father said Old Church was the prettiest in the parish. How he knew, Kaisa had no idea. In the past few weeks, he'd been full of surprises.

The stone-clad church was empty when they wandered down the narrow aisle. Kaisa shivered; the air inside seemed colder than outside. It was strange to think she'd stand here in a few months' time, arm in arm with her Englishman. There was so much to do before she could get away, and be with him for forever and ever. Kaisa moved her gaze from the simple altar, with its two silver candlesticks, to her father. He stood perfectly still, with his hands in the pockets of his light-grey overcoat. His shoes were unpolished. Instead of his smarter work clothes, he wore the same shabby jogging pants and cardigan that he did when lazing around in front of the TV at home. His eyes met Kaisa's. 'What?'

'Nothing,' she said.

Her father had been in a funny mood all morning. In the car he'd asked Kaisa how long they'd be away, as if he had some other, more important, appointment to go to. Had he changed his mind about paying for the wedding? But Kaisa wasn't sure he had any idea of how much it would all be, and neither did she.

Kaisa walked out. She was afraid someone, a pastor or a warden, would come out of the recesses of the church and start asking questions. She wasn't ready for that; she didn't even know the date of the wedding yet.

'We have to be in Bastvik in fifteen minutes,' Kaisa said to her father over her shoulder.

The Bastvik Manor House faced a central courtyard, with a

converted barn on either side. There were bedrooms in each of the outbuildings for the use of overnight guests. The ceilings were low and the furniture antique. It all looked perfect, even if there was just one bathroom in each corridor for the guests to share. Surely Peter's family wouldn't mind? The woman who showed them around the rooms smiled. Back at the Manor House she checked a large book and confirmed there were still dates available for a function in the summer. 'How many wedding guests are there going to be?' she asked Kaisa's father.

'Not too many, I hope,' he sneered.

The woman's smile froze.

Kaisa looked down at her hands. 'How many can you accommodate?' she asked.

'The maximum number is seventy-five.'

'That many!' Kaisa's father said.

'That should be more than enough,' Kaisa quickly added.

'Good, good,' the woman tried to smile at Kaisa's father again, but she ended up smirking in a futile effort to lift everyone's spirits.

Kaisa and her father didn't speak on the way home in the car. As they got closer to his house, Kaisa's anger rose. After being so keen on the wedding, and so normal, this morning, he'd embarrassed her in front of the woman in Bastviken. What must she think of them? How was Kaisa now going to arrange the wedding with her? She looked at the leaflet the woman had given her. The rates seemed reasonable. After Kaisa's father's comment about the number of guests, the woman had suggested a domestic sparkling wine for the toasts and a cheaper meal option. No fish course, and chicken instead of veal as a main.

Kaisa sighed.

Later the same day Peter called. Kaisa feigned excitement when he told her the news. 'I've got the whole of my programme set out for the next twelve months. First at the NATO base in Naples until the last week of May. Then two weeks off and the rest of the year I'll be based in Pompey. So, our date could be Saturday the 2nd of June!'

'The 2nd of June.' Kaisa tasted the date on her lips. Could this be true? Would it really happen?

'So when can you finally come over to England for good?' Peter asked.

'My Professor says I can take the final exams at the Finnish Embassy in London, so I can come over as soon as I have arranged everything here. I think perhaps the middle of February.'

'Great! I'm going to Italy in March, but you can stay in the house in Southsea. I'll be home every other weekend at least.'

The words 'I'll be home' rang in Kaisa's ears for the rest of the evening. How would it be to wait for Peter to come home in England when he was away? Would Kaisa be as lonely there as she was in her father's house in Espoo? Though more often than not Kaisa was glad her father stayed away, especially today after their disastrous outing.

At least it would be warmer in Southsea, Kaisa thought. And she'd be working just like Peter's sister-in-law and sister, taking the bus or the train to an office, where she'd do important work. As yet Kaisa had no idea what that job would be. First she needed to marry the man, she thought, and pulled out the *Yellow Pages*. She ran her finger down the names of printers. Now Kaisa knew the date, she could have the invitations made. And she needed to let everyone know. Kaisa lifted the receiver and dialled her mother's number in Stockholm.

KAISA SET the date for her move to England for 25th of February, 1984.

She'd take the train through Europe, just as before, and then cross the Channel over to Harwich. This way she could send all her worldly possessions separately to her new home country, rather than be limited by the number of suitcases she could take on a flight. The only snag was that instead of taking the ferry from Helsinki she'd have to start the journey by rail from Finland. This meant travelling to Turku on the Western coast of Finland and taking a ferry from there to Stockholm. This was the official Finnish Railways route and as much as Kaisa tried to negotiate, there was no veering from official policy. The man in the ticket office at the Central Station reminded Kaisa of Matti. With his neatly cut hair and same beige uniform, he could have have been his double. So Kaisa didn't argue with the official. Besides, personal luggage sent this way was free, whereas sending it by international mail would have cost money Kaisa didn't have. As it was, when in England she'd have to live off Peter's salary; something she tried not to think about.

Kaisa bought the train ticket at Helsinki railway station on a cold windy day. Afterwards she picked up two large cardboard boxes from Valintatalo, a cheap food and clothes store opposite her bus stop. She struggled onto the bus, and occupied two seats, getting disapproving looks from the other commuters. The last thing they needed was to lose a seat to a cardboard box.

Kaisa tried to ignore the other passengers and looked out of the window. It was just past three but already dark. The little snow that had fallen over the city after New Year had quickly disappeared, leaving Helsinki dull and rainy.

As she watched more passengers board the bus at the next stop, Kaisa thought about the items she'd take with her to England. The two large coffee cups and saucers that her mother left behind when she moved to Stockholm, the pestle and mortar her grandfather had made during the war when he worked at the ammunition factory in Tampere. All her books, including the thick heavy ones for the exams she was going to take at the Finnish Embassy in London, and all her LPs. Peter and Kaisa had discussed on the phone whether she'd need to take the ones they both owned by Earth Wind & Fire, Haircut One Hundred, Billy Joel or The Police. Peter thought Kaisa would be crazy to pack them, but she wasn't sure. These LPs were like her friends, they'd kept her sane at night when she was lonely and desperately missing Peter in her father's little house in Espoo.

THE NEXT day Kaisa went to pick up the wedding invitations. Peter and Kaisa had spent a long time on the telephone drawing up a list of guests. He'd come up with only ten, including his parents, godmother, sister and brother with their spouses, and Jeff, Oliver and Sandra, the friends with whom he'd shared the house in Southsea. He said the flights were so expensive that many of his friends couldn't afford to make the trip to Helsinki. The same conversation with Kaisa's father was fruitless. 'You must decide. How am I supposed to know who wants to come to your wedding?'

Then, after he'd been sitting in front of the TV for half an hour, he shouted, 'Invite my mother and my step-sisters. I guess they'll want to come now that old bastard is dead.'

Kaisa sighed. He would always have to put someone down. Her father was referring to his step-father, who'd refused to feed and clothe him when his mother remarried. She'd heard the story so many times: how the man had promised her grandmother that her illegitimate son would be educated and have his own room in the home he'd built for his new bride. And how, after only one week, he had threatened to throw out the new wife, too, if the boy stayed. Kaisa had often wondered what her father had done to receive such treatment. Or was the new husband just as evil as her father claimed. Kaisa had never met him; her father didn't see his mother again until after the evil step-father had died.

The conversation about the wedding guests was more enjoyable with Kaisa's mother. Over the phone, they made a list of over thirty people, including grandparents, aunts, uncles, cousins and Kaisa's friends from school and university. As usual when she spoke on the phone with her mother, she'd made sure her father was out. Kaisa couldn't bear the nasty things he would say about her afterwards, when he heard who was at the other end of the line.

Kaisa had a long conversation with her mother about the wording of the invitations, too. Peter had given Kaisa the text used in the UK, but she wasn't sure whether the Finnish translation should reflect the official tone of 'Mr and Mrs so-and-so have the pleasure of inviting you to the wedding of their daughter and Sub-Lieutenant Peter Williams, RN.' There was nothing similar in Finnish that wouldn't sound pompous and old-fashioned. Eventually they settled on a simple wording, in slightly more formal Finnish.

The printers were in Lauttasaari, in a small industrial park at the far end of the island. As she passed the street where her old block of flats stood, Kaisa felt a little sad. Life with her old boyfriend, or fiancé, had been dull but it was safe. When she saw a light in her old window, and a new set of dark curtains, Kaisa couldn't but wonder whether she was making a grave mistake. What if England turned out to be a difficult country to live in? What if people were unfriendly – even prejudiced – against foreigners like her? What happened at the Dolphin Summer Ball could happen everywhere Kaisa went, on the bus, at work, in the pub in the evenings. What if she didn't get a job at all and ended up being a Navy housewife like Lucinda in Scotland? What if the Englishman, once married, turned out to be as possessive and jealous as her former fiancé? What if Kaisa found married life as unbearable as Martha Quest had in Doris Lessing's books?

AT THE printer's, a man with ink-stained fingers pulled out a copy of the invitations for Kaisa to see. He left two dirty fingermarks in a corner of the card, embossed with heavy, beautiful gold lettering. She reread the text and blushed. Was this really for her? If only her family lived up to the fine wording and look of the invitation. The 'Mr and Mrs have the pleasure of inviting you to the wedding of their daughter' struck Kaisa as false. She wasn't even sure her parents would be able to sit in the same room without falling out, and here they were portrayed as the most united of happy parents, inviting family and friends to their daughter's wedding.

When Kaisa's father came home from work that evening, she showed him the invitations. Kaisa knew he'd be glad the number of guests wouldn't exceed fifty. It was at least twenty-five fewer than the maximum he was expecting. He sat down heavily in one of the plush comfy chairs and perched his reading glasses at an angle on the end of his nose.

'What's this?' he said holding the card and looking at Kaisa over his glasses.

She was standing next to him, but now sat down. For some reason her heart started to beat a little faster. 'The wedding invitations.'

He looked down at the single card Kaisa had handed him, frozen to the spot, saying nothing.

'It's in English as well as in Finnish, because...' she started. He must be offended by the bilingual text. 'We speak Finnish in Finland,' he'd often say when Kaisa's Swedish-speaking friends came to visit the house.

'No, what's this?' he said, pointing his fine long finger at the sentence, 'Mr and Mrs Niemi have the pleasure of inviting...'

'It's the English text. I thought, since half, or in fact it's much less than half, but all the same, they don't understand Finnish, so I thought, being that it is...' Kaisa was stammering now, her heart was beating so fast she could hardly get the words out. Her father looked extremely angry.

'Not that!' he said, loudly. 'It's me who's inviting these people, not your mother.'

'Yes, I know that...' Kaisa was puzzled, what did he mean 'not your mother'?

'It's me who's paying for it.' His pale-blue eyes, over the wonky glasses, were on Kaisa. His lips turned downwards. His hand, holding the card was trembling.

'What?' A chill ran down Kaisa's spine. Even before she heard him say it, she had a premonition about what he was going to say.

'I don't want that bitch on the invitation.'

Kaisa said nothing. Her throat felt dry, and she felt faint.

'And I don't want her anywhere near the wedding,' Kaisa's father said, handing back the card.

There was a long silence. Kaisa struggled to find the right words. 'You mean my own mother can't come to my wedding?' she eventually asked. She willed her voice to sound normal, or firm, but she could hear the tremble in it.

He said nothing for a while. Then there was a dry final comment, 'I'm paying for everything. Not your mother. Me. And I don't want to see that bitch there. That's my final word on the matter.' He took his glasses off and turned the volume up on the TV set.

Kaisa ran out of the room, clutching the plastic bag of invitations. The hate she felt for her father at that moment was even greater than the love she felt for Peter.

Back in her room Kaisa thought she might kill him.

Twenty-two

KAISA WAS lying face down on her bed, with her head spinning, trying to make sense of what had just happened, when she heard the front door slam shut. She waited for a few minutes. It was quiet. Kaisa crept out of her room and walked into the darkened kitchen. The parking space where her father's Saab was usually parked was empty. She took a deep breath and wiped her face with the threadbare tissue she had in her hand. She went to the telephone in the hall and lifted the heavy receiver.

'Mum?'

'What's the matter?'

Hearing her mother's concerned voice brought up the tears again, but Kaisa tried to stop the flow. 'Dad, he...' Holding back the tears took such an effort she couldn't finish the sentence.

'What's he done now?' Kaisa's mother sighed heavily.

But suddenly Kaisa hesitated. How much of what her father had said could she tell her mother? She didn't want to upset her, but then she needed to speak to someone. 'He said you wouldn't be allowed to come...' Now Kaisa couldn't hold back. Tears were running down her face. The cream-coloured receiver stuck to her chin.

'He said because he's paying, you are not welcome at the wedding. He said I'm not to invite you.'

'What!' Kaisa could almost hear her mother get up from the chair in the hallway of her flat, and then straighten her back, in readiness for a fight. She was like a lioness when it came to her daughters. Kaisa felt a little better; a little safer.

'Oh Mum!' Kaisa was crying now, there was no stopping her. What would she do? Get married in England? But how could they pay for the wedding? There was no money and she couldn't ask Peter's parents. Without Kaisa's father there was no way she'd be able to marry Peter.

There was a short, shocked silence at the other end of the phone. Kaisa heard her mother's quick intake of breath. 'I cannot believe it.'

'I know.' It was such a relief to hear that her mother felt equally strongly about what her father had said. And she hadn't even heard the awful words he'd used. Perhaps she guessed.

But very soon Kaisa's mother recovered, 'Don't worry, I'll pay for your wedding.'

'But you don't have the money!'

'I do. It's not a problem.'

Kaisa leant her weary body against the wall and sat down on the floor.

Her mother continued, 'I knew he was going to be trouble. Always the same, he just doesn't change.'

Half an hour later Kaisa got a call from her sister.

'Bastard!' Sirkka said. 'But don't worry, mum and I have discussed everything. We'll organise the wedding in Tampere, it's where you were born after all. You can stay at grandmother's place and the English guests can be in a hotel. I'm thinking of the Cathedral for the wedding. I can't imagine the date is a problem, we have nearly six months to organise things. I also think that we should have the reception at Rosendahl Hotel by Lake Pyhäjärvi, it's perfect for foreign visitors.'

Kaisa's sister went on; she had ideas about the menu, the wines and champagne they were going to serve. Kaisa listened and relaxed. She hadn't realised that, of course, as a qualified *maître d'* she was perfect for the job of organising a wedding. Kaisa smiled as she thought how her big sister liked nothing more than to direct things. Why hadn't she thought of that before? Sirkka said all Kaisa needed to do was turn up; she'd take care of everything.

Kaisa's mind started to wander and her thoughts turned to the gown. A schoolfriend, Heli, was a good dressmaker and had promised to make it. Kaisa couldn't wait to consider designs with her. She'd saved several magazines and patterns. At Stockmann's, dress patterns were sold next to the fabric department, where she'd worked at the weekends. Kaisa had only two Saturdays left there. The lady in charge of the patterns concession gave Kaisa several pictures from the ones she sold, including a Vogue pattern of a simple silk tulle dress. That was Kaisa's favourite, but she had no idea if her friend could make it or where she'd find the correct fabric. There was nothing even close at Stockmann's. There must be places in London where that sort of soft, feathery tulle fabric is sold, Kaisa thought.

'You still there?' Sirkka's voice was concerned.

'I'm just tired.'

'I'll call you tomorrow,' she said and hung up.

Kaisa went off to bed and slept soundly for over nine hours.

The next day there was no sign of Kaisa's father. She had to be at Heli's place at nine, so Kaisa hurried out of the house. She hoped her father would stay at his girlfriend's, where she presumed he was hiding, as long as possible. Kaisa didn't think she could endure one more evening with him. She couldn't wait to leave his house and Finland for good.

THERE WAS little snow left on the ground, just a few dirty patches on the side of the road. But there was a harsh northerly wind as she walked along the streets of Lauttasaari, where Heli lived. For the second time that week Kaisa was back on the island, and walking past her old flat. Was this some kind of torture designed to make Kaisa consider the consequence of her actions? She shrugged off this fatalistic thinking, although sometimes she wondered how many obstacles would be put in the way of her and Peter.

Would they ever walk down the aisle together?

KAISA SPENT her last few days in Helsinki arranging the practical details of a move to another country.

On the Thursday she had an oral examination in methodology with the professor at Hanken. Kaisa was ill-prepared for the exam. The old man, with his untidy grey hair and small round glasses, had to prompt her several times to extract the correct answer. At the end of the session, Kaisa was surprised when he told her she'd passed. He shook Kaisa's hand warmly as she left his stuffy office on the top floor of the School of Economics building. 'Don't be a stranger,' he said and smiled.

Closing the door behind her, Kaisa stood for a moment in the wide, empty hall. It was suddenly flooded with bright sunshine through the large windows to one side of the sixties-style building. Kaisa realised this could be the last time she'd stand here. When she first stepped inside this building, four years previously, she'd been proud to get a place here, but scared of not being accepted by the other students. Kaisa had known next to nothing about the Swedish-speaking community in Finland and was full of prejudices. That her life would be turned upside down during her first year there never occurred to her, nor that it was the start of the end of her life in Finland. How much older and wiser she felt now; yet as Kaisa stood there in the empty space, listening to the familiar echoing sounds from the stairwell, of students milling about on the floors below, she was more unsure of her future than she'd ever been in her life.

Kaisa glanced at her watch and saw she was running late. For old times' sake Tuuli and Kaisa were going to go to the university disco that evening, even though they went there rarely these days. Tuuli had finished her degree, and was now working in a bank in the centre of Helsinki. She still had the flat in Töölö, a couple of tram stops away from Hanken. Kaisa was due to be at her place in five minutes' time. When Tuuli had suggested that Kaisa stay the night she hadn't hesitated. Kaisa didn't want to spend any more nights in her father's house than she had to.

Kaisa ran down the stairs, taking two at a time and headed out of the glazed double doors of the Hanken building. She just made the tram approaching the stop on the other side of the street. The yellow and green vehicle screeched as it took the sharp corner from Arkadiankatu to Runeberginkatu and headed downhill towards Töölö.

Later that same evening, when Tuuli and Kaisa were walking up the windy Arkadiankatu to the disco, Kaisa said, 'This is not goodbye. I'll see you in June, before the wedding!' She'd be back for at least two weeks, to allow for the fitting of the wedding gown and a hen party, which Heli and her other old schoolfriends had already started planning. Kaisa was freezing in her tight-fitting, white velvet jeans and satin blouse. Her suede coat had never been the same after six weeks of rain in Edinburgh.

'Of course,' Tuuli said, and she put her arm around Kaisa's shoulders. 'But you promise to write, yes?' She turned to face Kaisa. She'd stopped walking.

Kaisa looked at her friend's serious face. 'I promise.' Kaisa took Tuuli's arm and they hurried to the warmth of the disco.

THE FOLLOWING day, Friday, was Kaisa's last working day at Stockmann's. When she saw the familiar faces, Kaisa realised that even though she'd been wishing for so long to be away from Helsinki and Finland, to finally leave it wasn't so easy. The doubts hovering in her mind about the seriousness of the decision didn't help. Her colleagues questions about what she was going to do in England, when she was going to get married, or where she was going to live, exhausted her, and Kaisa wished the evening would speed along. Half an hour before closing time, the floor manager gave Kaisa a card and a present – a pinnie made out of blue-and-white checked fabric, the colours of the Finnish flag. Kaisa hugged them all in turn before returning her name badge, uniform and discount card to the personnel department on the top floor.

When Kaisa returned home later that evening her legs ached. But she was relieved the house was dark and quiet; her father would not be home tonight either. Kaisa had just sat down in front of the TV and put her feet up on the sofa when the phone rang.

'What's up?' Peter said when he heard Kaisa's voice.

Kaisa couldn't explain how she felt to him. They'd been talking about the day she'd finally move to England, for so long, she wasn't able to explain to him that she now felt sad that the much-awaited day was nearly here. Instead, she started talking about the wedding. That they'd finally be able to be together forever was the only thought that kept Kaisa going now. She talked about the arrangements for the big day: Sirkka, she said, was telephoning her daily with updates and questions on guest lists or table placements.

'Oh,' Peter said absentmindedly. 'Where did you say this was again?'

Kaisa was silent. She'd told him on several occasions about the changed venue, why it had happened and how upset she was with her father.

'You there?'

'Yes. Look, I'll call you from Stockholm on Sunday, OK?' Kaisa put the receiver down. She felt stupid for getting upset over such a small thing and was glad she hadn't actually had a fight with Peter. What was the matter with her?

That night, when already in bed, Kaisa heard the front door go. Her father walked into the house. He kicked off his boots, rattled the clothes hangers in the hall and used the lavatory. Then all went quiet. Kaisa looked at the time; it was well past twelve o'clock. She wondered if he was drunk. His movements had seemed quite controlled though; perhaps he was sober and had come by car from his girlfriend's place. Kaisa tossed and turned in her bed for hours. She didn't want to see her father ever again. She'd managed to avoid him since the night when he'd refused to invite her mother to the wedding. On the Monday, rather than ask for help with the car, she'd taken a taxi to transport the two cardboard boxes containing her belongings to the railway station. They would take a month or so to arrive in Portsmouth, but the cost was included in the train ticket through Europe to Harwich. The taxi journey to Helsinki station had cost more than the transport to England, but it was worth it if Kaisa didn't have to see her father. But here he was now, at home. And tomorrow would be Saturday and he'd be free from work. How in this small house was Kaisa going to avoid saying goodbye to him?

Suddenly she remembered the stolen books. While living in his house, she'd occasionally referred to two expensive volumes of Finnish/English dictionaries her father had. In her fury at his betrayal, Kaisa had packed both volumes in one of the cardboard boxes. They were in a container ship somewhere in the middle of the Baltic now. What if he noticed the large gap in his bookshelf where the dictionaries normally stood?

Twenty-three

KAISA FINALLY fell asleep around three o'clock in the morning. She dreamt she'd hit her father with a large ice-hockey stick and drawn blood. He'd been trying to lead Kaisa into a darkened room. She woke with a start and heard movements in the kitchen. Her alarm clock showed it was five to seven in the morning. There was a strip of light under the door to the bedroom.

Kaisa found her father in the kitchen, sitting at the table looking out of the window. It was the day she was due to board the train to the ferry port in Turku, then the ferry to Stockholm and onwards through Europe to Harwich, leaving her country of birth for good. Kaisa saw her father was in his nightwear: a pair of long johns and an undershirt. He had a cup of coffee without a saucer in front of him. It was still dark outside; she was wondering what he was looking at when he spotted Kaisa's reflection in the window. He gave her a sheepish smile, which she didn't return. She didn't care if this morning he was being nice Dr Jekyll again. Soon she'd be away from here and never have to deal with his dual personality ever again.

'Coffee?' he asked.

Kaisa sat down in spite of herself. She was so angry she wanted to take his cup and pour the hot coffee over his head. That he tried to appease her with that boyish smirk of his, as if all he needed was to be nice to her again. Kaisa briefly wondered if he had vodka in his coffee, but she didn't get any hint of alcohol from his breath when he poured her a cup. He sat heavily back in the wooden chair. Its faint creak was the only sound in the kitchen. Kaisa's father's eyes were still on her, but now he'd stopped smiling. She tried to avoid his glance.

'So you're off today, then?' he said.

Kaisa nodded.

'I'll drive you.'

Kaisa opened her mouth to say there was no need, but hesitated. His blue eyes were red-rimmed with dark circles around them. He was unshaven and his hands shook when he fiddled with the ear of the coffee cup. Kaisa looked at her own hands and realised she'd inherited his bone structure. She chased the thought away; she wasn't going to fall into that trap again. This time Kaisa wasn't going to forgive him for the hurtful things he'd said about her mother, or for backing out of organising the wedding. Sirkka said he'd only done it to get out of paying for it, and Kaisa was beginning to suspect this was true.

'No, I'll take a taxi,' Kaisa said.

'Nonsense, you need to save your money. I'm taking you. No discussion.' His eyes were serious now.

Kaisa shook her head. She didn't know what to say, so got up and left the kitchen. She trembled as she sat on her bed. What was her father playing at?

'What time is your train?' he shouted after Kaisa.

'Three o'clock,' Kaisa shouted back before realising this was an acceptance of the lift he was offering. She put her head into her hands and looked at the alarm clock: twenty-five minutes past seven. In eight hours' time she'd be on the train to Turku and in twenty-four hours' time she'd be with her mother and sister in

Stockholm. Kaisa decided to get dressed quickly and go to say goodbye to a schoolfriend who lived nearby. She could cycle to her house in ten minutes, then come back via the shopping centre in Tapiola, where she needed to draw all the money from her bank account.

That would take a couple of hours from the day; the rest could be spent in her room, finishing the packing.

When Kaisa returned, the house was empty. Sighing, she went to the telephone and dialled her mother's number.

'Calm down. If he wants to take you, let him.' Her mother sounded so strong. Kaisa wished she was already with her in Stockholm. She felt so incredibly tired. Wasn't this supposed to be a happy time? The time before marrying the man of her dreams, the love of her life? Why was everyone trying to make it as difficult as possible? Or just her father. Why was he trying to make it so hellish for her?

Kaisa finished the conversation with her mother and went to wash her face. She had to pull herself together.

Kaisa's father returned half an hour before Kaisa had to leave. She was already wondering if she should call a taxi, when she heard the front door go. Kaisa had no idea where he'd been but was glad he'd stayed away. Evidently he didn't want a long-winded goodbye either. Kaisa was ready, sitting in the kitchen eating a rye sandwich and drinking a cup of coffee, when he walked in. Her stomach churned when she saw him and she didn't want to finish the sandwich. But she knew what her father's opinions were on leaving food uneaten, and forced down the last piece of bread and cheese.

'All ready?' he said. He stood in the doorway, and nodded at Kaisa's suitcase in the hall.

'Yes'

'We'd better be off then.' Kaisa's father took hold of the suitcase and said, 'Oh, oh!'

Kaisa couldn't help herself and let out a short laugh. It came out more like a snort. She knew the case was heavy. She'd bought some wheels in Stockholm, to make it easier to to transport. Otherwise she knew she'd not manage the long walk between the railway station at Turku Harbour and the ferry terminal. Briefly, she felt relieved that her father was driving her. He'd help to lift the case onto the train at Helsinki, which a taxi driver would not do. Or at least that's what Kaisa hoped. You never knew, her father might be equally unwilling to park the car at the station.

Kaisa soon regretted not taking a taxi.

It started in the car on the long bridge by Lauttasaari Island. In the dim light of the car interior Kaisa's father said, 'So what's happening with the wedding?'

She couldn't believe her ears.

'We're getting married at Tampere Cathedral. Mother's paying for the wedding. So you needn't worry.' Kaisa hoped he detected the sarcasm.

'She can afford it, can she?' he sneered.

Kaisa looked at his profile. His eyes were on the road and his lips were set in a straight line. He looked a little tidier than he had that morning; clean-shaven and wearing his striped Marimekko shirt with dark blue cords. This was the outfit she'd chosen for him when he'd asked Kaisa's advice on clothes shopping a few years ago. It had been a strange day. Her father had once again behaved as if he was a normal, loving, funny man, taking his daughter out shopping and then to an expensive restaurant for lunch. Once again, Kaisa wondered how he could change from one extreme to another so quickly.

It was as if he'd read her thoughts. 'It all went wrong with us when you moved in, you know.'

'Really!' Kaisa's anger rose again.

'Yes. And I bet it was your mother's idea?'

'What?'

'Yes, it's all her nasty plan, I'm sure. You and I have always got along, unlike your sister...' here he had the sense to stop. But he continued with his incredible thesis. 'Your mother knew living together would cause a rift between us and that's exactly what she was after.'

Kaisa was silent for a long time. They were waiting at the traffic lights at Hietaniemi. She looked at the red lights and counted to ten. But ten wasn't a high enough number.

'So it's nothing to do with the fact that you're a selfish, nasty bastard who doesn't love anybody and will never be happy? You're mean and don't want anyone else to be happy either. You don't think of anyone else but yourself. You never have. You and I have never "got on", as you put it. Have you forgotten how you tried to hit me? You weren't satisfied with hitting mother black and blue in Stockholm, you had to strike your sixteen-year-old daughter too. I guess I was just a little annoying, wasn't I?'

Kaisa's father turned his face away from the road and faced her, 'But I didn't hit you!'

'No,' she said quietly, when her father was once again looking at the road and not her. 'But you came very close, raising your hand. That's enough.'

Kaisa heard her father's breathing grow heavy. In silence they passed Arkadiankatu and the university disco.

Kaisa spoke into the silence. 'And another thing: last year when I was really ill and phoned you from hospital, you didn't want to help me. You stayed away just so that you'd not catch the stomach bug. When I was so poorly, you made me take the bus all the way into town to collect money from you. Who were you thinking about then? I had salmonella poisoning and, frankly, needed to be looked after. Where were you? Hiding at your girlfriend's place, that's where!'

Kaisa's father said nothing. Kaisa, too, was now quiet while he drove down Annankatu, past the bus station, crossed Mannerheim Street and parked outside the railway station. When she got out of the car, she saw her father was already by the boot, lifting up her suitcase. Kaisa hurried out and reached her hand towards the handle of the suitcase, not looking at him. But her father nudged

Kaisa's hand away with his elbow, locked the car, and struggling with the heavy luggage, began walking towards the station building. Kaisa stood still for a moment. Why wouldn't he just leave her? She'd told him what she thought of him now. She didn't regret one word, but she had nothing more to say to him. She picked up her Marimekko shoulder bag and the wheels for the suitcase and followed her father into the station.

Looking meek as a lamb, with his shoulders hunched, his eyes trying to search Kaisa's, her father stood next to his daughter on the platform. There was a bitterly cold wind blowing through the station. Kaisa had told him what carriage her pre-booked seat was in, but those were the only words that had passed between them since the car journey.

'Go on,' he now said, motioning with his head towards the door of the train carriage. There were beads of sweat on his forehead, but Kaisa had no pity left for him. She was still angry, and jubilant with it. She couldn't wait to tell her mother what she'd said to him, how at last, after all these years of biting her tongue, Kaisa had been able to let rip and tell her father exactly what she thought of him.

When Kaisa found her seat on the train, her father went to lift the heavy bag onto the parcel shelf. 'No,' she said and motioned towards a space between the seats.

'Right,' Kaisa's father said, and he looked at his daughter.

This time Kaisa returned his gaze. She felt strong. She was in the right. He was a mean bastard, just like Sirkka always said.

But her father moved towards Kaisa and gave her a bear hug. She froze. Holding her tightly, he said, 'I'm sorry.' He let go of Kaisa and hurried out of the door.

The last leg of Kaisa's train journey across Europe, from Harwich to London's Liverpool Street Station, seemed to take forever. She was dead tired from three days of travelling and had not slept a wink during the Channel crossing. By the time she got to the train at Harwich it was full, with the only free seat in the smoking compartment. Sitting there among people puffing at their cigarettes, Kaisa suddenly fancied one herself, even though she only smoked when she had a drink. It might perk her up a bit. But the unopened carton of Silk Cut that she'd bought in the tax free shop, mainly for Peter, was inside the Marimekko shoulder bag on the parcel shelf. Kaisa lifted her eyes to the bag and looked at the gangly boy who had the seat next to her. He was fast asleep, with his head resting on his chest and his mouth open. His breath smelled of alcohol. His long body was blocking Kaisa's way to the aisle, and she had no wish to wake him. She tried to forget about the cigarette and looked out of the window. But she couldn't close her eyes and snooze. The train was moving through a startlingly green landscape. Unlike the barren fields she'd left behind in Finland, there was no snow and the sun was shining brightly. Kaisa leant her head against the seat. Only two hours until she'd see Peter. Only two hours until she'd officially moved to England.

When the train at last pulled into Liverpool Street Station Kaisa waited until most people were out of the carriage. The gangly boy carried her heavy suitcase down the steps and onto the platform. Kaisa smiled a thanks and he gave her a nod. 'No problem, Hen,' he said in a Scottish accent.

Once she'd fixed the wheels onto the suitcase, Kaisa quickly wheeled it down the long platform, towards a busy station concourse. She looked around and tried to spot the tall Englishman. But she couldn't see him. Kaisa waited for five minutes, then began to worry. People were looking at her and she became conscious of her appearance. She felt shabby in her dark-blue jeans and tennis shoes among the smartly dressed businessmen in their pinstripe suits and dark overcoats.

There were several phone booths in the middle of the station, and after another ten minutes had passed Kaisa wondered if she should join the queue. But who would she phone? Kaisa didn't want to talk to Peter's mother in Wiltshire, and she guessed his mother wouldn't know where Peter was anyway. Kaisa didn't know if anyone was at home in the house in Southsea. Had she written down the telephone number of the house? She'd never used a phone booth in England. It was bound to be completely unlike the Finnish or Swedish ones. Everything – trains, the Tube, buses, banks and shops – worked differently here. They even drove on the wrong side of the road. Kaisa looked at the long queues snaking out of the two phone booths in the middle of the station concourse. She dreaded to think how impatient the people behind her would become when she tried to work out the telephone system. No, using one of the booths wasn't an option.

Kaisa decided to stay put and wait. Perhaps the train had been early, she'd not checked what time it was due to arrive; all she knew was that it was mid-morning on the Wednesday. Perhaps Peter had got the wrong day? Kaisa was sure she told him the day clearly, when he'd phoned her in Stockholm on Monday. Peter had made Kaisa smile when he'd said how much he was looking forward to staying in the house together, even if it was for just a couple of weeks. He was leaving for his NATO job in Naples in only ten days' time. Perhaps something had happened and he had to go early? But surely he would have arranged for word to be sent to her, or for someone else to come and meet her instead?

As time passed, Kaisa began to feel angry. Why was he late this time of all times? On the telephone from Stockholm, she'd told him about the awful goodbye with her father, and everything else she'd endured before leaving Finland. Surely he must have known how important this time was for Kaisa? She imagined how delighted her father would be to see his stroppy daughter now. 'I told you, foreigners can't be trusted,' he'd say. Next, standing there in the middle of the station concourse, feeling shabby and foreign, blocking the way of the people hurrying past her, Kaisa pictured the satisfied face of Matti, her ex-fiancé. 'See, he's left you in the lurch, just as I told you he would.'

Kaisa took a deep breath.

She saw a row of plastic seats by the side of the stairs and made her way to them. She sat down opposite the station clock and looked up at it. She dug a packet of Silk Cut out of the Marimekko bag and lit a cigarette. She decided to stay calm and wait until two o'clock. That was over an hour from now. If Peter hadn't turned up by then she'd take a taxi to the nearest hotel and take a room for the night. Kaisa had just about enough money for that. She tried to convince herself that it wouldn't come to that. Any minute now Peter would appear in the centre of the station concourse, look around, spot Kaisa, run to her, and fling his arms around her, apologising profusely.

But the Englishman was nowhere to be seen.

Twenty-four

KAISA SAT and waited on the orange plastic seat at Liverpool Street Station for over three hours. It was a chilly February day, and as the light began to fade in the late afternoon, she finally saw a tall man running through the throng of people, dodging an old woman pulling a large suitcase, and several men in smart suits carrying small black briefcases.

'God, I'm so sorry!' Peter was panting. He took Kaisa into his arms. 'I was afraid you'd gone.'

'I have nowhere to go,' she said. Now the tears she'd been holding back for several lonely hours began to roll down her face. Kaisa wiped them away, trying not to smudge the mascara. She took in his smell and rested her head on his shoulders. They kissed.

'You poor darling,' Peter said and took Kaisa's face into his hands. He kissed her again and hugged her for a long time. 'You're safe now,' he said. Kaisa let her body relax in Peter's arms.

Peter explained how he'd been waiting at Waterloo. After an hour he had enquired about the trains from Harwich and to his horror realised Kaisa's was arriving at Liverpool Street instead.

'The traffic was awful and I couldn't find a parking space anywhere,' he said, as he lugged her heavy suitcase down the busy street outside. It was already dark and Kaisa realised it must be rush hour. 'It's a bit of a hike,' Peter said, taking Kaisa's arm.

'Are you OK?' Peter said, as they walked along one narrow street after another. He looked so miserable, Kaisa couldn't be angry with him, even if she wanted to. The warmth of his fingers around her cold hand was such a sweet sensation, she didn't care about anything else. 'I'm fine,' Kaisa said and smiled in spite of herself.

THEY SPENT the ten days together, just the two of them, in the little house in Southsea. Peter's friend, Jeff, who owned the place, was still in Ireland, and a new tenant wasn't due to come in until later.

'It will be nice for you not to be all alone here,' Peter said.

Kaisa's new companion was another Navy friend, whom she'd met only once before, but remembered as a well-spoken and well-mannered guy. 'James's father was an admiral,' Peter said. James had been with the Australian navy for the past three months and needed somewhere to live in Portsmouth while on a course at the base. 'He's a skimmer, but alright.' Peter said.

'But Jeff is a skimmer!' Kaisa laughed.

Peter kissed her. 'You'll make a good submariner's wife yet.'

She threw a pillow at him. They were sitting in bed on the Sunday morning. James, the admiral's son, was due to arrive that evening and Peter was going back to Naples early the following day. Kaisa was trying not to think about having to say goodbye to him again so soon.

'HOW DO you do?' James said when Kaisa opened the door to him. He shook Kaisa's hand timidly and didn't take off his coat nor put his bag down until Peter noticed him standing awkwardly in the cold, dark hallway. 'Come in and make yourself comfortable!' he said. As they sat in the living room Kaisa suddenly noticed how shabby the house in Southsea was. James in his crisp, well-pressed navy trousers, striped shirt and cashmere jumper looked far too tidy to perch on the lumpy three-piece suite Jeff had inherited from his parents. Apart from the old furniture in the front room, there was a TV on a cardboard box in the corner, a record player with two large speakers either side, and no coffee table. That explained the stains on the worn-out mustard-coloured carpet around the sofa.

In spite of its appearance, it was a happy house. People came and went, and everyone renting a room there was immediately taken into the ever-expanding group of Peter's friends. It was as if being in the Navy, or being the girlfriend of a Navy man, allowed entrance to an exclusive club, one that those outside the services weren't allowed to join.

However correct and formal the new recruit to the Southsea house gang was, Kaisa appreciated his presence. As she waved Peter goodbye at the train station the next morning, and took the bus home, she was glad she'd not be alone in the little terraced house.

KAISA SPENT most of her first months in England studying for the final exams she was to take at the Finnish Embassy in Chelsea. Before Peter left Southsea for Naples, he'd set up a small office for Kaisa in the unoccupied middle bedroom. They'd found an old trestle table in the lean-to conservatory at the back of the house, which Kaisa wiped clean and then set all her books and papers on, as well as the old typewriter she'd lugged with her all the way from Finland.

Now sitting at the rickety table, Kaisa gazed at the neighbour's garden beyond their narrow one. The house opposite looked identical and was occupied by a young family, the mother always at home. Kaisa often saw her during the day, washing dishes at the kitchen sink, or hoovering in the living room. She usually wore a skirt and a blouse, but never looked up from her chores. Kaisa guessed she was too busy to worry about her neighbours.

Kaisa wondered if her life was going to be like that a few years after she'd been married. Sometimes she even daydreamed about having Peter's children, then, horrified at herself, turned back to her exam revision.

The new lodger, James, was rarely at home; he spent his days as well as many evenings at the base in Portsmouth. Occasionally he'd come back to his rented room early in the afternoon and offer Kaisa a cup of tea, which she accepted. Kaisa had decided to start drinking tea, even though the smell of the milky drink made her wince. During the three times she'd stayed with Peter's parents in the country, Kaisa found she couldn't consume as many cups of coffee a day as the English did tea. Besides, she wanted to surprise Peter when he returned with her new, very British habit.

One evening in early March James got back from his course before Kaisa had gone to bed. She'd stayed up, hoping for a call from Peter. It had been three days since they'd last spoken and Kaisa was dying to talk to him. As usual, James made them both a cup of tea, then perched on the worn-out sofa next to Kaisa. After talking about the weather – it had been raining every day that week – he finished his tea and fiddled with his empty glass mug. He glanced at his watch and yawned. 'Guess it's time to turn in,' he said but didn't move. It was past midnight.

Kaisa picked up her half-drunk tea and his empty mug and took them to the kitchen.

'Right,' James said and half rose from the sofa.

'Goodnight,' Kaisa said, and she started to walk up the narrow stairs.

Kaisa heard him cough and turned her head towards the living room.

'Hmm, if you don't mind, I was going to make a phone call...'

'OK,' Kaisa said.

'You're not expecting...?'

‘No, I don’t think he’ll phone tonight.’

‘In that case,’ James lifted his eyes to her. ‘It’s long-distance...a girl I met in Australia.’

‘Ah,’ Kaisa said and smiled. She felt like an old, experienced woman. As she lay in bed, trying not to listen to the muffled telephone conversation below her, Kaisa thought how far Peter and she had come. From meeting at the British Embassy four years before, to walking down the aisle together in less then three months’ time. Kaisa thought about all the happy and tearful phone calls they’d had; the heart-breaking goodbyes and the blissful reunions; the many misunderstandings and then the realisation that they couldn’t live without one another. Kaisa’s stomach tightened when she thought about the wedding. She could hardly believe it was going to happen.

But the invitations had been sent. The English guests had all replied; there were going to be ten of them. They had even bought their flights, and Sirkka had booked the hotel in Tampere. Kaisa’s flight back, two weeks before the wedding, was booked, as was Peter’s. He was to fly with the guests a few days before the ceremony. All he had to do was to get a Certificate of Non-Impediment so that he could marry in Finland. All Kaisa had left to do was find a suitable silk tulle fabric for her dress and send it on to her dressmaker friend. Kaisa had planned to do that after her first exam in London. She knew exactly what she wanted to buy and had the addresses of three shops that sold fabrics near Oxford Street.

Before he left, Peter had given Kaisa a map of London and told her how to take the Tube from Waterloo Station to Sloane Square. Being alone in London was scary but exhilarating. Kaisa followed Peter’s directions and found the right line and the right stop on the Tube. Emerging from the dark tunnels, carrying her black leather briefcase and dressed in a sombre black suit, Kaisa left the station and walked fast in what she thought was the direction of Chesham Place. It was around noon on a Tuesday in mid-March. She tried to match the steps of the people rushing around her, wanting to pretend that she, too, was part of the hub of the city. Kaisa didn't want to appear a tourist and avoided looking at the map.

The Finnish Embassy turned out to be just beyond a large green park, fenced off with freshly painted wrought-iron railings. There was a sign that read 'Private'; Kaisa presumed the right to use the park belonged to the owners of a long row of white stucco-fronted houses. They had tall windows draped with heavy curtains. Along this wide street there were fewer people about, so Kaisa slowed her pace and at last dared to look at her map. She was very close, and turning a corner she saw the Finnish flag.

Kaisa travelled to London five times in all during March and April. The embassy staff got to know her and Kaisa got to know the front room with a small desk where she spent three hours each time, writing down her answers. The exams always came in a sealed envelope. When she pulled out the exam papers from the brown envelope, the same Finnish lady would stand by Kaisa. She had brown hair and dark-rimmed glasses. Her make-up was always quite heavy but carefully applied. Even when the weather got warmer in April, she still wore the same tweed skirt and white blouse, often with a blue-and-white silk scarf tied loosely around her neck. When she closed the door and left Kaisa alone, she'd say, 'Good luck, see you later.'

On Kaisa's last visit in late April 1984, when she was ready to go, the lady with the tweed skirt said, 'It's our staff sauna night, perhaps you'd like to stay?' She told Kaisa how one of the previous ambassadors had built a Finnish sauna in the basement, and that evening was the regular bathing night for the female employees. They had one once or twice a month, if the Ambassador wasn't entertaining. Kaisa had not brought a towel, nor a change of clothing, but they said they had some things for guests, so Kaisa spent an hour or so alone in the dimly lit basement where a wood cladded sauna stood. The smell inside the sauna of pine and soap, and the heat on her skin as the *löyly* water hit the hot stones made her suddenly very homesick. When she left, the secretary hugged Kaisa and made her promise to come and say hello to her when she needed to apply for a new passport.

Usually when Kaisa left the Finnish Embassy she felt tired but glad that another exam was over. She was in a hurry to get away, whether it was to go shopping on King's Road, or to take the train back to Southsea. Feeling fresh and relaxed from the sauna, Kaisa was now reluctant to leave. It was as if another tie to her mother country was being severed. Even though the embassy would always be there, Kaisa knew it wouldn't be the same to come back as an ordinary expatriate to renew a passport. She'd never again be offered a sauna, or sit in that little room, officially a part of Finland, feverishly writing, straining to remember anything she'd learned at the temporary desk in the little house in Southsea.

On that last exam day, the sun was shining. As Kaisa hurried to catch the next train from Waterloo, she remembered she was to meet the naval padre the following day. Her new life as a naval wife was getting closer, so there was no point in mourning the old one. The padre was to issue a Certificate of Non-Impediment to the Englishman, the final piece of red tape they needed for the wedding to go ahead.

THE PADRE wore a dark suit with a white dog collar. He was a tall man and his dark form loomed large over the front door of the terraced house. He offered Kaisa his hand and held onto her palm for so long she felt trapped by his grasp. But he continued gazing into Kaisa's eyes and smiling, until she pulled her hand away.

'And how may I help you, dear?' he asked, after Kaisa had made him a cup of tea. They were sitting facing each other on the sofa in the front room.

'I am from Finland. My English fiancé, a lieutenant in the Royal Navy, and I are getting married there next month. He said you can issue him with a Certificate of Non-Impediment.'

'Ah,' the padre said, and he drank his last drops of tea. For a moment he looked for a table on which to place his empty cup and saucer, and then put it carefully down on the floor. He crossed his hands and said, 'There may be a little problem with that.'

'A problem?'

'Well...what is the date of the happy occasion?'

Kaisa told him they'd be married the first Saturday in June, in just under five weeks' time.

'Hmm...well, oh dear. You see, I don't issue these certificates. What happens in England – this may be the same in Norway –'

'Finland,' Kaisa interrupted him. She was getting a strange feeling in the pit of her stomach.

'Of course, yes, Finland.' He gave Kaisa a sheepish look and smiled. She noticed the expression in his eyes did not change when his lips moved. He reached his hand across and touched Kaisa's knee. 'For your fiancé to get a Certificate of Non-Impediment he needs to have the bands read in his home parish.'

'Yes?'

'Has he had his bands read?

'No, I don't think so.'

'Well, then he needs to do that. But it takes six weeks.'

Kaisa stared at the padre. She held her breath.

The padre squeezed Kaisa's knee harder. She pulled her leg away. The padre placed his hands carefully on his lap; not looking at Kaisa, he said, 'Can you perhaps change the date of the wedding?'

Kaisa thought how much her sister had organised for the day. How all the English guests had bought their expensive flight tickets. How Peter's mother and godmother had already bought their outfits and matching hats. How the Cathedral in Tampere had been booked, how the hotel for the reception had been reserved, how the menu had been decided. 'No...' she said.

'I understand, dear,' the padre said, but the expression on his face remained unchanged.

Kaisa knew she needed to say something but her mind was

suddenly blank. She couldn't think at all. Did this mean they couldn't get married? The pastor in Tampere had said that without this certificate he couldn't marry them. Kaisa had never heard of any 'bands'.

'The purpose of the bands being read in the groom's home parish is to establish that he's not been married before...' the padre hesitated when he saw Kaisa's face, 'which I'm sure he hasn't been, of course, but when a young man marries abroad the foreign – or in this case the Fi...Fin...'

'Finnish.'

'Ah, yes, the Finnish church has to be certain that he is not committing a crime.'

'But...' Kaisa was staring at this vision of the devil in a clergyman's clothes. What the hell was he telling her?

'We don't have six weeks.'

'Well, no,' the padre said and went for Kaisa's knee again.

Kaisa moved her leg away just in time.

The padre coughed. 'What you could do is have a civil ceremony here in England, at a registry office,' he pronounced the last two words carefully as if Kaisa was half-witted, 'and then have a blessing in the church abroad. The wording of the ceremony is almost the same, and in the eyes of God you'll still be married in the Church in...hmm...your country.' The padre gave Kaisa another of his half-cocked smiles. 'I have the telephone number here somewhere.' He rummaged in his worn-looking leather satchel.

After the padre had left, Kaisa immediately went over to the beige-coloured telephone under the stairs and dialled the number for Portsmouth Registry Office.

The friendly man who answered the phone listened to Kaisa's rambling explanation of the situation. How her fiancé was in the Navy and stationed abroad, how moments ago she'd only just found out that the wedding they'd planned for months may not happen, and how the only solution the naval padre had suggested was to have a civil ceremony in England and a blessing in the church in Finland. Occasionally he said, 'Oh dear,' or 'I understand,' or 'Yes, yes.' When Kaisa finally finished the tale, he said, 'So would you like me to have a look in the diary to see what dates we have before the 2nd of June?'

'Yes please!' Kaisa realised she could have just asked him to do that straight away, but felt so much better for having told someone about the catastrophe. She exhaled slowly and waited for the man to come back to the phone.

'Well, I do have a date this coming Friday, but then the next weekend date I have is the 9th of June.'

It was Monday 30th of April 1984. Kaisa had woken up that morning remembering it was Walburgh Night and felt very homesick. That same night all her friends in Helsinki would be going out to celebrate, wearing their student caps and drinking too much. Meanwhile Kaisa was trying to organise something that felt very much like a shot-gun wedding. Then it dawned on her: she'd be married this Friday, in four days time, not in five weeks time!

'Would you like me to book this?'

Kaisa thought for a fraction of a moment. 'Yes, please.'

The man went through the cost and asked if Kaisa could post a cheque as soon as possible.

Next Kaisa called the number in Italy that Peter had given her. They never telephoned each other during the day and Peter sounded surprised when he heard Kaisa's voice.

'Are you OK?'

Kaisa realised she was unbearably annoyed with him. She'd been nagging Peter about the certificate during almost every phone call from Finland, and again when she arrived. Then he didn't get around to doing anything about it until he was already in Naples. And then he'd only managed one measly phone call to the naval padre.

'No, I'm not,' Kaisa said.

'Really?' Peter sounded worried.

'The padre told me this morning that he can't issue the certificate. You know the Certificate of Non-Impediment you need in order to marry me.' Kaisa told Peter the whole sorry tale.

'We'd be getting married this Friday?' Peter said. He sounded very calm, considering.

Kaisa was even more furious now. Didn't he understand how serious the situation was. Or was he having doubts? 'Yes.'

Neither of them spoke for a moment. Then, trying to control herself, Kaisa said, 'This was the ONLY thing you needed to organise, and you couldn't even be bothered to do that!' She was holding back tears. She wanted to scream at him. She wanted to tell him that if he didn't want to marry her, he should say so. While Kaisa listened to Peter's breathing, she felt cold. Peter had been late at the train station when Kaisa arrived in England. He'd been posted abroad as soon as she arrived in Southsea. Now he'd not bothered to get the certificate. Was it possible he was subconsciously trying to stop the wedding from going ahead?

'I'm really sorry,' Peter said. His voice was barely audible. 'Look, I'll call you back in an hour. I need to arrange a pass. But I'm going to do it, don't worry, everything will be alright.'

'Yes?'

'Yes, it will. And,' Peter put his lips very close to the receiver. Kaisa knew he was trying to say something without being overheard, 'I love you, don't ever forget it. And I can't wait to be married to you. The sooner the better.'

Twenty-five

TWO DAYS after the padre came to visit Kaisa, exactly one month before they were due to marry in Finland, Peter came back from Naples. He stepped out of the taxi as the evening sun was about to set at the end of the tree-lined street in Portsmouth. He looked tanned, and so handsome in his Navy jumper and trousers that Kaisa had to catch her breath. The anger she felt for him dissipated. Peter kissed Kaisa outside the front door, dropping his brown holdall on the pavement. He took her upstairs and before they had a chance to talk, they made love. His eyes seemed darker against his tanned skin and his body more taut.

Afterwards, as Peter and Kaisa lay in bed and she was resting her head on his shoulder, taking in his scent, which included something new, an addition from the heat of the Italian sun, they talked about the wedding.

'So this time on Friday you'll be my wife,' Peter said and kissed Kaisa again. Then he jumped out of bed. Kaisa watched him in silence as he opened a new carton of Silk Cut and lit one. 'Sorry, I've been smoking a lot more in Italy, everyone on the base does.'

Kaisa smiled. Italy suited him; his body was bronzed and

muscular; the black hairs that covered his legs had turned slightly lighter. The effect was mesmerising. Peter came back to bed and started telling Kaisa about his journey from Naples to Rome, where he'd caught a plane to Heathrow. 'The driver they gave me was Italian. He drove like a maniac, on roads that had sheer drops down to the sea, littered with tunnels and traffic lights, which he ignored. He scared the living daylights out of me. He drove through all the red lights. He said you didn't have to follow traffic signals in Italy, that they were just advisory. My God, I though I'd never make it to you alive!'

Kaisa looked at him and laughed. But the thought that she could have lost him in a stupid car accident made her fall silent. What difference would an early ceremony in a registry office have made then? Wouldn't she rather have her Englishman hopelessly disorganised than not have him at all?

'What did the others say when they found out about the certificate?'

'The Italians just shrugged their shoulders and the English said what a prat I was.' Peter gave Kaisa a sheepish look.

'They were right.' She play-punched his side.

Peter took Kaisa into his arms and kissed her, 'But I'm happy because it means I can marry you sooner.' He got out of bed and put on his boxer shorts and a worn out T-shirt that he dug out of the wardrobe.

Kaisa had tried to arrange their clothes as best she could, though there was very little room for their things. Once they were married, Peter said, they'd get a large three-bedroom married quarter right in the centre of Southsea, though he didn't know exactly where. Kaisa couldn't wait to move into their own place.

'Thank goodness we're alone this weekend,' Peter said. James had gone to see his parents somewhere in the country. 'I'll phone around to let people know and then we'll go to the pub, shall we?' Peter was halfway down the stairs and shouted to Kaisa as he took them two at a time. She stretched herself on the bed and listened to his footsteps. Through the open door, she heard him dial a number and talk to someone, 'Yeah, this Friday, can you make it?'

ONCE AT home, Peter sprang into action. His second call was to his best friend, Jeff, who was also his best man. He was going to try to get weekend leave from his posting in Northern Ireland. His friend's parents, who owned the house they lived in, also ran a pub and B&B in Old Portsmouth and they offered to give Kaisa and Peter a small reception after the registry office wedding, in the breakfast room upstairs.

Peter laughed when he told Kaisa how the conversation with his friend had gone, 'Me: Listen, I'm getting married. Him: Yes I know; I'm your best man. Me: No, I'm getting married this Friday. Him: WHAT?'

In all Peter managed to gather about twenty people for the wedding. Kaisa was amazed by his capacity to get things done, and she watched in silence as he made his phone calls, laughing with people, joking with them about his inability to organise the certificate, and about how angry Kaisa was.

'But I'm not mad at you anymore,' she said to him after one such jokey call. She'd put on a pair of jeans and one of Peter's old submarine jumpers.

'I know, darling,' he said, looking at her, 'My clothes suit you.' He gave her another quick kiss. Then, leafing through his black notebook, he dialled a number. The truth was, Kaisa wasn't even slightly annoyed any more. She was simply blissfully happy; happy to watch him organise everything, happy just to hold him, happy to be married to him sooner than planned. Then it occurred to her; what would her mother and sister say? How could Kaisa tell them she was already married when she walked down the aisle in Tampere Cathedral?

***

THE DAY of the registry office wedding was gloriously sunny. During the two days of frantic organising, Peter had managed to enrol the help of their neighbours in Southsea, a couple who lived opposite, people whom Kaisa hardly knew. The husband had deep sideburns and grey hair. He'd got very drunk at the parties she'd been to in their house, which was a mirror image of the one they stayed in. In his inebriated state, he'd get his guitar out and sing. His wife was a short, jolly woman called Sally. She was in her forties and had jet-black hair, with white roots at the parting. Sally was incredibly kind to Kaisa. When she found out about the wedding, she immediately crossed the street from her house opposite and demanded to know if Kaisa needed her help.

'You have to have something, old, something blue and something borrowed,' Sally said, ushering Peter out of the way. The next day, she took Kaisa shopping on Palmerston Road, a small high street in Southsea, and said she'd be over the night before the wedding to make sure Kaisa had company. Peter was planning to go out with his friends, 'to celebrate his last night of freedom.' He was going to stay the night in the bed and breakfast rooms Jeff's parents had above their pub. 'It's bad luck for you to share a bed the night before your wedding,' Sally said.

Peter squeezed Kaisa's shoulders, 'You going to be alright on your own?'

She nodded. She'd lived in the house in Southsea more or less on her own for months. Why would this one night be any different?

But on the night before the wedding Kaisa was glad of company. She and Sally sat on the velour sofa in the front room of the terraced house and emptied half a bottle of Smirnoff that Sally had brought with her. 'I remembered you saying Finns drink vodka.' Kaisa told her about her old fiancé, Matti, about the night at the British Embassy when she met Peter, about his 'accident', about the tennis player, about her father, and about her mother and sister. Kaisa had never told anyone so many secrets before. Sally held Kaisa's hand and listened.

The next day, in the back of the neighbour's car, clutching the posy of white and pink roses Sally had ordered for her, Kaisa took her hand and thanked her. When Sally noticed that the whole of Kaisa's body was shaking, she put her arm around her shoulders. Her husband, who was driving, turned around and gave Kaisa a worried look. She felt the black curls of her new friend's hair touch her cheek and smelled the strong musk perfume she wore, 'You'll be fine, girl. You know you love him and he loves you, so there's nothing to worry about,' Sally said and smiled.

Sally's husband nodded vigorously from the front seat, as if to confirm her words.

Kaisa smiled. She knew they were both right, but suddenly in the night, alone in the large bed, listening to the empty house creak all around her, she'd panicked. It dawned on her that in the morning she was going to marry and there wasn't going to be a single person there who knew her – if you didn't count a neighbour who'd known her for only a matter of days. Kaisa was abroad and utterly alone. She'd not had the heart to tell either her sister or mother about the wedding. She didn't want the real wedding in Finland to be spoilt for them, but when Kaisa lay there, drunk on the vodka and wide awake, she realised that the next morning was the actual wedding. This was going to be when she and Peter would be joined together in law.

Forever.

'You look lovely,' Sally said and gently helped her out of the car. Kaisa was wearing a new white hat she'd bought while shopping with Sally and a white skirt and top Kaisa's friend in Finland, Heli, had made. The blue in Kaisa's outfit was a lacy garter that she'd bought at the same time as the hat. Her white shoes were the old item; they were the same shoes she'd worn to the cocktail party where she'd met Peter. Finally, Sally had lent her a gold bracelet, which was the only item of jewellery, apart from a set of pearl earrings and her diamond engagement ring, that Kaisa wore.

Outside on the pavement there were a few smiling faces she

knew. When the guests saw Kaisa, they hurried up the steps to the registry office and disappeared inside.

But Kaisa's nerves would not let her be. When she saw Peter standing next to Jeff, his best man, at the top of the mahogany staircase, her legs almost gave way. He kissed Kaisa lightly and said, 'You ready?'

Kaisa looked into Peter's eyes and held onto him. She couldn't speak but nodded instead. He placed Kaisa's hand in the crook of his arm and nodded to Jeff, who disappeared behind a set of double doors.

'We'll wait here just for a second, and then we go in,' Peter whispered in Kaisa's ear.

Twenty-six

KAISA AND Peter fell sound asleep in the vast bed at The Portsmouth Hilton Hotel at about five in the afternoon. They were both exhausted after the ceremony at the registry office, where, with her trembling voice and in his confident, sure words, they'd promised to love and honour each other for as long as they lived. When at the end of the ceremony Kaisa had been told to sit down at a desk and sign a large book, she was glad to rest her trembling limbs. Peter took hold of her shoulders and, bending over Kaisa, also signed his name. There were pictures; everyone wanted to take one. At the end of the day, when they'd stood at the reception to receive the congratulations, had lifted their glasses of champagne for the hundredth time, and had cut the cake with a naval sword acquired by Jeff, Peter's best man, Kaisa's jaw ached from all the smiling.

But most of all Kaisa was relieved she'd been able to go through with the day without bursting into tears or collapsing in a heap. She'd worried she was going to somehow forget to breathe, that she'd not be able to say anything at all during the ceremony or afterwards at the reception. Kaisa was afraid the right words would not come out of her mouth when she spoke to all the kind and happy people who'd gone to such trouble to make the day special for her, a foreign girl no one really knew, and Peter.

Everything had been new to Kaisa; she'd never been to an English wedding. The sword, which should have been bought with the money the Navy had given him for kitting himself out (spent on other things, ' beer and cigarettes', as he reluctantly admitted to her), was the traditional way for a naval officer to cut his wedding cake. The cake itself was different too; it was dark and fruity, a tea cake rather than a sponge, which was usual in Finland. The ceremony, Kaisa guessed, was the same; although as soon as she'd said the words she forgot them. The small paper flowers that were thrown over them, 'confetti', Peter had called it, was also different. In Finland they threw rice at the newly-weds.

Then there was the strange tradition of spoiling the bed at the hotel. Jeff had somehow got into the hotel and put sand between the sheets. 'It's what you do,' Peter laughed, as they stripped the bed. Lying on the duvet cover, unable even to drink the champagne the hotel had left for the newly-weds, they fell asleep.

When Kaisa awoke early the next morning, the first thought that entered her head was that in only a few hours' time she'd have to say goodbye to her new husband. It was pitch-black in the room and for a moment she had to remind herself where she was. A thin strip of light came from somewhere between a set of dark, heavy curtains.

'What time is it,' Peter murmured next to her.

He got up and fell over, 'Bloody hell!'

Kaisa giggled. He cursed once more and after a few minutes finally managed to crawl into the bathroom and switch on a light. When he pulled open the curtains Kaisa could fully appreciate the vast size of the bridal suite. It occupied the corner of the top floor, with large floor-to-ceiling windows on two sides. The hotel itself was ugly; a seventies high-rise situated on the outskirts of Portsmouth, but it was the best one in the city. It had been a complete surprise to Kaisa when, at the end of the lunch reception, Jeff had led Peter and Kaisa into a taxi. A small holdall had been packed for her, and Peter said, 'I'm taking you for the shortest honeymoon in the history of naval weddings. It will only last 24 hours but I promise it'll be memorable.'

Now that the honeymoon was nearly over, Kaisa went and stood next to Peter as he gazed out of the window towards the harbour. The sun was about to rise and the sky was separated into steel-grey clouds at the top and bright-white light below, where it dipped into the sea. Peter put his arm around Kaisa's shoulders. She pressed herself against his body, 'What time do you have to go?'

'The flight leaves at five thirty.' Peter's body shifted and he turned to face her. He looked into her eyes and said, 'But I'll be back before you know it.'

AFTER THE registry office wedding Kaisa suddenly became somebody in England. She had a banker's card and a chequebook, which her new husband had organised for her. Kaisa also had a title, Mrs Peter Williams, which immediately brought respect, whether she was paying with her brand-new chequebook in the local butcher's or arranging driving lessons over the telephone. During the following two weeks, which Kaisa spent in the house in Southsea, with the occasional company of the polite and friendly James, she forged a new life, a new set of rules to live by. Gone was her solitary life with her father, her nights out with Tuuli, the long hours spent in the Hanken library, cramming for her exams. Instead Kaisa spent the mornings writing her thesis with her grandmother's old typewriter on the rickety table. At around noon she'd walk down to the end of the road to buy food for the day and post that day's letter to her husband. In the evenings she'd either watch TV, or pop over to the neighbour's house, where they'd chat, sitting at her kitchen table. Kaisa would tell her the latest news on getting a married quarter. Peter was waiting to hear when they could move in and, more importantly, where. Even with her elevated position as a naval wife,

Kaisa still couldn't find out from the Navy's housing officer which flat they'd been allocated. She wanted to know where their new life as a married couple would truly begin; to picture their home together. Continuing to live in the terraced house in Southsea seemed like being in limbo.

Three days after Peter had returned to his posting in Naples, the phone rang. It was Sirkka, Kaisa's sister. 'Have you thought about who's going to give you away?'

She sounded breathless, as if she'd been running.

'No,' Kaisa said and was surprised she hadn't thought about her father, or that his absence from the wedding meant there'd be no one to hand her to Peter. It was such an antiquated tradition anyway. After the ceremony in the registry office Kaisa hadn't given much thought to the wedding in Finland. It didn't seem that important anymore. But, of course, she couldn't tell Sirkka this; no one in Finland knew that when she walked down the aisle in Tampere Cathedral, she'd already be married to Peter. Kaisa now regretted she hadn't been brave enough to tell her sister or mother about the registry office wedding. Telling them now would not only spoil the day for both of them but would also make all their hard work seem unimportant. Also, telling her friends behind her family's back seemed wrong. In any case, she'd not had any contact with anyone; Kaisa's new life in Sunny Southsea seemed far removed from Helsinki.

'Well, you said you didn't want to invite him…' Sirkka now said.

'No, I don't.' Kaisa interrupted her. Had Sirkka changed her mind about the bastard?

'Yes, well, in that case... Mum was wondering if she should ask our uncle?'

Kaisa agreed. Sirkka then went into a long conversation about the hotel she'd booked for the English visitors. She also thought it would be nice if everyone would get together for a meal on the day Peter's family and friends arrived in Helsinki. 'It would be a good way for everyone to get to know each other,' she said. Neither

Kaisa's mother nor Sirkka had yet met Peter's family, not even his parents. She'd decided on Sahlik, the Russian place where Kaisa's father had taken her and Peter all those years ago. It was a good choice – the food was unusual and they could accommodate a large group. Kaisa had not been back since that evening there, and wondered if it was going to bring back bad memories. But Sirkka wasn't one to be easily swayed by woolly emotional issues like that, so Kaisa decided not to object to her sister's choice.

ONE LATE afternoon, a few days before Kaisa was due to return to Finland to prepare for the church wedding, she got a phone call from a girl called Samantha. She'd been invited to the registry office, where she'd hugged Kaisa warmly even though she'd never met the girl before. 'I'll call you and take you out sometime when he's away,' Samantha had said and winked at Peter.

Samantha was a large-bosomed girl with streaky blonde hair. She rang the door bell and confidently stepped inside before Kaisa had had a chance to ask her in. She kissed Kaisa on both cheeks, rising on tiptoes as she did so. Samantha was shorter than Kaisa remembered. She must have read Kaisa's mind because she laughed, 'Oh God, don't look at these,' she pointed at her shoes, 'I just wear these flats to drive in; my proper ones are in the car!'

Kaisa looked down at Samantha's feet for the first time, 'Oh.'

'So you ready?' Samantha said, her heavily made-up eyes wide. She had bright red lipstick, and Kaisa felt underdressed in black cropped trousers and a simple top she'd made herself from a piece of faux-suede fabric. Kaisa looked like a boy compared with Samantha with her flowing, deep-cut dress.

Samantha had decided they'd go to the naval base where, on Wednesday nights, there was a bar and a disco. Kaisa had been there once before with Peter. He'd told her it was an after-hours place for young naval officers to go and find a date, and that it was full of nurses looking for officers. Kaisa remembered the saying about nurses being easy, so she didn't tell Samantha this. It felt strange for Kaisa to go to a place like this without Peter. As they sat at the bar, Kaisa felt more and more uncomfortable under the searching looks that some of the young officers gave her. Samantha raised her eyebrows at Kaisa after a blonde guy asked if she wanted a drink, even though Kaisa already had a full glass of wine in front of her. 'No thank you,' Kaisa said, lifting up her left hand and flashing her rings. The diamond had now been joined by a simple gold band, still producing a strangely heavy sensation on Kaisa's finger. 'Ah, sorry,' he mumbled and moved away.

Quite of lot of the men were drunk already when Kaisa and Samantha arrived. After only two drinks Samantha decided she wanted to go and asked if Kaisa needed a lift home.

Sitting next to her in the small car on the way back from the base, watching the already familiar streets whiz past, Kaisa felt relieved the evening had gone well. It had been the first time she'd been out in England without Peter. Kaisa looked warmly over to Samantha and asked if she wanted to come inside for a coffee before driving home.

Samantha looked surprised, 'Yeah, sure.'

Kaisa went through to the kitchen and asked Samantha to sit down on the sofa in the front room. Kaisa made instant coffee with milk for Samantha and black for herself. As Kaisa handed her the mug, Samantha said, 'It's jolly decent of you to be friends with me.'

Kaisa looked at the girl in the now wrinkled cotton dress, 'Why?'

'Well, you know…' she gave Kaisa a sheepish look and lowered her eyes to the carpet.

'I don't know – what?' Kaisa said.

Samantha stirred her milky coffee and lightly shifted her position on the sofa . She wasn't looking at Kaisa and suddenly she knew what Samantha meant. In a flash, images of Peter – Kaisa's new husband – and this voluptuous girl with the perfect English upper class accent filled her mind. This was the girl; the 'accident'

Peter had so wanted to hide from her. Her face grew hot and Kaisa wondered if she'd blushed.

'Look,' Samantha said, 'it really didn't mean anything, honestly…'

Kaisa couldn't think of what to say. Her throat was dry and she doubted she'd be able to speak even if she'd known the words she wanted to utter.

Samantha's eyes met Kaisa's, 'You did know, right?'

At last Kaisa was able to speak, 'Yeah, of course, don't worry.'

Kaisa's heart was beating so hard she wondered if the girl, the 'accident' sitting with her legs crossed, wearing her 'driving shoes' at the end of her little plump legs, might hear it. Kaisa concentrated on breathing normally and added, 'He told me right away.'

Samantha's eyes flashed at Kaisa. She straightened her back and lifted up her bosom, 'It was a total accident. We were both so bloody plastered; I mean, it could've been anybody.'

Kaisa forced her mouth into a smile. The girl had used that word, that same word Peter had used. Had they agreed what to tell Kaisa afterwards?

'We've known each other for donkeys, and of course we were friends, because you know, I went out with one of his Dartmouth pals.' Samantha babbled on. 'And don't take this the wrong way, but the last thing I want to do is to marry a naval officer.'

Kaisa wasn't listening. She just wanted to shout at Samantha to shut up and get the fuck out of her house. Instead she sat at there with a fake smile on her face until at last Samantha finished her coffee and left.

FOR THE next two days Kaisa couldn't work on her thesis. She tried to write to Peter but as soon as she started a letter, she tore it into bits. James was away again and Kaisa was alone in the house. The only person she could talk to was her neighbour. Sally patted Kaisa's hand kindly and said, 'But it happened once, and that's it. I know him, he's a good man, he won't make the same mistake twice.'

Kaisa knew what she felt was wrong. When it happened they'd been far apart and had had a fight. Even she was unsure if they'd broken up at the time. And Kaisa had been with somebody too. But it wasn't the actual act that made her feel so bad, it was the fact that 'the accident' was here, close to Kaisa. She had come to the wedding and had even tried to make friends with Kaisa. By insisting on not telling her who it was, Peter had allowed that to happen. What kind of fool did he take Kaisa for? Did he really think she wouldn't find out who the person was? Besides, why had he invited Samantha to the wedding? All this Kaisa wanted to ask him, but she couldn't find the right words to put into a letter to him without sounding madly jealous, or hypocritical. But more than those things, she was afraid for the future. What if Peter just couldn't be faithful? What if that was the reason for his previous doubts about the future, why he'd said what he did on that sunny day in Hyde Park? And if so, what had changed his mind and made him want to marry Kaisa after all?

Twenty-seven

'YOU'VE LOST weight,' Kaisa's old schoolfriend said. Heli's eyes were sharp under newly blow-dried short hair. They were standing in front of the hall mirror of Kaisa's grandmother's house in Tampere. Heli was much shorter than Kaisa and had to stand on tiptoe to zip up the bodice of her white silk tulle wedding gown. Kaisa was hot, even though she had nothing but her knickers on underneath the dress. The stagnant air held specks of dust afloat in the old, wooden house. Kaisa wondered if she could ask someone to open a window.

The temperature in Finland had suddenly soared the day before the English party arrived in Helsinki. At the airport, Peter's mother had carried her trench coat on her arm and said, 'Is it always this warm here in Finland?' Kaisa smiled and said the summer weather was very much the same as in England – it could be cold and rainy or hot and sunny.

When her eyes settled on Peter at the airport Kaisa had felt exactly the same as she did when she came to meet him that first time three years before. They kissed and hugged as long as they could in front of everybody without any embarrassment.

'I love you more than ever,' Peter whispered into Kaisa's ear. Jeff went to hug Kaisa too and she smelled beer on his breath. The English people looked out of place in Helsinki. Kaisa directed the group onto the Finnair bus and when at last all the luggage was in, including the two hatboxes Peter's mother and auntie had carried as hand luggage, Peter nodded to a set of two seats at the back of the bus. Kaisa and Peter sat next to each other, holding hands, and Kaisa wondered if she should mention Samantha. She looked into Peter's eyes and he smiled at her. 'God, I've missed you,' he said.

'Me too,' Kaisa said.

Later in his hotel room, where they'd escaped together, Peter – her husband – took Kaisa into his arms. But she pulled away and looked down at her hands.

'What?' he said and bent down to see Kaisa's face.

'I went out with Samantha a few weeks ago,' she said.

Peter slumped onto the bed. He ran his fingers through his thick black hair and sighed. It was dark in the room; brown curtains had been pulled across a wide window. 'Come here,' he said and patted the silky bedspread.

Kaisa crossed her hands over her chest. How easy it would have been to just give into him. To sit next to him and be loved. But she had to know what really had gone on between him and that girl. 'No,' Kaisa said and went to stand by the window.

There was a loud knock on the door. 'What are you two doing?' somebody shouted from the other side. Peter gave Kaisa a quick glance, raising his eyebrows. She nodded and he went to open the door. Peter's best friend and Kaisa's best friend burst through the door, arm in arm.

'This is strickly *veerbooteen*,' Jeff said. He was wiggling his finger at Peter. Tuuli was giggling. Jeff turned to her and said, isn't that what you say in Finnish? He was drunk, slurring his words. 'You can't be doing it – you're not even married yet.' He winked at Peter. Jeff had been under strict instructions not to breathe a word of the registry office wedding to anyone.

Tuuli stopped giggling when she saw Kaisa's face, '*Förbjuden'*, she said, 'and it's Swedish, not Finnish,' She loosened her arm from Jeff's grip. 'I told you.'

'What's up?' Tuuli said coming over to Kaisa. Tuuli was dressed in cotton trousers and a short-sleeved top. Her long arms were tanned and she seemed even taller than usual. Kaisa looked into her eyes – she'd had a drink too. Kaisa touched Tuuli's arm and said in Swedish, 'It's OK, we just need to talk for a bit.'

Tuuli nodded, turned on her heels and took hold of Jeff's arm again, 'Come along you Englishman, there are beers to be drunk.'

When Peter shut the door behind their friends, he said, 'They seem to be getting on very well.'

'Yes,' Kaisa turned her face away from him. She needed to stay firm, not to give in to the false lull of happiness. Not now she'd finally dared to talk to Peter about the 'accident'. Kaisa sat down on the bed. The dark, dusty heat in the room was oppressive. 'I need to know,' she said quietly.

'OK,' Peter sighed. He sat next to Kaisa on the bed. She looked at his face. His eyes were serious and round. He opened his mouth to say something but then seemed to change his mind.

'Why did she come to our wedding?' Kaisa asked.

Peter stood up and went to the window. His hands were hanging either side of him, 'I don't know. She must have heard the rumour about our quickie wedding,' Peter turned around and gave Kaisa a boyish grin, then growing serious again, continued, 'You know what the Navy is like...I couldn't believe it when I saw her outside the registry office.'

'She said she'd gone out with your mate when you were at Dartmouth.'

'Did she? I didn't know.' Peter came over and kneeled in front of Kaisa. His eyes were so wide and his face so sad she knew she'd forgive him anything at all. 'Darling, you've got to believe me when I tell you it didn't mean anything. I was drunk, she was drunk. If I could rewrite history, I'd give anything for...' Peter buried his head in Kaisa's lap. She stroked his short black hair. There were curly strands growing on the back of his neck. Kaisa pulled his face up and kissed him. She felt the harsh stubble on her cheek. 'I love you, Englishman,' Kaisa said.

After she'd left for Tampere, two hours north of Helsinki, the English party spent a few days sightseeing in the capital. Sirkka had organised a trip out to the archipelago, as well as the train tickets to Tampere for all of them later on in the week. Peter had kissed Kaisa long and hard at the station. 'I can't wait to be married to you again,' he whispered in her ear and grinned.

In the evenings in Tampere there was a slight sea breeze coming from the two vast lakes bordering the city, but during the day the sun burned Kaisa's shoulders as she sat in the garden of her grandmother's house. Kaisa hadn't visited the place of her birth in years; the memories of her childhood there flooded back and Kaisa had to keep herself in check not to give into a maudlin sense of loss. For not only was she marrying; she was also leaving her home for good this time. The old Finlayson cotton factory; the sombre stone statues guarding the Hämeensilta bridge; the people, whose faces seemed more familiar to her than those in England, or even Helsinki, all seemed to point a finger at her and ask, 'Why are you leaving your homeland?'

As Kaisa walked around the old Stockmann's department store in the centre of town, she remembered how, as a child, she'd spent her pocket money there, on toys and little packets of chewing gum with cards of ice-hockey players in them, and how she'd been allowed to go Christmas shopping there for the first time on her own at the age of ten, just for half an hour. Kaisa's grandmother's dishes of semolina pudding, blueberry pie and dill meatballs took Kaisa back to her childhood, as did the burgers her sister and she had in the old Siilinkari café opposite Stockmann's.

The three days Kaisa spent in her grandmother's house brought her close to revealing what had happened in England four weeks previously. But each time she started to tell her mother or sister about the English registry office wedding, she drew back and decided it would be better for them not to know. The padre in England had promised the service would be no different, and when Kaisa had telephoned the Finnish pastor from England, on that frantic day of arrangements in May, he too had assured her that no one would notice the difference between an actual ceremony and a blessing.

'Have you been starving yourself or what?' Heli now said and tutted. She was biting her bottom lip and had her hands crossed over her chest.

Kaisa looked at herself in the mirror. Her friend was right; the top was a little loose, 'Sorry, I hadn't noticed.'

After assessing Kaisa's image in the mirror, with her head cocked slightly to one side, Heli got a needle and thread out and started sewing an extra seam to tighten the fabric around Kaisa's body. The bodice fell off her shoulders and she felt bare in her nakedness. When Heli disappeared with the dress Kaisa put her hands across her breasts and reached for the T-shirt she'd been wearing before.

Kaisa's mother had also been standing behind her daughter, watching the final fitting of the dress. She and Kaisa's grandmother had been ready for ages: Kaisa's grandmother in her leopard-print outfit; her mother in pale blue with a straw-coloured wide-brimmed hat with a few matching silk flowers pinned to it. Kaisa had helped her mother choose the outfit in Helsinki, during the week before the Englishmen's arrival. She smiled at her mother in the mirror and noticed she had tears in her eyes. Kaisa remembered the picture of her mother and father on their wedding day, displayed on the bookshelf in Kaisa's grandmother's living room. She, too, had worn a simple white dress and a long veil. The black-and-white photograph of Kaisa's mother was the most beautiful she'd ever seen of a bride.

Kaisa wondered if she'd been full of hope on that day or whether she'd already feared that the marriage wouldn't last. Had her doubts been similar to the ones Kaisa was now having? Kaisa shrugged off any such thoughts and turned her eyes back to her own image. Heli had finished with her sewing and, with the needle and thread between her teeth, asked Kaisa to once again step inside the bodice. 'There!' she said triumphantly, as she zipped up the gown. Carefully, she arranged the veil on Kaisa's head and pulled it down over her face.

There was a gasp from the small group of women behind Kaisa. Her mother and grandmother had been joined by Sirkka, wearing a stylish black-and-blue dress and matching hat, as well as by Kaisa's Polish 'aunt', who was wearing a bright-red suit and high-heeled red shoes. 'Oh la, la!' she said, and came closer to Kaisa. She stretched her arms as if to squeeze Kaisa, but stopped just in time, 'Ah, I cannot touch you, but you look beautiful!'

'What time is it?' Kaisa spoke into a silence in which all the women were staring at her, as if in a trance, through the mirror.

'Goodness,' Kaisa's mother said, and she rushed to the kitchen window, 'the cars are here already!'

Kaisa's grandmother and sister went off in the first car with Heli, all air-kissing Kaisa in turn as they disappeared out of the door. Sirkka looked as nervous as Kaisa should have been. She took Kaisa's hands into hers and said, 'See you after the ceremony!' Kaisa guessed that for her the most difficult part was to come. She'd arranged everything concerning the wedding reception, stuff Kaisa didn't even know to think about.

'Are you ready to go?' Kaisa's mother said. Kaisa could see she was fighting tears. She nodded and they started to gather up the veil into Kaisa's arms. Suddenly Kaisa stopped. 'I think I need the toilet,' she said.

'What?' Kaisa's mother turned sharply at the door.

For a moment they all stood still in the hall, wondering what to do.

'You can't wait?' Kaisa's mother asked.

Kaisa felt like laughing out loud, 'Of course not – what if...?'

‘No worry,’ Kaisa’s Polish ‘auntie’ said. She opened the door to the little downstairs cloakroom and took hold of the veil. ‘You sit, we hold, and how do you say, what do you call it…you…?’

Kaisa struggled to get herself free of the layers of fine tulle fabric and onto the toilet seat. But with all the fabric, it was impossible to shut the door. ‘OK, now,’ Kaisa’s mother said and smiled. They’d all been giggling and now grew quiet.

But it was no good. After a few minutes, Kaisa said, ‘I can’t go when you’re watching.’

Kaisa’s mother looked at her watch. She lifted her eyes to her Polish friend, whose face suddenly brightened up, ‘We close door so, and we go here.’

The two women arranged the veil and the overflowing fabric of Kaisa’s dress so that the door could be left just a little ajar. Still holding onto the veil, they moved themselves behind the door. Finally Kaisa could let go.

In the car the women giggled like schoolgirls. Kaisa’s Polish ‘aunt’ was sitting in the front seat, her hat touching the roof of the car as she turned her head back and forth.

‘That will be the one thing you remember about this day,’ Kaisa’s mother said, and she squeezed her hand. ‘Just like the time when you were a little girl. When Father Christmas came you were on the lavatory, nearly missing the whole visit!’

Kaisa laughed, ‘But it was only my father dressed up as Father Christmas!’

Kaisa’s mother looked down at her hands. Her smile waned and they fell silent in the back seat.

The car pulled into the bridge over Tammerkoski. Kaisa saw the fast flowing water of the steep rapid. She remembered how, as a child, she’d been afraid she’d fall into the foam created by the water and be lost forever in the strong current. They drove slowly through the edge of Tampere centre, onto Satakunnankatu, and then turned up the hill towards the Cathedral. Kaisa’s mother squeezed her daughter’s hand and Kaisa realised she thought Kaisa was nervous. She still didn't know that Kaisa was already married. Kaisa smiled at her reassuringly and pulled the veil over her face while she waited for the others to get out of the car.

Kaisa's uncle's smiling face was waiting for her on the steps of the church. He was a tall, slim man with slightly thinning, fair hair. Kaisa hadn't seen him for years and it seemed strange that it was not her father who was waiting for her. Kaisa swallowed the sudden tears and nodded to him.

'Well, this is an honour indeed,' he said and offered Kaisa his arm. Slowly they made their way up the steps. At the doorway Kaisa had to stand still for a moment to adjust her eyes to the darkness of the church. The organ started playing Mendelssohn's wedding march. As they began the long walk down the aisle, Kaisa could see Peter, looking smart in his dark suit, start towards her from the top of the aisle. When he moved forward, his mother also got up and took hold of his sleeve. Peter whispered something into her ear. Kaisa now suppressed a giggle; she guessed no one had told her that in Finland the bride and groom meet in the middle of the aisle, where the bride is handed over. She must have thought Peter was about to make a run for it.

When Kaisa and Peter walked out of the church, now properly man and wife in the eyes of God as well as law, Peter whispered into her ear, 'You look stunning.'

KAISA'S FATHER stood alone, a little to the side of the path leading up to the church. As Kaisa and Peter stepped out into the bright sunshine she saw him right away and found that his presence didn't surprise her in the slightest. It was as if Kaisa had known he couldn't possibly keep away. She wondered briefly how he'd known the time of the wedding. Had he waited there all day? He wore a light-grey suit and was carrying a camera case. He smiled to Kaisa and lifted his hand as if to wave, then changed his mind and lowered his hand again. As Kaisa and Peter walked down the steps, followed by the wedding guests, her father met them half way down. He was standing two steps below the couple, squinting against the sun.

'I brought you a wedding gift. It's just money but I thought you might find a hole for it.' He gave Kaisa a boyish grin and moved towards her. He was holding a white envelope in his outstretched hand. Kaisa looked at his hand.

Kaisa's father took another step towards her, then turned to Peter instead and said in English, 'For you.'

Peter took the envelope, 'Thank you very much,' and shook hands with Kaisa's father. He nodded to the Englishman and turned his eyes to Kaisa again. She loosened herself from Peter's grip and took a step closer to her father. They were now at the same level on the steps of the Cathedral. He put his arms around Kaisa and squeezed hard.

'Congratulations,' he said. His voice was dry and low; Kaisa could hardly hear him. His eyes looked pale blue, almost grey. Kaisa felt something fall onto her shoulders and realised it was a combination of rice and confetti. The noise from the crowd behind them grew stronger. Kaisa smiled, wiped a tear away from her eye and slipped her hand through Peter's arm.

When Kaisa turned back towards her father again, he was gone.

Coffee and Vodka

You may be interested to read Helena's second novel, *Coffee and Vodka,* which is set in Finland and Sweden. It tells the story of Eeva, who together with her family move from the small town of Tampere to the Swedish capital, Stockholm.

Eeva is excited when Pappa declares the family will move to Stockholm, a city where 'everything is bigger and better'. But in Sweden Finns are reviled and despised by the more affluent Swedes. While Mamma finds feminism and Eeva's feisty older sister, Anja, quickly learns the language and pretends to be Swedish, the domineering Pappa grows angry and resentful of his family's new-found independence. The two teenage daughters bear witness to a drink-induced, violent family drama and Eeva's world falls apart.

Thirty years later when Eeva, now a teacher of Swedish to foreigners, travels back to Finland, she dreads seeing Pappa again. But she finds a grief-stricken old man. Eeva is confused and worried for her grandmother, when Anja enters the room. Her sister, who never hid her disgust for Pappa, has been seeing him for years. If Anja has been able to forgive and forget, will Eeva too?

Coffee and Vodka is now available.

The Red King of Helsinki

Helena's third novel, *The Red King of Helsinki*, a tale of spies, lies and gymnastics, is now out.

The year is 1979 and the Cold War is all but over in Helsinki, the playground of the Russian KGB, when a former British naval officer Iain goes undercover to investigate Vladislav Kovtun, a violent KGB spy. This is Iain's first assignment, and when he discovers there are bodies in Kovtun's past, he quickly gets embroiled in danger.

Pia has two goals in life: she dreams of a career in gymnastics and she wants Heikki, a boy with the dreamiest blue eyes, to notice her. When her gym teacher announces there's to be a competition with a Moscow school, Pia is desperate to take part. Then her best friend Sirkka, the daughter of an eminent Finnish diplomat, goes missing, and Pia begins to investigate what's happened to her friend.

Unbeknown to Pia, Kovtun, The Red King of Helsinki, is watching her every move.

The Red King of Helsinki is now available.

34018199R00150

Made in the USA
Charleston, SC
29 September 2014